THE TIME IS NOW

BETTY BREUHAUS

ISBN: 978-1-6847-1313-4 (sc)
ISBN: 978-1-6847-1314-1 (e)

Lulu Publishing Services rev. date: 11/13/2019

ACKNOWLEDGEMENTS

MANY THANKS TO *my* Woodford Harbor for their support in making the first in the Woodford Harbor Mystery series, *A Curious Corpse*, so rewarding and fun. A shout out also goes to Pepper who still adds so much life to everything. Also thanks to the entire "crew" down at the Driftwood, my day would not start without you. And again, kudos to Amy Brown for recognizing what was lacking, and telling me. Marty Riskin has again created a beautiful cover, and added drawings, creating new insights into Woodford Harbor. And, as always, many many thanks to Margo W.R.Steiner, my Editor Extraordinaire.

DEDICATION

TO BILL...
...who spent a lot of time in Woodford Harbor with me

CHAPTER
ONE

I T WAS A peculiar moment to have a Jimmy Buffet lyric running through my head.

> According to my watch the time is now
> Past is dead and gone
> Don't try to shake it just nod your head
> Breathe in, Breathe out, Move on

My personal "now" seemed exquisite. I was enveloped with love, surrounded by every person who defined my life and gave it meaning. Those who had come before me, those I had brought into the world, and all those who were living life alongside me. We were gathered in a sacred spot we all shared.

All of us had blossomed and grown right here in Woodford Harbor. Ours was a quintessential small town nestled into a crook of the Maine coastline, just twenty minutes north of Portland. Its rugged and rocky shore gives testament to its strength, and the graceful curve of its harbor speaks to its gentle beauty. The salty air and the clanking of sailboat halyards are our heritage.

Today, we stood on freshly mowed grass overlooking the water. The warm autumn sun bathed us in a golden haze, and Dr. Nielson's low, melodic voice bound us together. The stones surrounding us bore the names of families who had called this little town home for generations; most of them could also be found on street signs downtown.

Pulling myself out of my reverie, I focused again on reality. I engaged the lowering mechanism and watched along with everyone else as the ornate and beautifully-carved box that held their attention descended into the ground. The fragile, elderly body it housed was going back to Mother Earth, but the spirit it released was dancing around the assembled folks. I again found my mind wandering, which was not good. As head of Bainbridge Funeral Home I was more than just a witness to this moment—I was directing it.

I stood next to Dr. Nielson as he completed his blessing and looked heavenward. All eyes were riveted on the casket. I suddenly felt an unexpected jolt as his arm, seemingly intentionally, brushed mine. I looked toward him for an explanation and followed his eyes. Now it was my turn to gasp. A body in a casket at a cemetery is one thing—something one expects—but one crumpled behind a nearby headstone is something else again.

Fortunately, my professionalism kicked in. My sole responsibility right now was to Thistle, the grand lady whose casket was disappearing from view. Flowers had to be laid on her casket and final farewells said. This was *her* moment and her loved ones' moment, and it was my obligation to make this happen. Dr. Nielson gave me a quick nod, and I knew we were both on the same page.

I picked up a basket of beautiful sunflowers and offered one to the first of Thistle's three sons. He took it, looked down, and gently laid it upon his mother's coffin. Others followed suit, their total absorption in the moment leaving them fixated on the task at hand. As the line slowly inched around the indentation where the body lay, I realized my Uncle Henry would be the last through. This was ideal. I gave him a conspiratorial nod as he passed and directed my eyes back up the hill where, of course, the body remained.

I had known Uncle Henry my entire life, and our wordless communication system was well developed. His eyes gave me a knowing look, and he nodded his head. Uncle Henry would be the man in charge of this disaster; as the sheriff of Woodford Harbor it was on *his* plate. I suddenly realized how easy my job was in comparison. And speaking of that, I now had to get to Thistle's house to organize the refreshments.

The crowd walked slowly and quietly to their cars. Nearly all headed to Thistle's. Most everyone in town had sat around the large grinding stone from the old mill that Thistle had converted into a table in her backyard. Always the perfect hostess, her laugh, energy, and lively spirit enlivened everyone who crossed her path.

I waited until all the cars had begun their progression out of the cemetery before I turned back to join Uncle Henry. Mr. Stanley and two other men from the Bainbridge Funeral Home were seeing to the final details of the burial and didn't need me. So engrossed were they in their work that they didn't even notice I had stepped back to speak with Uncle Henry.

"Oh my, my, my," I stammered, at a total loss for words.

Uncle Henry looked at me. "Yes, dear, he is dead. Looks to be Ty Waters. That shovel over there might well be what smashed him in the back of the head. Bit of a mess. Even his sneakers are messy. Imagine Ty Waters with dirty white sneakers!"

It seemed inappropriate to be snarky about a recently murdered man's shoes, but it *was* funny given Ty's obsession with grooming. His blond hair was so perfect you suspected he used designer gels, and you just knew he employed a hair dryer to make the end effect just so. Perfectly fitted jeans, a fresh polo shirt, and pristine white sneakers always completed his 'look'. As a tennis teacher, that footwear defined him somehow. He had always been handsome and had managed to age gracefully, maintaining his youthful smile into his sixties. A caricature of a tennis pro, he wasn't looking very snappy now.

"Uncle Henry, I have to go to Thistle's for the reception. Is there anything I can do for you?"

"Thank you, dear, no," he replied. "I have a call into the state police. I'm sure they will send out one of their haughty, imperious, pretentious officers to take over. Most probably Lt. Daniels, the arrogant, self-important twit. Having to deal with him is almost worse than the murder in my mind."

I quickly raised an eyebrow, implying that perhaps he was going a bit overboard. "Yes, what a thing," I said. "A murder right under our noses at the cemetery."

Death, regardless of how expected it may be, is akin to having a baby in my book. You know the child will be born, but when it happens it still seems like such a surprise. Death is the same. You know a person is elderly, but when they die it's oftentimes still a shock. But this body, smashed and crumpled up against a tombstone? Now that's a surprise on steroids!

CHAPTER
TWO

I GOT INTO MY Jeep and headed for the reception, beyond happy to be in my own controlled, familiar space. I smiled. The car makes me happier than it probably should. It takes me wherever I ask it to go and, with the top down and the wind ruffling my hair, gives me a feeling of freedom beyond compare.

I began focusing on my next task, the reception. Much of the healing process for those who remain begins at these post-funeral gatherings. Family and friends share memories and reassure each other that the deceased did, indeed, matter. The bereaved are surrounded by love and support. It was my job to facilitate this ritual.

Bode, Thistle's oldest son, was my main concern. Although not formally married, we are as close to soulmates as can be. We grew up together in Woodford Harbor as best friends, but romance never entered our minds. We shared bicycle rides all over town, sailed in little Optimists, swam across the harbor together, and even built an awesome tree house. We ate together most every night, at his house or mine, depending on the better menu.

We went our separate ways after high school. Bode ended up at Dartmouth in New Hampshire, an inevitable choice as his parents were both very active alumni. Both his younger brothers graduated from Dartmouth as well.

Bode settled in Boston after graduation and was working at an investment house when his father suddenly suffered a heart attack and died on a fishing trip with his mother. All the brothers came home immediately, but Bode was the one who stayed behind, ostensibly to help his mother. Breathing the air of his beloved home town again brought a certain clarity to Bode. Truthfully, Boston had never really captured his heart. It had been a grand adventure, to be sure, but with his father's death he realized he belonged in Woodford Harbor. He once again took up lobstering—his summer job as a student—and made it his vocation. The circle was complete.

As I walked into the house, people were still arriving. Most entered the rarely used formal front door. They filled the house and were already spilling out into Thistle's lovely garden.

"Lizzie, that was a wonderful service. Dr. Nielson's voice is so lovely that I swear he could read the phone book and it would sound profound," smiled Carly, the owner of our local breakfast spot, The Driftwood. In another corner sat the entourage from The Old Port, Woodford Harbor's favorite watering hole. I looked outside and saw representatives of all the garden clubs knotted together. The ladies from the Congregational Church's bell choir chatted quietly, and practically the entire membership of the Chamber of Commerce mingled nearby. Thistle had touched many lives, and everyone seemed compelled to honor her.

Thistle's family, of course, was the center of attention. Her two younger sons and their wives were setting out casseroles on the dining room table, looking a bit out of place. They seemed to be searching for familiar faces from their childhood. Bode was at the beer cooler, making folks feel at home.

Thistle and James had been very social, entertaining and being entertained almost every night, and were loved by many. After her husband's death, Pammy—her given name—had to reinvent herself to survive the loss of her partner. She turned to what she knew best, gardening, and opened The Thistle. She was so ensconced in the shop that it wasn't long before she and the shop were one, and the moniker 'Thistle' became hers. She spent long and successful days in the shop, chatting with everyone and, of course, knowing everyone's business. It fit her to a tee. Her extensive knowledge of flowers combined with her devotion to wild flowers made her arrangements magical.

After ten wonderful years in the shop, Thistle suffered what the elderly fear most, a broken hip. Although the injury broke her body, it could not break her spirit. She moved into Woodford Pines, the town's assisted living facility, and quickly became its unofficial social director. Although she was failing physically, her spirit remained positive and strong. She seemed bigger than life, and it was hard to imagine she would ever leave. But last week her heart finally gave out.

It seemed that everyone in town was here to celebrate her life. Indeed, the gathering did have the feel of a celebration. But for those whose lives she had created—her beloved sons—it was a monumental loss. All three had the same look of disbelief and sadness in their eyes.

Bode sat on the bottom step of the porch and distributed cans of beer, but I could sense that his thoughts were far away. Perhaps he was thinking back to the time his mother had bandaged his left elbow after he fell out of our tree house. Or to the many roast chicken dinners she had created. A death can be many things, but to those closest to the departed it is an unimaginable loss.

Interrupting my reverie, Bode's brothers approached and thanked me for organizing the service.

"Lizzie," said Jonny, the middle brother, "it seems both strange but inevitable that you're taking care of this event. Your father and your grandfather ran Bainbridge Funeral Home before you, and I guess we knew you would inevitably step in and take over one day. Seeing you in your element is very impressive. You're still the sweet little girl we always knew, but now you're a grown woman taking care of the people in our little community. You've been a wonderful friend to the family forever, and we're so grateful for the way you've helped us through this."

"It's true," added Bill, the youngest of the three. "I feel like my father saying this, but it seems like just yesterday we were all tumbling around at Darling Park. Fast forward and here we are. Who would have guessed? Makes me think of the John Lennon lyrics, 'Life is what happens to you while you're busy making other plans.'"

"I know," I replied. "But we're all so fortunate with the choices we've made."

Just then, two little cousins, sons of Jonny and Bill, came running up to their fathers. "Can we go down to the beach around the corner?" they asked. The circle of life was lost on no one.

I gave Jonny and Bill big hugs; I could muster no other words.

Perhaps it's time I introduce myself. My name is Lizzie George and, as you have probably surmised, I am the funeral director at my family business, Bainbridge Funeral Home. I had a wonderful childhood in Woodford Harbor, and was always welcome at my father's office. Although it may seem peculiar to some, my childhood reality included corpses, so entering the business was a natural progression for me.

I'm an only child and if I was spoiled or doted upon I don't think it did me any harm. I had the run of this simple seaside town with my best friend, Bode, and I loved it. I'm afraid I took my beautiful surroundings for granted sometimes, though. Like most kids, I was sure there was something better beyond. I excelled at school and was exceptionally good at math and testing. It was a great combination and got me into the University of Michigan in Ann Arbor. I imagined that glorious town as the enchanted place of my dreams and thoroughly enjoyed the years I spent there—perhaps to an extreme.

After consuming outrageous amounts of beer, attending numerous insane football games, and trying pretty much anything offered me, I somehow managed to graduate. Fortunately, I had the good sense to know what I wanted to pursue post-college, and enrolled in the mortuary science program at Wayne State, in Detroit.

As often happens, though, my life veered slightly off course. No one was more surprised than I when I discovered I had somehow conceived a child. None of the three candidates who might have been responsible for this little bump in the road seemed like worthwhile candidates for a lifetime relationship, so I treated the event as I had pretty much everything else that had presented itself to me in the past. I had the child and expected to continue on my merry way.

Such was not to be the case, however. For one thing, this tiny little breathing thing I had produced consumed far more time than I had anticipated. In return, though, the unexpected love that came back to me was astonishing. And then there was this sudden desire to be with my mother—and my father—and all the good folks in Woodford Harbor whom I suddenly realized were also my family.

Little Charlie and I picked up and drove straight back to the happy little hollow in the ledge that is Woodford Harbor, and there we settled in. That was over sixteen years ago. Today, I cannot imagine my life other than it is right now. Charlie and I make a great team and use all the love surrounding us to grow and thrive. And it's kind of fun—she looks just like me!

CHAPTER
THREE

I LOVE WHAT I do. My work at Bainbridge Funeral Home allows me to see people through a very difficult time in their lives, and this gives me a real sense of accomplishment. Not all clients are as gracious and thankful as Bode's family, of course, but I do my best with everyone. As I heard all the chattering around me, I knew I had orchestrated a successful funeral today. In sharing stories and memories of Thistle's life, each guest confirmed—in his and her own way—her immense value to her family and her community.

I needed to see Bode, though. When I finally managed to sidle up to him, I was awarded a quick whack on my butt; his special stamp of endearment. He smiled, but I could tell he was running on adrenaline at this point. Unfortunately, it would have to last him a couple more hours.

"Hey Z, this is really nice," he offered, looking out over the gathering. Not exactly a wizard with words, his brief comment contained much gratitude; this I knew—and appreciated. He also has a penchant for giving people nicknames, mine being merely

'Z'. There is something about the way he utters the sound, though, that conveys a huge dollop of affection to me.

"The service at the church was perfect—the ladies playing 'Amazing Grace' on the bells, the poem you picked out for Jonny to read, and all her grandchildren walking her casket in and out of the church. I'm sure Dr. Nielson's eulogy was great too, but I don't think I even heard it. I could feel Mom right there throughout and didn't need words to remind me of her. The flowers people put on her casket were beautiful and would have made her so happy.

"I still feel like there's a hole in my heart, but this helps, I guess."

It is awful to see someone you love hurting so much. Unfortunately, there was nothing I could do or say to make it go away. I might be able to lessen it a wee bit in the coming weeks and months, but the pain will have to run its course.

I was fairly bursting with my desire to tell Bode about the debacle at the cemetery, but I knew I had to let him attend to his guests. My news would have to wait.

Suddenly, I noticed the trio of Jonny, Bill, and Daniel Dunkirk coming towards us. The latter is one of the more prominent lawyers in Woodford Harbor.

Lawyers, I'm afraid, are generally not my favorite people, and Dunkirk is no exception. He's a lawyer with a less-than-stellar reputation, and his fixation is on the wealthy. He tends toward bow ties and fidgets with them mercilessly. The word around town is that the devil came to him early in his career and proposed a deal.

You can win every case you try for the rest of your life, Satan told our barrister. Your clients will adore you, your colleagues will stand in awe of you, and you will make piles of money. All I want in exchange are the souls of your wife, children, and parents.

Dunkirk reportedly thought for a moment and asked only, What's the catch? That about sums up the local lawyer who now stood in our midst.

Pushing somewhat rudely into the center of our space, he fixed his beady little eyes on Bode and addressed the group.

"Boys, I'm sorry for your loss," had a decidedly hollow ring.

"As I am sure you know, your mother retained me to execute her will and take care of her final wishes. I'd like to meet with you at my office sometime tomorrow morning to iron out the details. Would 8 a.m. be good?"

Bill, who practices law himself, stepped up to Dunkirk. "I think 10 tomorrow morning will do nicely." Though decades younger than Dunkirk, he wasn't at all intimidated by him. He can smell a rotten fish anywhere.

Dunkirk gave a curt nod and was off. The three brothers exchanged woeful glances and sighed. Although Bode, Jonny, and Bill don't display any remarkable physical resemblances, their loyalty to each other is strong. It would be important tomorrow.

Although Thistle had raised her boys in Woodford Harbor, only Bode remains. Jonny had followed in his father's footsteps and become a doctor. He had fallen in love with Beth, another medical student at Rush Medical College in Chicago, and eventually they—and their two boys, now 10 and 12—ended up in Seattle.

Bill chose the law after graduating from Dartmouth, and practices in Boston. He and Spicy, his adorable, curly-haired wife, produced two boys as well. It seemed wrong somehow that this little sprite had all boys living with her, but they follow her around like the alpha dog she is. The boys are 6 and 9, with curly hair springing out at all angles.

Bode is the tallest and most solid of the three. Unlike the rest, whose hair is both thinning and receding, he has a great head of bushy blond hair. His work in the outdoors shows in his large, square face; a face both tanned and wrinkled by the sun. Partial as this may seem, I think he is the kindest, smartest, and most gentle of the three as well.

Soon, people began the inevitable exodus, and the family was about to be alone. Charlie had been handling the boys during the reception, and I saw her corralling them into the TV room for some quiet time. While Beth and Spicy organized the leftover casseroles and various desserts, they put on water for macaroni and cheese to feed the boys.

From some distant place, I heard myself saying, "I think we have had enough nibbles for one day. How would it be if I were to bring a nice dinner back in about an hour? I think it's time to put our feet up and enjoy a meal of real food with a nice wine."

"Oh, Lizzie, that would be great."

"Sounds perfect to me."

Feeling like Julia Child herself, I walked over to Bode to say good-bye. As our eyes connected, I leaned in and and said quietly, "I have to tell you something. When we were at the cemetery, there was a dead body lying against a tombstone up the hill towards the water. Dr. Nielson saw it first. I alerted Uncle Henry, but I don't think anyone else saw it. Uncle Henry thinks it's Ty Waters. I didn't look very closely, but I'll take his word for it."

Bode gazed back at me and mumbled rather numbly, "Too bad."

I guess it was sensory overload for him. Really, why should he care if the local tennis pro is lying dead in the cemetery? He'd just buried his mother. I got it.

Charlie bade farewell to the boys and joined me. We gave a final wave and jumped in the Jeep.

"So Mom," she asked, "what exactly are you going to bring to all those people that resembles real food? Your hamburger stroganoff doesn't really qualify, and plain hamburgers probably won't fly either."

Okay. I am not renowned for whipping up gourmet meals—or really much of anything in the culinary department. My heart was in the right place, though, when I had made the offer.

"Don't be silly, Charlie. It will be fine!"

Deep within my brain, though, my inner voice screamed, "Oh, dear, dear, dear, dear, dear..."

CHAPTER
FOUR

I T WAS A quiet ride home. My mind, however, was on fire. What
to bring for dinner? What to tell Charlie about Ty Waters? I also
couldn't get rid of the image of Daniel Dunkirk wringing his hands
in anticipation of a billable two hours tomorrow morning.

I decided to cross one problem off the list right away. I turned
to Charlie. "Honey, a terrible thing happened at the cemetery today.
A dead body was discovered resting against a tombstone just up
the hill from where we were gathered. I met Uncle Henry up there
after everyone left, and he thinks it's Ty Waters."

"The Grinning Tennis Pro?"

"Is that what people call him?"

"Sure. He always has a group of women standing around,
gawking at him. He can schmooze six women at a time, I think!
Poor guy, he doesn't seem to notice that he's old." This from a teen-
ager who probably thinks 30 is ancient!

"Was he murdered? A real body right up the hill from us? Wow!"

I was a bit appalled at her lack of compassion for the deceased, not to mention her enthusiasm about a murder. I like to think she is a caring and empathetic human being, but then it occurred to me that she's just sixteen. Why should she care whether or not Ty Waters comes down to breakfast tomorrow? I would have to save that lesson for another time.

Suddenly, inspiration struck, and the second item on my list was stricken. "I know!" I exclaimed. "I'll order a roast chicken and mashed potatoes from Brown's and pick it up on my way back!" Brown's is our local market, and they make a mean roast chicken and heavenly mashed potatoes.

"Brilliant," said Charlie. "I have to admit you are good under pressure. Can you get string beans there, too? And how about a pie and ice cream?"

I liked knowing she was on board with my genius.

"Pie and ice cream are excellent suggestions, but I think I'll buy the beans and steam them there. It will give the illusion I'm cooking."

We jumped out of the Jeep in unison and headed up the railroad-tie steps to our front porch. It is not a spacious house, but it is beyond perfect for us. We live in the oldest section of Woodford Harbor, right across the road from a small cove called Little Harbor. Local lobstermen moor their boats here, accessing them with dinghies they lean up against an old rock wall. A boat ramp gives them entry to the water, and also gives me passage into the Atlantic when I swim in the summer.

Our tall, lanky house welcomed us. It sits back from the road and is flanked by Burial Hill on one side and an old dirt lane on the other. Out back, it's all woods. Our front porch affords us a classic peak of the water.

Charlie headed straightaway to the stairs just inside the front door and made her way to the third floor, her little kingdom. The tiny little room to the left of the entranceway, although only the size of a decent area rug, is the space we live in most. Blessed with a fireplace, a love seat, and an overstuffed chair and ottoman, it's really all we need. A roaring fire and a television to watch Jeopardy and the Red Sox complete our world.

Charlie owns the chair, and Bode and I fit perfectly on the little sofa. White-beaded wainscoting bisects the room's soft white walls two-thirds of the way down and makes this a happy little room. Coral-striped fabric and a massive palm tree are the colorful accents that tie it all together.

A bar separates this room from the kitchen, where sparkling white cabinets and periwinkle walls continue the cheerful ambiance. The two banks of windows that overlook our little back garden let in a wonderful, welcoming brightness.

What should be the living room on the opposite side of the house is dominated by a ping pong table, which fills the entire room. A tiny dining room completes this side of the house.

I followed Charlie as far as the second floor. Not only are the winding stairs joining these two levels small and pie-shaped, they have uneven risers. Fortuitously, I installed a grab bar reminiscent of a boat on the inner wall. I need it for a secure grip to ascend.

I quickly changed out of my business attire of formal black pants and white shirt. Both require dry-cleaning. My everyday black pants and white shirt look just the same, the only difference being that they're washable. In the cooler months I add certain accoutrements for comfort. Generally, it will be crew-neck sweaters or, on more casual days, a flannel shirt. Comfort is paramount. For funerals, though, it's always a well-tailored black blazer. I like to keep my life as uncomplicated as possible. Don't sweat the small stuff was scripture to me at a young age—and still is.

I'm reasonably content with my overall appearance. I'm medium height, weigh in at the middle of my acceptable weight chart, and have attractive brown hair that bleaches to a lighter shade in summer. Trims are haphazard at best; I usually just pull it back in a ponytail. My eyes are attractive in a simple, unadorned way. It would probably serve me well to apply some pricy cosmetics to these unremarkable features, but that's not my style.

However, my smile! Frankly, I think this is my best feature! It's engaging, though not sultry, and brilliant, but far from breathtaking. I can always work a little magic with it if I need extra help at the Registry of Motor Vehicles or want extra salt at McDonalds. Oh, yeah, I can turn on the charm when necessary.

Dressed now in black yoga pants, a white polo shirt, and a coral crew-neck sweater, I crawled my way up to Charlie's room. Twangy country music greeted me as I reached the landing. It's not my favorite, but I suppose it's preferable to what passes as popular music these days. Bode's a country music buff, although his tastes tend more toward traditional classic country. When I see Charlie using Bode as a role model like this, it warms my heart, and my judgement about their taste goes out the window.

"Hey, honey! What are you up to? I'm leaving for Brown's to pick up the chicken and things for dinner, then I'll head back to Bode's. Are you going to join us there?"

She looked at me with the pained expression that is ubiquitous on sixteen-year-old faces around the world.

"Really, mom? I mean, those kids are cute, but I did just entertain them all afternoon. And..."

"And you don't want to listen to the memories of three middle-aged men about their 83-year-old mother?" Much as I loved it when our worlds overlapped, I recognized that maybe this was an instance to respect her place in all this.

"I completely understand. You'll be fine here, Charlie. There are turkey burgers in the freezer and leftovers of some sort in the fridge. I won't be late. I'm exhausted."

"Thanks. Mom." She smiled. "I'll probably work on some homework."

I recognized that 'probably' was the operative word here and kissed the top of her curly hair, loving the familiar smell. She could do anything she wanted. Goodness, I love this girl.

CHAPTER
FIVE

M Y TRUSTY JEEP took me straight to Brown's Community Store. I spend an inordinate amount of time in this little market, perhaps because it's the social center of Woodford Harbor, especially around dinner time. You'll always find a gaggle of townies there comparing notes on meal plans and generally catching up with the day's events—and gossip. I hopped out and headed for the entrance. Before the door was completely open, I found myself assaulted by a loud, lusty voice. "Lizzie!" it roared, "What's going on?!"

I wasn't as astonished by this verbal assault as you might think, as it happens with some regularity with this friend.

"Let me guess, Pepper. You've heard the news from the cemetery."

"Damn straight! What is the world coming to when Ty Waters is found clobbered behind a tombstone in broad daylight at Woodford Harbor Cemetery! You can't write this stuff!"

She seemed entirely too gleeful. No doubt the investigative reporter in her had already clicked in.

"What the hell? Didn't anyone at Thistle's service even notice? How do you have eighty people standing forty feet away from a dead body? And Ty's body at that! He always loved being the center of attention. Actually he might have kind of liked this, now that I think of it."

"Come on Pepper, that's a bit much. The stone was behind everyone, and it's not like folks were perusing Woodford Harbor Cemetery looking for crumpled bodies. Dr. Nielson saw him first. I looked up at about the same time and told Uncle Henry about it as soon as I could. I didn't really take a good look, but he said it was Ty. You're right, though. What in the world?"

In a strange way, talking to Pepper about this was somehow reassuring. The woman calls a spade a spade.

Pepper has her own way of addressing the world and the events that surround life. Although a Woodford Harbor native, she forged her own path when she left after high school. A true proponent of taking the road less traveled, she skipped college and enlisted in the WAVES. She spent years traveling the world as one of their first female journalists. Her wanderlust finally quenched, she returned home, where she now writes for the local paper, the *Woodford Reporter.*

With very few major news events in town, Pepper is generally left to report on predictable small-town politics. She does, however, have her own weekly column; here she holds court on any and all things that capture her fancy. That can vary from picking up dog poop, to liquor licenses, or to reporting on a boat stranded at low tide. Her tanned and weathered face seems a caricature of a female naval enlistee, and her strong, stocky build is a sure sign she's not to be messed with. She must have worn a lot of khaki and navy blue while in the WAVES, because it's her daily wardrobe of choice now. Short, sensible hair completes the package that is Pepper.

When the woman speaks, she looks you right in the eye. Ferociously. Believe me when I tell you you'd better look right back. I'm always on my toes around her. What you don't see in this crusty, somewhat sassy exterior, though, is that inside she is as loyal and loving as it gets. If Pepper has your back, you're good to go.

Her true passion, no question about it, is food. She sees every meal as an opportunity—and she gives each meal an inordinate amount of attention. Her very descriptions of a meal make you want it. Need it. Crave it. One of her favorite sayings, as a matter of fact, comes from George Bernard Shaw: 'There is no sincerer love than the love of food.'

Her tolerance for my lack of culinary skills lets me know she loves me. This is just one of the reasons I chose her as Charlie's godmother. If I am gone, I want someone like Pepper to inspire my girl.

"After you've talked to your Uncle Henry," she tells me now, "let me know pronto, Tonto, what's going on. We haven't had a headline this exciting in years! Ty as victim! Ha!"

"Pepper, keep your voice down. I understand the irony, but …" She is one of the few people on earth who can put me at a loss for words.

"Well then," she continued, not missing a beat, "what are you having for dinner?"

"I'm bringing dinner to Thistle's house for Bode and his family. I'm picking up a roast chicken, mashed potatoes, blueberry pie, and chocolate chip ice cream."

"And you'll bring green beans to cook there so you look like you're preparing the meal," she said with a knowing smile. It's scary when someone knows you too well.

I headed off to pick out my chicken before she could begin what would certainly be a lengthy, detailed description of her next meal.

There was no line at the deli counter so I had Phil all to myself. When he gave up his local gas station he moved to Brown's, where he currently rules the meat counter. His gas nozzle became a butcher's knife, which was quite a change, but one thing has remained constant; he still has the pulse of the town and knows everything worth knowing. His round face and warm, sparkly eyes, grounded by a neat grey beard, is comforting; it somehow makes you want to tell him everything. He plays that card well.

Because he's one of the folks who support me in my cooking

adventures, I seem to need his help almost daily. Today was no exception.

"Phil, I'm doing takeout for Bode's family tonight, and I need some help."

"Help with takeout?" he asked, looking at me somewhat quizzically. I don't suppose he gets that question very often.

"Oh, don't give me that! I need help with quantities. We'll be seven adults and four children who don't count—except for dessert. How big a roast chicken should I get? How many pints of mashed potatoes? Will two blueberry pies be enough? Two quarts of ice cream? I can eyeball the green beans myself."

I am always a little apprehensive when figuring quantities of food for a group and, truth be told, this group intimidated me just a little. I have known Bode and his brothers basically all my life, but the addition of two wives and little kids running around changes the dynamic. I wanted to be sure I would have enough food without looking like I'm trying too hard to please everyone, which of course I am.

Good old Phil put a large roast chicken and mashed potatoes in a box and suggested I get one blueberry and one apple pie—and perhaps two different kinds of ice cream. I smiled my thanks and picked up two blueberry pies and two quarts of chocolate chip ice cream. I may listen, but I don't always comply.

Pepper was in front of me as I checked out. She wished me godspeed with the meal and was out the door.

I gathered the box and bags in both arms, then put the box on the ground to open my passenger door. I put both bundles in, rounded the front of the Jeep, and climbed into the front seat. As I started to turn the key, I heard a shout. "Lizzie!" To my left, Pepper's face was pressed rather unattractively against my window. I quickly put the window down in the hopes she would stop screaming.

"Get this! I had my police scanner on in the car and heard there's a manhunt going on! Apparently after everyone left the cemetery this afternoon, Ollie appeared to supervise the closing of the grave and saw Henry and his crew standing around Ty's body. He promptly took off!

"And there's more. The murder weapon appears to be the shovel he uses to dig graves! This is getting better and better!" Before I could gather my wits to reply, she was back in her car, speeding away.

This piece of news was disconcerting. Ollie, you see, is Ty's twin brother. He is also the caretaker at Woodford Harbor Cemetery, and lives in a cottage on the grounds with his wife, Alice. I don't know a lot about twins, but I do know that Ty and Ollie have to be fraternal. There's no way they could have shared a common egg. Ty's egocentric, brash personality has always been diametrically opposed to Ollie's reclusive, quiet make-up. Ty's hair is blond, whereas Ollie's is brown. Ty's physique, the result of an inordinate amount of time at the gym, is the complete opposite of Ollie's diminutive constitution. Ty's eyes were always darting and searching, whereas his brother wears a permanently downcast semi-frown. They are opposites on all fronts.

Neither were they close. It's hard to even think of them as friends. I can't imagine Ty, for instance, going to Ollie's cottage for Thanksgiving dinner; his oversized sense of self would dwarf everything else in those confined quarters. For someone like Ty, obsessed with wealth and the wealthy, Ollie held little attraction.

As easy as it is to imagine Ollie wanting to whack his brother with a shovel, I couldn't believe him capable of such a thing. Even if he did, why would he run? It's just not Ollie. Ty was no brain surgeon, but Ollie has always been even slower. He's not so much honest as afraid of dishonesty. The whole matter seemed more and more perplexing by the minute. Thankfully for me, though, it had no impact on my world.

CHAPTER
SIX

I WALKED UP TO Bode's back door and peeked in. The three brothers were gathered in the kitchen, and my slight shove on the door announced my arrival. All three turned toward me. My eyes, however, rested on Bode and stayed there. It's so hard to watch someone you love in a situation like this. The family is blessedly functional, but the death of your mother is devastating. I beamed him a warm look, and hoped he understood its import.

"Hey, you guys. Can you help me with the stuff in the car?"

"I'll get it, Z." Bode walked to the car with me and began to gather the parcels.

"How are you doing?"

"I guess I'm okay, but I am just so tired. Going through the church service, the whole cemetery thing, and then having all those people talking in my face has been exhausting. I get it that they're being nice, but really, I just need some time to wrap my brain around Mom being gone. I still think she's going to walk through that door and tell us all to get out of the kitchen so she can get dinner ready." I hugged him for a good long time. We both inhaled some fresh air then and carried everything to the house.

Jonny and Bill were leaning against the counter. They seemed uncomfortable there, but apparently found it preferable to sitting. "Hey, Lizzie, some red wine?" If this offer was a nervous need for something to do, I didn't care.

"I sure would," I smiled. And I meant it.

The television was on in the living room, and I heard Spicy and Beth speaking in low tones in the dining room. I stayed in the kitchen, thankful to have a task. I turned the oven on and put the chicken and potatoes in to warm. The ice cream went in the freezer, the pies on top of the stove. I began the arduous task of preparing the green beans.

Jonny arrived with my glass of merlot. Turning to Thistle's three "boys," I held my glass high. "To your mom!" Each held on to the moment and raised his beer can. It was quickly apparent that these weren't the first beer cans to have touched their lips today.

"Remember when Mom would ring that cow bell on the back porch, and we would haul ass as fast as we could to get home?" Jonny was looking off into the distance with a faraway look in his eyes.

"And how about if we were still out when the streetlights came on? Now *that* was raw fear." Bill's face reflected not nostalgia, but sadness as he reminisced.

"It's comforting to remember how we looked up to both our parents. To us they were like supreme beings," added Bode. "Omnipotent! Maybe everyone feels this way about their parents. When you get to be an adult, though, and recognize what really good people they were, it's amazing. Accomplished, loving, honest . . ." Bode's thoughts went unfinished, for just at that moment a 130-pound beast crashed through the swinging door from the dining room.

"Hi, Bob." I caressed his giant head. There was no need to stoop; Bode's massive Bernese mountain dog's head is even with my waist. Bode selected him from a litter at eight weeks old, and the two of them have been inseparable ever since, sharing large—yet gentle—personalities. Bob goes lobstering with Bode every day; the two of them are so graceful as they bait the traps and haul and measure the catch that it's almost a ballet. Bode will haul up a pot, clean out the old bait, measure a lobster if there is one, and band the keepers. Turning gracefully, he'll grab a new piece of bait that Bob holds aloft in his generous mouth and put it in the bait bag. I sometimes think if Bob were a person he would be Bode; likewise, if Bode were a dog he would be Bob. I love them both.

Bob retreated to his water bowl and started slurping water. This exercise never ceases to be comical and with everyone amused at his antics, the melancholy mood was broken.

Beth and Spicy joined us. I took one look at them and felt no guilt about handing my empty wine glass to Jonny for a refill. I could see that these poor folks had been at it for hours; I both needed and wanted to catch up.

A small rap on the door turned everyone's head. A small, slightly wizened figure stood beyond the screen. We all jumped, almost to attention. It was as if a real adult had just entered the room, and we children needed to be respectful.

As the woman entered, Bill pulled out a chair from the kitchen table, and the diminutive figure sat down. Her grey hair, somewhat wispy and very curly, framed bright blue eyes and encircled the folds of her fragile skin. She looked at all of us hovering. "Perhaps someone would get me a glass of Chardonnay," was all she said.

"Oh, Aggie! It's so nice you're here!"

"Aggie, dear, how good you are to come!"

"It makes everything feel complete with you here, Aggie."

The assembled multitude paid its respects to Agatha Hawthorne, Thistle's BFF, as though she was visiting royalty.

"It is lovely to see you. I couldn't imagine not being here with all of you, so I grabbed a ride over. How I wish your mother were here. I can almost see her over at the sink! But then again, she wouldn't have allowed us all to be in here, would she? This kitchen was her sanctuary." Aggie smiled. "And she liked to create her magic in peace and quiet—alone."

"She'd love to be here with that roast chicken in the oven and the blueberry pie warming on the stove—and, of course, all of us," ventured Bode.

I raised my glass again. "Here's to Thistle!" I said in the cheeriest voice I could muster. As glasses were raised, so too were spirits. Spicy and Beth offered to set the dining room table. Although I was more familiar with the lay of the land, I understood their need to do something and didn't protest.

The chatter in the kitchen grew more and more boisterous as we drank and watched the beans steam. I unwisely accepted a third glass of merlot, vowing to myself to drink a glass of water before downing it. Aggie was in rare form, most likely because she was surrounded by all the people who had been a part of her life with Thistle.

As the bean steaming came to an end, I took the chicken, with great ceremony, out of the oven and presented my masterpiece to the troops. I had already transferred the mashed potatoes to a ceramic casserole, which gave them a homemade appearance.

Draining the beans, I raised my voice to soprano, giving it a Julia Child effect, and announced dinner's arrival. The mood lightened further as everyone dove in.

The meal suddenly became a real party, which is just what we all needed. Wine bottles were scattered around the table, available for refills; with every refill, our memories of Thistle became more fun and less sad. She was somehow with us all, and we knew that. Jonny went into the living room and brought out old photo albums that we quickly passed around the table.

"Look at that! All of us as babies! I was just born, Bode looks about three, and Jonny's a tiny two-year-old!" Bill laughed with pleasure.

"She adored each and every one of you. I was there for every birth and even their September wedding. What a stunning pair your mother and dad were—and so much fun!" added Aggie.

In another photo Thistle and James held a fat blond baby.

"Ha! Mr. Big Shot! Bode as an only child! Gosh, Mom and Dad look so young," Bill remarked.

"But they weren't really that young," added Jonny. "Dad was in medical school at Dartmouth, and they were sensible enough to wait before getting married."

"How old *were* they when they married? Mom, I think, would have been 31, and Dad was 33," said Bode. "So when I was born in April of '72 they must have been . . ."

The muddled minds around the table dug out their phones as dates were thrown out. I had an interesting thought rolling around in my mind but decided to keep it to myself.

Suddenly Jonny squealed. "Wait a minute! Bode, you were born seven months after they were married!"

"And that's not the half of it!" added Aggie, almost giggling.

"What are you talking about, Aggie?" Bill mumbled in a beer-driven haze as he looked to her.

"Not only was Bode a surprise," she whispered conspiratorially, "no one was ever certain whose surprise he really was!"

Bode's fork was hanging in midair, a gasp escaped Bill, and Spicy blessed us with her nervous, gurgling laugh. Jonny and Beth sat stock-still, their mouths agape. Valiantly, I searched for a diversion, but came up empty.

Apparently oblivious, Aggie went on. "Thistle had quite a crush on Ty Waters back then. It was crazy times, believe me. But, oh my, everyone did love that little Bode!"

No one seemed to know quite what to do. It wasn't a topic that was going to lead to a coherent discussion at this point, so we abandoned it in favor of action—action of *any* kind! I jumped up from my seat, grabbed as many dessert dishes as I could balance, and headed for the kitchen. Spicy and Beth started toward the living room to corral the children and usher them upstairs to bed. Bode grabbed whatever he could and joined me in the kitchen. To Jonny and Bill was left the task of escorting a rather wobbly Aggie back to Woodford Pines, where she resided.

Bode and I cleaned up the kitchen like the well-oiled machine we are, grabbed Bob, and headed to my house. No good nights to anyone, just out the door.

The drive home was awkward at best. The elephant in the car was suffocating, but I felt I should wait for Bode to speak. As we reached my house he finally said, somewhat softly, "You know Z, this is just too much. I'm trying to process my mother being gone, and now my father is thrown into the mix. I'm going to surrender to a big glass of Grand Marnier, which will, I hope, lead me to where I want to be. Sound asleep."

I love a man who knows his mind.

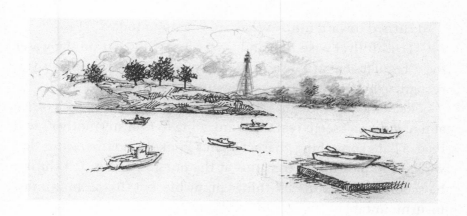

CHAPTER
SEVEN

I FELT THE MORNING sun on my eyelids and enjoyed the moment. The warmth suffused my face, the body lying next to me gave me comfort, and a certain lazy fuzziness enveloped me in pure bliss.

But wait! On a normal morning, Bode was up and out before I came to my senses. Pleasant as it was to find him still next to me, it meant something was wrong. And then it all came crashing down on me. The reason he was still sleeping had to do with yesterday and was not a good sign.

Poor guy. His 220 pounds felt softer and more vulnerable this morning—and no wonder. The combination of death and the chain of startling revelations he experienced yesterday would bring even the strongest man to his knees. I knew Bode was strong. I just hoped he had the resiliency to deal with this.

Bode stirred next to me now and moved closer. We stayed this way, welcoming another ten minutes of sleep, then rose to greet a day that promised to be difficult at best.

I turned toward him. "What are you up to today?"

"Truthfully, I wish Bob and I were just going out on the water for a regular day of lobstering. It's days like this that make you recognize how wonderful your day-to-day life is.

"Realistically, though, I have to be at dingbat Dunkirk's office at ten. It doesn't seem real that I am going to hear my mother's will read. That's something characters in a book do, not me. After that we have to pick up Mom's stuff at the nursing home. Z, I think I have done a lot of difficult things in my life, but this seems almost insurmountable.

"Will you come with me, Z? You're included in Mom's list of those invited to the reading, as well as Beth and Spicy. She loved you and thought of you as part of the family. I love that about her and you.

"Jonny and Bill are going to Woodford Pines this morning," he continued, "to take what they want. Will you go over with me later this afternoon?"

"Of course, Bode. I'd do anything for you. I feel a little awkward going to Dunkirk's office, but I *was* included. And I am more than happy to help you with Thistle's things—honored, actually."

Bode suddenly flipped over on his back and looked up at the ceiling.

"How about Aggie last night? She *is* a bit daft and certainly had a lot of Chardonnay, but what the hell? She acted like everyone in the world knew about something going on with Ty Waters and Mom.

"This just boggles my mind! You don't think much about your parents having sex, but an illegitimate affair? My *mother*? With *Ty Waters*? Forty-some odd years ago? It's ludicrous! And to even consider Dad not being my father? No. No, no, no. I understand the irony, but I sure as hell don't see any humor in it."

I spoke up. "Maybe it was just Aggie trying to be the center of attention and the life of the party. She loves to think she's still a sparkling twenty-year-old entertaining the crowd."

"I don't know, Z. For now I just need to get my ass out of this

bed and deal with the rest of the day. That'll be enough for me."
This is the Bode I know, full of eternal optimism.

I heard Charlie running water upstairs. It reminded me of my
own responsibilities.

"I'm heading home to see what's going on there. Do you want
to meet down at The Driftwood after you drop Charlie off? I'll see
if anyone at the house wants to join us," Bode offered.

"Great, see you there," I answered.

After he left, I ducked into the bliss of my morning shower
and wondered what the day would bring. I felt more than a little
awkward going to the reading of the will. Our unmarried status
is clear as a bell to Bode and me, and we're content with it. People
on the outside don't necessarily understand, though. Are we not
married because we don't truly love each other? Can't commit for
a lifetime? Have some underlying distrust of each other? So much
speculation.

These are their issues, not ours. Even so, there are times I want
to grab someone and shout in their face that they are wrong—not
that it would help. So on I go, keeping my thoughts behind my
closed mouth. It's not exactly what I do best, but I'm working on it.

I slipped into my "dress clothes," preparing for the meeting at
the lawyer's office and a later meeting with Cam Johnson's sister.
She was coming to plan the funeral for the beloved bartender from
The Old Port. Fortunately, things were in good order, for Cam,
a confirmed bachelor, had come to me about five years ago and
bought a prepaid funeral package.

Rocky, the owner of The Old Port, had called me when Cam
passed away and offered to help out however he could. He's an
old-fashioned employer who treats his staff like family. If he was
willing to step in as a father figure for Cam, it was wonderful for
everyone. But I had to wait on his offer until after I had met with
Cam's next of kin.

I was only one step ahead of Charlie getting downstairs, but
managed to pop her English muffin in the toaster before she
arrived.

"I have an algebra test this morning, my chemistry lab this afternoon, and soccer practice after school. Oh, and an English project on meaningful quotations. Our first quotation is supposed to be about family. I'm thinking 'Today is the first day of the rest of your life'."

"Charlie, I think you can come up with something a bit better than that—maybe something relating more towards family, as the teacher requested. Let's talk about it," I replied.

"Really? Well, not now! Can you put some peanut butter on that thing? I'm going to grab the orange juice."

I burned my fingers getting the blasted bread circles out of the red-hot toaster, slathered them with peanut butter, and put them on a paper towel. No time for a plate with this girl. Her juice gulped down, we were out the door in nothing flat.

Our drive to school is lovely.

"Charlie, look how still the water is in the cove. It's high tide, and it looks like a lake out there. Redmond Island looks so pretty in the morning light."

No response from Charlie.

"You know, there are lots of kids on their way to school right now who see nothing but replicas of their own houses, manicured trees planted in rows, and no water whatsoever."

She was still mute.

"'All that I am or ever hope to be I owe to my angel mother.' Abraham Lincoln," I spouted.

"Mom! Not now! I'm focusing on algebra!" squealed my little intellectual prodigy. I am almost sure she will become a reflection of what I imagine my own glowing, philosophical self to be. With time and some divine intervention, that is.

CHAPTER
EIGHT

I TURNED LEFT TO head back toward the harbor and The Driftwood. I knew I had a difficult day ahead, but having Woodford Harbor beneath my feet gave me confidence. My town, you see, is more than just a collection of old colonial houses and a picture-postcard harbor. The houses are owned by real people who can paint them any color they want and live as they please. And they do.

These differences give us our strength. Not everyone loves or even likes everyone else, but I do think we have a healthy dose of respect for each other, and that makes it all good. Most of the time.

The town does a stellar job with the Fourth of July, including a harbor illumination defined by lighted flares that circle the perimeter at sunset. When it is dark, a barge in the middle of the harbor sets off fireworks, paid for by donations left in large mason jars around town from townspeople. Memorial Day is given its due with an early ceremony at the town landing that pays homage to all branches of the military. We honor the fallen by casting a wreath from each branch into the harbor. This is followed by a parade in which the selectmen, the Girl Scouts, the Boy Scouts, and the high school band march through town to the cemetery. There, Dr. Nielson says a few words while a bugler plays taps, giving everyone goose bumps.

Then, of course, there are the singular events that draw us together from time to time. Last winter, for instance, we celebrated the tenth anniversary of a terrible blizzard that shut the town down for almost a week. Residents came together to help each other with shoveling, and we enjoyed impromptu neighborhood potluck dinners. It was an occasion on which we made lemonade out of lemons. Ten years later, we're still celebrating the unique event that bound us as a community.

I pulled into the parking lot at the town landing, next to The Driftwood. I don't like bacon much, but the smells that emanate from this beloved breakfast spot are irresistible. Pushing the latch on the door down twice, I gave it an extra shove and was in. The smells that attracted me outside were child's play compared to the varsity sports of aromas inside.

At this time of year tourists are in the minority, and the regulars seem to be where they belong. Those who perch on the stools at the counter may change stools daily, but once a stool person always a stool person. The tables along the outside wall today were filled with an assortment of town residents: the bank president, a librarian, a dressmaker, a bartender, and a couple of fishermen. Even the almighty Daniel Dunkirk was here, head bent over a stack of documents. I grabbed a table, and Jennie arrived promptly with my iced tea. Her smile, though warm, seemed distant.

I poured in a packet of Splenda, gave the tea a stir with my straw, and enjoyed my first taste of iced tea for the day. Pepper was seated at a table not far away. When she saw me she felt compelled to fill me in on the news of the day.

"Hey, Lizzie," she called in the throaty voice I'd recognize three streets away. "Ollie's on the loose, huh? Poor kid! Maybe we should start a pool on when he'll get caught! This will certainly give the *Woodford Reporter* some exciting meat!

"Maybe Henry'll be the one to capture him and bring him in. That would be a front-page photo! Fact is, though, that Ollie isn't the scariest-looking varmint to be bringing in! Still, handcuffs are handcuffs. I don't think we've seen them around here since Fat Jack drove circles around the baseball field, and they put cuffs on to bring him in!" Her monologue was cut short by Bonnie, one of the regular waitresses.

"I'm so upset! We just heard about poor Ty! How could such a thing happen to such a wonderful man? It's so violent, and Ty was such a sweet, gentle guy. I don't think he ever hit a tennis ball hard enough to hurt anyone—and he was so helpful with my backhand. How could this have happened to him?"

Yeah, I think. I can just imagine those big strong arms of his around her back, both hands cupping hers as she swung away. Must have been great for both of them.

I've got to stop this. Talk about not speaking ill of the dead! Here I am raking him—and poor Bonnie—over the coals, when all Bonnie is doing is waiting tables at The Driftwood.

I decided to ignore Pepper, as well as my thoughts, and focus on Bonnie, who continued to wail.

"It *is* shocking, Bonnie. Had you been taking tennis lessons from him?"

"Oh, yes, for almost three years. Right after I moved here I joined the tennis club as a way to meet people. Since I wasn't much of a tennis player, I thought lessons would be a good idea. That's when Ty and I hooked up. Well, not hooked up in *that* sense, you know. I started taking lessons twice a week. He was almost my therapist. I told him everything, and he always listened and was so understanding. Oh, dear . . ."

I didn't allow my mind to contemplate how much her tennis had actually improved in those three years.

Bonnie was standing in the middle of the restaurant, oblivious of the customers; she seemed to have lost track of the fact that she was working here. Luckily, Jennie was also on duty today. She wove with ease in and around Bonnie to deliver omelets, pancakes, and hash. She shot me a look that was accompanied by a slightly raised eyebrow. With that one gesture, we had an entire conversation.

Jennie has worked at The Driftwood for what seems like a lifetime, but she never changes. Back in the day, we played softball against each other in the Woodford Harbor Women's Softball League. I remember dreading any game in which she was on the opposing side. We called her The Roadrunner and with good reason. She would smack the ball and run, run, run. And she's still pretty sprightly on her feet!

Just then the old door behind me received an extra shove, and the familiar presence of Bode filled the room. He was sans siblings which was fine with me. There was an awkward atmosphere in the room as everyone nodded to Bode. Acknowledging the death of someone's mother or other relative can't always be addressed sufficiently in five seconds, but in social situations like this it was sometimes all you were allowed. The quick greetings didn't last long, and Bode was gracious enough to acknowledge them all with a considerate nod.

"Where is everybody?" I asked.

"They're getting a slow start. The boys are a little feisty after being here for four days, and it's obvious they're all ready to leave. Nice as it is to have everyone around, I must admit that a little peace and quiet right now will be welcome. Oh, Z, this is just exhausting."

"Bode, I'm so sorry about Thistle," Jennie said to him. "I was one of her biggest fans. She loved our family. We had so many girls, and she did the flowers for all the weddings—beautiful flowers! It must be so hard."

Bode nodded, a sad smile his reply.

"So, what's it to be for breakfast?" Jennie was quickly back to business.

"I'll have a single-egg omelet with cheese and salsa and a dry English muffin," I replied.

I am trying to be sensible as I come precariously close to my fortieth birthday. I only have French toast, for instance, on weekends.

Or on days that are cloudy. Or sometimes when it is too hot. I am doing my best.

"Two eggs over easy with bacon and raisin toast." Bode said it almost as one word.

We took a breath and began to settle in. That's when Pepper plopped down at our table.

She didn't waste time. "Nice service yesterday, Bode. Your mom would have loved it. The sunflowers covering her casket at the end was marvelous, and she and I both lean toward the King James version of Bible readings. You did her proud, my friend."

He sat up three inches taller, and I secretly blessed Pepper. Sensitivity is not always her strong suit.

"Isn't it shocking about Cam," she continued. "Such a dear fellow, and an excellent bartender to boot. He'll be a real loss to the town. He was always so even tempered with all the characters that inhabit The Old Port. A local pub is not an easy place to navigate, but he was connected to everyone. He probably heard more dirt than me. Damn shame he should drop dead at that age."

I concurred. "I couldn't agree more, Pepper. I'm not sure what's going to happen with his funeral service, but his sister is coming in today to meet with me. Hopefully, she'll have some good additional information that will give us a more complete picture of our Cam."

"Have you talked to Henry about all the goings on surrounding Ty?" Pepper asked. "Talk about a lightweight! I can think of any number of people he annoyed, but really . . . whack him with a shovel? Cam would have been a good suspect if he was still around. There aren't many people Cam ever had to shut off, but Ty was a frequent offender.

"All the ladies would secretly buy him drinks then coo from a distance. And he would sit there and suck them down until he could hardly hold himself up. When Cam shut him off he didn't even have the good taste to leave. He would just wobble unsteadily on his chair, catatonic in the midst of all the twitttering. It drove Cam nuts, which wasn't easy to do. But I guess we can count Cam out."

Pepper wasn't finished. "I tell you, those tennis students of his seem inordinately upset. How many ladies did he have under his charismatic charm, and what do you think really went on on those clay courts? I don't belong to the tennis club. I never had any interest in hitting a green fuzzy ball—or a hard white dimpled one either, for that matter. There are too many great classic movies to watch on the weekends to bother with all that."

I obviously did not share my newfound interest in Ty with Pepper. Instead, I told her I was going to go over to see Uncle Henry to check in.

"Who do you really think would do such a thing?" I asked her in parting.

"It's kind of fun to think about that," said Pepper, and I sensed a certain maliciousness in her tone. She loves this kind of stuff.

CHAPTER
NINE

P EPPER HEADED FOR the door, leaving her bombshell on the table.

As she departed, Bode spoke up. "Is this really happening? My mother is gone, and I'm supposed to wonder if Ty Waters is my father? To make things even more ludicrous, some unknown person whacks Ty with a shovel and kills him. Really?"

Bode has a great handle on life. He's no drama queen and generally takes everything in stride. Then suddenly I had a thought; I wished it was last week when none of this had happened, and everything was so simple. But of course it wasn't last week. So much for wishful thinking.

Our plates arrived, and we grabbed the silverware that was thrown down on the table and started in. Our meal was interrupted throughout by folks expressing their condolences to Bode. Such nice gestures, so inadequate, and yet so important.

After we finished, Bode had another cup of coffee, and I refilled my iced tea glass with water. We sat over our drinks in a kind of haze. Daniel Dunkirk passed by our table on the way out and lifted his chin towards us. I guess it's his way of wishing us good morning. Wouldn't you know he'd lift his chin rather than nod downwards. The man displays arrogance in every gesture! Oh, brother! I've *got* to reign in this snarkiness.

I'm really trying to look at people more kindly and cut them some slack by recognizing that they are 'doing their best'. It's my new mantra, but it doesn't come easily to a person with my occasionally overly judgemental brain. It's a real wake-up call sometimes to realize that what I'm seeing actually *is* the best a person can do.

Bode arose from the table. "I guess I'll go home and check in on everyone. We'll all go over to Dunkirk's office around 9:45. Can you be there then?"

"Sure, but I still feel kind of awkward doing this."

"Lizzie, the legal, formal vows of marriage didn't carry much weight with my mother. You know how she loved having you come visit, especially when you brought those little bottles of wine for her. She trusted you to take care of her garden. She's known you all your life! I suppose it isn't nice to say this, but really, I don't think Beth or Spicy hold a candle to you in her heart. They reproduced, but that's their primary claim to fame. Yes, you belong there this morning."

Over brimming eyes, I nodded my thanks for what he had just shared.

"Okay. I'm going to see Uncle Henry first, then I'll meet you there."

After settling the check, Bode headed off in his truck, Bob hanging out the window. I hopped into my Jeep and made the short drive up State Street to Uncle Henry's office. Unlike other towns, the Woodford Harbor police station is not red brick with bad landscaping and a little American flag out front. Here, it is housed in the basement of the Old Town House, a yellow clapboard building dating back to the 1720's. The fact that it is still in use speaks to the pragmatic nature of Woodford Harbor. It's a sturdy, dignified building that sits smack dab in the middle of town. It was confiscated by the British during the American Revolutionary War and today houses a Civil War museum and serves as the town's polling place.

I opened the little door off the street and there was Uncle Henry, savoring a cup of coffee and some obscene frosted gut bomb on a napkin.

"Missed you down at The Driftwood, Uncle Henry, but it seems you're more than making up for it." I gave him a big smile.

"I can't show my face down there! The whole town is buzzing with Ty Waters' murder and Ollie Waters' flight. I don't know which is worse. Poor Ollie. He came out of his cottage to finalize the burial details, only to find a group of us circled around his dead brother and holding his shovel. It was just too much for his limited mind to handle," Uncle Henry explained.

Ollie is a very nice fellow, albeit a bit on the slow side. He graduated from high school with some difficulty, and was hired to take care of the town-owned Woodford Harbor Cemetery. It affords him housing and an adequate salary, and this suits him perfectly. He married his classmate, Alice, and the two enjoy an easy relationship that works for them both. Alice is a hard worker and very down to earth. Together, they care for the cemetery, Ollie doing the physical labor and Alice seeing to the record-keeping and accounting. Their only son is in the merchant marines, creating a good life for himself.

"How do you live in the same small town with a twin brother like that?" asked Uncle Henry rhetorically. "As honest and straightforward as Ollie is, Ty has a slippery personality that I never trusted.

"Whoever murdered Ty dropped the shovel right next to him. The only blood on it appears to have come from the front of Ty's head where it hit the stone. There is a deep gouge in the grass right behind the gravestone; this must be where Ty slipped when he was startled by the shovel. We're checking the prints on it, but I don't think we'll find much. There must be prints from every guy who works at the cemetery on that shovel.

"They'll do the autopsy down in Portland; hopefully, that will shed some light on all of this."

"And then the body will go where?" I inquired, suddenly feeling apprehensive.

"I'm sure there will be a service somewhere, and frankly I can't imagine any venue other than Woodford Harbor. Hopefully, Ty has a friend somewhere who will step up to the plate and take care of that. I certainly wouldn't bet on his relatives.

"It leaves you in an awkward position as the owner of the funeral home," Uncle Henry finished. I didn't miss the slight smirk on his face. He has always been a bit hurt by my following in my father's footsteps and taking over the family funeral home rather than signing on as his deputy dog. He was definitely getting some pleasure from this.

No one, not even Uncle Henry, seemed terribly bothered by Ty's demise. As for me, I only knew him to say hello. During our occasional ten-second conversations he had always seemed perfectly fine to me. His sculpted blond hair and somewhat arrogant demeanor had amused more than annoyed me. That he was a tennis pro to the rich and famous of Woodford Harbor never much impressed me. He lived in Chillingsworth's stone gatehouse, adjacent to the impressive mansion; this *had* impressed me—impressed and puzzled me both. Having a tennis pro was a vital part of the very successful Abenaki Tennis Club that Arthur Chillingsworth built and owned, but was it necessary to house the pro, too?

It did give Ty airs, though. Whatever superior attitude he attempted to throw *my* way, though, missed its mark completely. I saw him most often at The Old Port, holding down a barstool. He always had lots of company around him, and yet he somehow seemed alone. Nonetheless, the curveball Aggie had thrown out last night had definitely gotten my attention.

I looked at Uncle Henry in a different way for a moment. He's my mother's brother, and we have a pretty close relationship. He never married and had long ago moved in with us. It was just me, my mom, my dad, and Uncle Henry. I loved it!

Parents have certain parental responsibilities that an uncle doesn't. This is probably why Uncle Henry and I enjoyed some great adventures. He'd let me do everything my parents wouldn't. We'd go camping and hiking and he even let me drive his car when I was thirteen. He also had an intuitive sense of what nefarious schemes I might have in mind, be it drinking beer, smoking dope, or skipping school. I wasn't a bad girl, but it was fortuitous to have an Uncle Henry to bail me out of my occasional predicaments.

"Aggie was at Bode's house for dinner last night," I told him. "She drank nearly a full bottle of white wine and was carrying on, as she does. But at one point she implied that Ty Waters might be Bode's biological father. Does that sound conceivable to you?"

"Come on, Lizzie, don't we have enough on our platters without that? Rumors *have* come up from time to time, but I've always discounted them as gossip.

"Don't forget, there were ten years between them and in those days that made a world of difference. Thistle and James were the ringleaders of that older group, which traveled as a pack and could be found at bars, restaurants, and each other's houses drinking and partying almost every night. Actually, the drinking part isn't really fair, as I'm sure there were people who drank more than they did—they just stayed home and did it.

"Aggie and her husband, Ralph, were part of that crowd, too, along with Gus Beethoven and his wife, and the Chillingsworths. What a bunch! They hung out at The Old Port, for the most part, and the Abenaki Tennis Club. In the winter, they vacationed as a group, too, heading to Captiva Island in Florida. Although much younger than they were, and in an entirely different class, Ty was in the middle of it most of the time, but was hardly a bona fide member. To my mind, he was more like background noise—and I think he resented it. He could come into the room, all right, but he wasn't invited to sit down.

"It makes sense that he would be watching Thistle's service from a distance. He probably didn't feel he should be a part of it. Frankly, Ty gave me the creeps."

"I know," I replied. "I can't conjure up any real sympathy for him, and I don't want him taking up my time and energy. If you think he gives *you* the creeps, imagine what this is doing to Bode."

"I have never understood the allure of whacking that fuzzy ball around on a piece of cement, but there certainly are plenty of people around here who seem taken with that tennis club Chillingsworth built." Uncle Henry scratched his chin. "The ladies of Thistle's generation played well into their seventies, and now Ty is attracting the ladies in their fifties and sixties as well.

"Your mom and dad and me were kind of stay-at-home poops. I was a built-in babysitter, but we were all content just being in that house."

That made me feel loved, which, while not exactly what he said, seemed like a natural interpretation to me.

"I have a mountain of paperwork to complete for the state about this murder. That's actually more difficult than catching the culprit sometimes," complained Uncle Henry.

"Well, I just might stick my little Nancy Drew nose in here from time to time. Aggie's contemplations are reverberating in my brain, and I can't seem to slow them down. I'll see what I can do," I offered.

"I'm going over to Ty's to have look around and see if there is anything interesting laying around. Maybe it would be a good idea for you to come along. You have good instincts for detail," said Uncle Henry. "I'll probably head over around one."

"I have an appointment at ten and a client after that, but I would sure like to have a look around with you. Quite honestly, I've always wanted to have a peek inside that little gatehouse."

"Great, but really," said Uncle Henry looking a bit anxious, "I don't much like thinking about murderers roaming around this little town."

CHAPTER
TEN

I DROVE HOME AND brushed my teeth, freshened up my mascara, and immediately felt more professional—to what end I wasn't sure. This was my situation: I'm the girlfriend of one of the deceased's sons, and his mother's will was being read in a lawyer's office. This was the big time. I knew I should have felt honored, but I hated it.

I took off for Bode's house where the assembled multitude had gathered outside. After final warnings to the boys to behave, we piled into two vehicles and headed to the law office of Daniel Dunkirk, Esq. Bode and I took his truck and enjoyed a largely silent ride until we pulled into the parking lot. "I hate this," I said as we pulled in.

"I hate it more," said Bode.

Dunkirk's office was predictable. Its walls were a moss green that missed tasteful by several shades. The wood trim was veneer, and the leather furniture was faux. The secretary, too, had seen better days, but I was sure she was 'doing her best'.

Dunkirk kept us in the waiting area for a few minutes. I'm certain he used the time to futz with his bow tie and polish his little spectacles. Finally, he buzzed Miss Doing Her Best, and we were shown in.

There was ample seating for all of us around his desk, which displayed at least four framed versions of the lovely Mrs. Dunkirk and the four little Dunkirks. That's pretty much all I remember, as after the introductions I zoned out and thought about other things. While I planned what to pack for an upcoming Florida trip and how to help Charlie with her quotations project, the meeting droned on. I was deciding between two pair of white shorts or one white and one navy when it all ended.

As we left the building it was decided to go over to The Old Port for a farewell lunch, but I begged off as I had a client meeting. I hugged everyone good-bye and hopped in Bode's truck for the quick ride back to my car.

"Z," said Bode then, looking into my eyes, "that was one of the nicest things Mom could have done. She showed not only that she loves us, but that she respects us and sees us as a working, functional couple. I don't say this often, but I love you, Z."

I must say this declaration left my head spinning.

"I'm sorry Bode, I'm not sure I understood all that," I apologized.

"Z, weren't you listening? The three of us were treated equally in the trust. But she left us—the two of us—the house. We've been taking care of it for almost four years, but the fact that she left it to you and me is so impressive. She treated you as part of the family. You *are* part of the family. Mom got it." Finished, Bode looked at me and smiled.

"Whoa!" I suddenly woke up. "What does that mean?"

Bode took my hands. "Nothing. It doesn't change anything. We'll still do exactly as we please, married or not, living together in that house or not. We will continue on exactly as we are until we decide to do otherwise. And we will do it together."

Wow! That seemed better than any marriage proposal on earth. I jumped over the console into his lap, and we laughed and hugged.

"'Life isn't how many breaths you take, it's the moments that take your breath away'," I said, throwing my head back. "Oh, what fun!" Maybe I should share that one with Charlie for her quotation project, I thought as I got out. Bode followed. We laughed some more, and I was off.

It was difficult to switch gears and re-enter my real life at the funeral home after that bit of excitement. As I walked in, Mr. Stanley was waiting for me. I was so wound up that I gave him a little hug; I fear he took it as a borderline assault. Mr. Stanley is very dignified, with clear boundaries. He's been at Bainbridge forever, working for my father and my grandfather before that. Mr. Stanley might not be the brains of the Bainbridge Funeral Home, but he certainly is the backbone.

Although his wiry, elderly body is not physically able to do as much as it used to, his temperament immediately soothes people, and his attention to detail is invaluable. I have always referred to him as Mr. Stanley, as did my father and grandfather. I think we all thought that the use of a first name for such a dignified and stately individual would be an indignity.

"Good morning, Miss G," he said, stepping back from my hug. "Mr. Johnson's sister will be here shortly. I feared you wouldn't have had lunch, so I have a nice egg salad sandwich for you downstairs. I heated up some chicken noodle soup as well."

"Mr. Stanley, that sounds just perfect. Thank you so much." I really cannot function if I miss a meal, and Mr. Stanley has an almost clairvoyant knack for feeding me when I need it.

We descended the small staircase to the left of the front door and entered the lower level. Having the embalming room down there may make it seem creepy to some, but the lower level fulfills other functions as well. Like right now. I smelled the heady aroma of soup emanating from the kitchen immediately and welcomed the wheat bread that accompanied it. The taste of the soup, I think, is only improved when one drags the crusty bread through what remains in the bowl at the end.

"Wasn't that a dreadful ending to Thistle's service yesterday?" asked Mr. Stanley rhetorically.

"It was," I responded. "I wasn't there for much of it, but the shock was awful. It's so nice we were able to send everyone off focused on Thistle rather than sidetracked by that mess. You did a wonderful job, Mr. Stanley."

"I must admit I didn't much like being around for it. Dead bodies are one thing, but mangled ones in that state I find unacceptable. I will leave you to your lunch and get ready for our guest."

I sat back and tried to wrap my brain around all that had happened in the past twenty-four hours. My head was spinning.

After consuming the delightful repast, I gave myself a few quiet moments to center myself for the task at hand. While I would not describe myself as a "friend" of Cam Johnson's, he was certainly a familiar acquaintance. I saw a great deal of him at The Old Port, but I was sure there was much more to him than that.

Being in Cam's company was always a pleasure. He had an upbeat, lively, and spirited personality. He owned a beautiful old wooden ketch that was the center of his universe. In the summer he lived aboard, sailing it every morning with almost no regard for the weather. Nights, after his shift, he could be heard strumming his guitar on the mooring, as content as is humanly possible, I think. He and the *Jolly Mon* shared life together. In the winter she was stored indoors, where Cam scraped, varnished, re-spliced her lines, and coddled her. The name *Jolly Mon* was in honor of the delightful Jimmy Buffet song and book. The two of them embodied the whimsical tale.

I smiled as I remembered him. Ascending the staircase again, I found Cam's sister waiting for me in my office. She was not what I had expected. Or, if I may, what I had hoped for.

She sat with her ankles crossed over sensible shoes. A cardigan sweater in a mousy brown topped a straight wool skirt in a similar shade. The stockings that enclosed her rather chubby legs were so opaque they were almost tights. And her face? Her lack of make-up made me look like a painted hussy, and her small turned-down lips were pressed together so tightly I wasn't sure they functioned. But unfortunately they did.

"Good afternoon, I'm Lizzie George. I'm so sorry for your loss. Cam was a wonderful addition to our community, and we all miss him."

"He was a bartender—one who did nothing but play music. Cam's was a meaningless life of decadence and frivolity. I fear he is damned."

That little monologue did me in.

CHAPTER
ELEVEN

I F THIS WAS Cam's sister 'doing her best,' heaven forbid running into her on a bad day. I didn't like her. Didn't like her at all. But of course that didn't deter her.

"I am Isabelle Johnson, Campbell's sister. Older sister. I live in northern Maine and am part of a community that lives with discipline. We refer to ourselves as Disciples of Discipline. Ours is a community that relies on one another, that reliance based on strict discipline. We live according to a few simple but steadfast rules. We know what is right, and we do right. Emotions are kept in check so as to not to cause unruly behavior. We are vegetarians, grow our own food, and have as little to do with the world outside our boundaries as possible. No alcohol, no music, no foolishness.

"Unfortunately, my brother and I had lost touch, but I received the message of his death yesterday. I understand that he has made arrangements with you for his disposal. However, I feel compelled to plan a service for him. Truth be told, though, I am not sure there is much in his life to commemorate."

My head was exploding. This creature and Cam had been created in the same womb? Chemically, it seemed impossible. Of course mine is not to judge, but...really? Before I could utter a word, she went on.

"If he has any friends that might be inclined to attend, perhaps you have a room here we could use. It seems diabolical to hold it in a house of worship—and I doubt this little burg has an appropriate one anyway.

"I'll lead this event. I will introduce myself, give a short family history, then read some verses from the Old Testament, perhaps from Hebrews: 'For the moment all discipline seems painful rather than pleasant, but later it yields the peaceful fruit of righteousness to those who have been trained by it.'

"I'll follow that with Revelation 3:19: 'Those who I love, I reprove and discipline, so be zealous and repent.'

"After that, there will be five minutes of silence to give people a chance to repent. That should be sufficient.

"Done."

No words sprang to mind because there were no words to adequately reply to this holy-roller nonsense. My brain was devoid of a response; it felt heavy and utterly empty.

Finally, I swallowed and found my voice. Or so I thought. I opened my mouth, but nothing came out.

I liked Cam way too much for this. I had a responsibility, and it was not to this insensitive creature awash with bogus religion sitting across from me. I wanted to send her back to whatever cave she had escaped from and cleanse Woodford Harbor of her presence, her poison mouth, her words, and her thoughts.

I collected myself.

"Perhaps this is not the place for you at this time, Miss Johnson." She couldn't possibly be married to someone, could she?

"I knew Cam, and I know that what you suggest would not be an accurate representation of who he was." Not accurate? Perhaps a borderline criminal misrepresentation, I thought to myself.

"I'm the person responsible for his funeral preparations, and I suggest you leave."

I stood up then and left the room, desperately looking for Mr. Stanley.

Bless his heart, he was right there in the hallway. Sputtering, I requested that he remove her. Faithful servant that he is, he nodded, nonplussed as always, and went in. I scurried down to the lower level in a less-than-adult fashion, running away from the confrontation. I knew I didn't have a rational bone in my body at this point, and it would be a lose/lose for everyone if I stayed behind.

I hid behind my desk until Mr. Stanley came down fifteen minutes later. As always, his dignity was intact, and there was no further discussion.

It occurred to me that as unpleasant as this encounter was, at least it left me time to join Uncle Henry.

"Mr. Stanley," I began, "I will probably be gone for the rest of the afternoon."

Just then there was a knock on the lower level's back door. Mr. Stanley was standing next to it. His eyebrow lifted quizzically. I nodded, and he opened it to reveal Bonnie. Giving a nervous little twitch, she said, "I wonder if I might give you this tennis ball to put in Ty's casket? We had this little thing, Ty and I. When I would have a really good lesson he would give me a special tennis ball. I would like to do this last little thing for him."

I have had odd requests from people in the past, but this one seemed a little out there. How close were they, I wondered.

"Of course, Bonnie," I said without hesitation. "I'll make sure it's in there."

With a short, final whimper she was gone, and I was alone with Mr. Stanley again.

"Actually, there have been three other women who have arrived with tennis balls," said Mr. Stanley. "And the body hasn't even been released yet."

"Oh my," was all I could muster.

"What do you think of this murder, Miss G?" he went on. "Ghastly, of course, but why would someone do such a thing? In broad daylight, in the middle of the cemetery? From what I can ascertain there are any number of people who might have considered such an act, but my goodness! To act on the urge seems rather barbaric."

"I agree with the 'rather barbaric' part," I told him. "I might actually crank it up a notch and consider it 'criminally insane!'"

"There is that," replied Mr. Stanley, and there his speculation ended. I wish I could rid myself of questions as easily. Indeed, why whack Ty with a shovel at the cemetery? Obviously he had provoked someone beyond the annoying stage. My own feelings about him had always been consistent: He was arrogant, lazy, and glibly smooth, and he always smelled vaguely of Coppertone. It gave him an endless summer kind of appeal—and I use the word 'appeal' loosely.

I couldn't get Aggie's speculations out of my mind. Bode's father, James, had always been very kind, quiet, and caring. He was actually the more nurturing of the two. Thistle was lively and fun but if something happened we always went to Bode's father. The two of them made a great team, balancing each other as parents and as a couple.

I soon found myself focusing on the differences between the three brothers. Bode was obviously the biggest and most athletic of the three and had followed a more physical vocation than the other two. All three were bright, but a doctor and a lawyer seemed more in keeping with James than his somewhat rebellious lobsterman son. Oh, stop with the generalizations, I told myself. It's not only a waste of time, but could prove counterproductive as well.

I found it ludicrous to even think of James as not being Bode's father. I tried to imagine how it made Bode feel, but couldn't. He's a strong, well-grounded guy, but this seemed really out there. To have this odd situation compounded by the discovery of Ty's body at Bode's mother's gravesite—well, it was just way over the top. It made me want to reach out and protect my love, eliminate the confusion as to his parentage, and find out who was responsible for the hideous act in the cemetery. The whole thing was, for lack of a better word, loony.

CHAPTER
TWELVE

I CALLED UNCLE HENRY'S office and caught him before he left for Ty's. We decided it was best to meet there as I only had an hour before I had to meet Bode at the nursing home.

It was a short drive to the Chillingsworth estate, which sits just over the town line. I think of it as "out of town," but that might be more a reflection of the house's persona than its physical boundaries.

Uncle Henry had contacted Dexter Welch, who was a caretaker of sorts for Arthur Chillingsworth and had a key to Ty's cottage. The Chillingsworths had already headed down to Captiva for the winter, and Dexter would soon follow, but at the moment he was still here finishing up some projects. He lived on the estate as well, on the second floor of the massive garage and stables.

The entire estate was constructed of beige stucco with white trim and black shutters. Matching slate roofs tied together the main house, the stables, and the gatehouse as a set. The landscaping gave the estate a certain dignity and cohesiveness and was a mix of regal old pine trees mixed with long established rhododendrons and azaleas, the whole connected by stately stone driveways. I headed for the gatehouse, which I always thought of as small. Up close, though, its diminished appearance was really just a matter scale; it was actually the size of an ample small house, and only appeared diminutive next to the massive main house. Its heavy, shiny black front door with brass knocker perfectly mimicked the main house's door.

Dexter greeted us with a shaky handshake at the entrance to the gatehouse. His face was decidedly pale.

"How could this have possibly happened?" he began. It was an obvious question, more rhetorical than literal. I was struck by the stricken look in his eyes.

"We were supposed to be driving down to Captiva next week," he continued. "I can't believe how things have changed so dramatically in just an instant."

Dexter, who worked for Arthur Chillingsworth year-round, had small apartments at both locations. A magnificent woodworker, he spent hours creating beautiful custom-made furniture at both estates. There were teams of gardeners at both properties, but it was Dexter who chose the plantings and was responsible for design. He had the talent, Chillingsworth had the money, and everyone was content.

Ty also spent his winters on Captiva, where he taught tennis at the local resort, and housing was also part of his deal. Both he and Dexter were accomplished tennis players, with an instinctual sense for placing the ball, and watching them compete was mesmerizing. With Ty being the more personable of the two, it made sense he was the teacher. Dexter was slighter in stature and almost withdrawn, but no less talented. It appeared they were travel companions as well.

Poor Dexter fumbled awkwardly with the key as he tried to unlock the heavy door. The situation seemed to have unglued him. Uncle Henry eventually took the key from him and swung the door open. I had an inkling of what I thought the inside of Ty's house would look like, and this did not disappoint. Neat, orderly, and clean would be understatements. Surgery could have been performed in his living room, and the kitchen was positively sterile. Nothing was out of place, not a stray shoe, sock, or magazine. It was as orderly as a showroom and twice as clean.

There was also a distinct lack of personal items. No half read book on the floor, and no family photos anywhere, just tennis trophies adorning the shelf space. But what was I expecting? Baby pictures of Bode?

I felt awkward and out of place. Dexter seemed to have recovered, though, and flopped down in an easy chair; I perched on the edge of the sofa. Although I had mentally been preparing myself to count the number of white sneakers in the closet, the reality of being in the newly deceased's living quarters made me feel uncomfortable. The only sound was Uncle Henry rummaging around in the bedroom.

Dexter and I sat in silence, but I kept gazing around the room, hoping to be of some assistance to Uncle Henry. I finally got up and wandered into the bedroom, where Uncle Henry was going through boxes on the closet floor. Under a shelf containing at least a dozen immaculate white polo shirts, folded like they were on display in Nordstrom's, sat rows of pristine white tennis sneakers. Uncle Henry stood up, a wooden box in his hands.

"Here, dear," he said. "Can you take this box? It was in the back, behind all the Adidas boxes."

I took it and opened it on the bed. Inside, we saw an 8"x10" black-and-white photo of a rock formation and a small box with a Ziplock bag of what appeared to be red sand.

"Hmmmmm," I heard Uncle Henry grumble. "Does that rock look familiar?"

"Let me see," I said, leaning forward. "Actually, it looks like that wall in Darling Park that we used to use as a backstop in softball when we were little. Now it would be behind the back wall of the Abenaki Tennis Club."

"But what's with the red sand?" speculated Uncle Henry. "It's so strange. Everything else in this place looks like it could be in a hotel room somewhere. So generic—and impersonal."

Uncle Henry picked up the box, and we went back to the living room. He did a cursory check of the other three rooms and seemed satisfied. Dexter sat immobile, staring at his shoes.

"How will I get to Florida now?" puzzled Dexter. The big picture seemed to be evading him. Shock takes different forms in different people, I knew. We prepared to leave, but Dexter was still frozen on the sofa. Uncle Henry cleared his throat and subtly nodded toward the front door. Dexter remained seated, so I gently put a hand on his shoulder to bring him back to reality.

He glanced up at me, took in Uncle Henry, and mumbled a few words while rising. "It's a real shock," I ventured.

"Yes. He was here yesterday, and we were planning our road trip. Now he's gone. How will I get to Florida?" he repeated.

We exited in a line, each with our own questions. I was sure Uncle Henry was immersed in the mystery of the photo and red powder. Dexter seemed obsessed with his Florida plans. And me? I was once again taken with the power of a life ending suddenly in midstream. Ty Waters had played his last set.

CHAPTER

THIRTEEN

W E EACH HEADED in our own direction. Uncle Henry departed for the station to research the red sand and photo.
Dexter stumbled back to his place, and I steered my Jeep toward
Bode's to join him for the trip to Woodford Pines. My mind was
churning on the short ride over. I felt like I had lived a week today,
and it was only three o'clock.

Bode was outside the back door, standing uncharacteristically
still. I wondered if he was remembering standing in that very spot
as a little boy, his parents getting ready to drive him somewhere. I
ached for him and again thanked my lucky stars that my parents
were still with me.

Bode looked up at the sound of my wheels on the gravel, and
his eyes brightened when he saw me.

"Want me to drive?" I offered.

"We probably should take my truck. I'm not sure how much
we'll be bringing back."

I agreed, and basked in a nice warm hug.

"I'm really not sure what we should bring back," said Bode. "Most of her things are here at the house. Bill and Jonny took what they wanted from the house, and they were at Woodford Pines early this morning to take what they wanted from there. None of us is in a situation where we want or need furniture or household goods. It's just the few sentimental things that strike a chord. They left me with the bulk of it: the photo albums, the clothes, the old dishes, and pots and pans. I haven't a clue how to deal with that."

"Don't worry, Bode," I reassured him, "we have plenty of time to think about it, and Woodford Pines will be very helpful. There are a number of charities they donate to and they also know people who resell items or use them directly. It's reassuring to know that clothing and possessions that your mother used and enjoyed will once again be in the hands of people who will appreciate them. Just take it all a step at a time."

We parked and walked toward the front entrance. I must admit it was sad knowing we were not going in for a visit. There would be no fun chat with Thistle, no game of cards, and no drinking wine we'd smuggled in. We were here together, but she would not be joining us. I knew Bode shared the same thoughts.

We put one foot in front of the other and entered the building. But only because we had no alternative.

The lovely receptionist left her desk and gave each of us a hug. We started down the hall to Thistle's room when it suddenly occurred to me that maybe we should stop in and see her dear friend, Gus Beethoven. Both he and Thistle's friend Aggie lived here, but I had noticed that Gus wasn't at the service yesterday. After his wife Emma passed away, Gus had moved to Woodford Pines; it wasn't much after that that Thistle moved in to rehab from her broken hip and never left. Aggie had been here for sometime as her husband Robert had succumbed to cancer years before.

I recalled again the four couples who had formed a group back in the day. Gus and Emma, Gloria and Arthur Chillingsworth, Aggie and her Robert, and Thistle and James. Arthur Chillingsworth was the king of the hill at the Abenaki Tennis Club, where they all played, and his large sailing yacht down south was their base on Captiva. It seemed borderline incestuous to me, but what do I know? There were just too many intertwined relationships for my simple mind.

Aggie and Thistle had been best friends growing up in Woodford Harbor, and when they married they brought their husbands home with them. While in Hanover, Thistle and James had convinced Gus and Emma to join them in the wonderful little town, and Arthur Chillingsworth, I have always assumed, found the harbor to his liking.

Thistle referred to Gus as Augustus. It had the most wonderful sound on her lips and indeed he was a gentle, wonderful man. We knocked softly on his door and were welcomed by a tall, stately, grey-haired man in fresh khakis, a starched shirt, worn cardigan, and the ubiquitous old man slippers. He had been an esteemed lawyer and retained his charisma even now. But behind his soft exterior was a hard-nosed lawyer respected for his diligent work and brilliant intellect. Many a high-profile case had featured Gus at the helm. His smile was gentle as he opened his arms to me. He felt big boned and soft in a worn kind of way. He turned and embraced Bode similarly.

"Come in, come in, you two," said Gus. "Sit down anywhere." Newspapers and old books were scattered on various surfaces about the room, but two worn tapestry-upholstered chairs were available. He settled down on his desk chair, and we all sat in companionable silence for a moment.

"I'm sorry I couldn't make the service yesterday. Thistle's passing has been a real blow to me. Emma and I had a wonderful marriage and lived a long and blessed life together. We raised three extraordinary children and when she died I felt I had, too.

"Then Thistle showed up here. What a delightful, loving, wonderful woman she was. When she walked into a room the lights got brighter, and her energy was contagious. She reopened a place in my heart I had feared was closed forever.

"I think everyone has always been a little bit in love with Thistle.

And, oh my, didn't she enjoy it! That rascal could flit from person to person in a room and leave each and every one with a lighter heart. Yes, I loved Thistle, and I miss her so.

"Does it seem wrong that I couldn't bear to say good bye to her in the company of others yesterday? Forgive me, but I just couldn't do it. At my age, I tire more easily than I used to and the thought of sharing my grief in public was too much for me.

"Bode, you are so lucky to have had such a mother. She loved both you and Lizzie so much. And what fun it was to find those little wine bottles you would sneak in to her. That was her! Break the rules, but leave everyone a little happier."

"You're so kind Gus," I began.

But he was having none of being interrupted while he went back in time. "Emma and I were in Hanover with your parents before they were married. We were married and had a little house, so when your father wasn't studying they spent a lot of time at our place. What a gay group we were. Robert was getting an MBA, and Aggie started having kids before any of the rest of us. We added Gloria and Arthur Chillingsworth to the group when we all ended up in Woodford Harbor. We were still so innocent and enjoying all life had to offer.

"And now, Bode, Aggie tells me what she let slip the other night. As an adult, I hope that you can understand that whatever may have happened was a long, long time ago. We were all having a grand old time, and your mother really was the supreme flirt. No one escaped her. That she was perhaps infatuated with that young, foolish tennis instructor is not the greatest travesty ever. But I don't believe for one minute that she ever would have committed any wrongdoing with him. She was just so playful—and people love to talk. It didn't help, I suppose, that you were born a bit before nine months after their wedding. Believe me, there is no greater evidence of the lifetime love Thistle and James shared than you.

"That Ty was just a twit and ever so annoying; he never left us alone. A pesky mosquito at best. Troublemaker would not be a stretch. He moved to Woodford Harbor and held court at that tennis club of Arthur's, and then, to make matters worse, he showed up on Captiva. How I wished that he would just disappear—and now, I understand, he has met his demise. None too early in my book.

"Bode, I knew your parents their entire married life. There was such great love between them, and their devotion to you three boys was extraordinary. I miss them both. I was lucky to see so much of your mother for the past five years.

"Now you two go on, and stop listening to the ramblings of a tired, heartbroken man. I sure would like it, though, if you could see your way clear to smuggling some of those little bottles of wine into my room sometimes!"

We bid him a heartfelt, but swift, good-bye and were off down the hall to Thistle's room. As we entered, I was relieved to see that the one item I had my eye on was still there-a small ornate frame that was one of Thistle's prize possessions. It held a handwritten copy of "Amazing Grace," done by Thistle's grandmother during the Civil War. The John Newton lines endure still.

> Amazing Grace, How sweet the sound
> That saved a wretch like me
> I once was lost, but now am found
> Twas blind but now I see

I am always struck by the timelessness of these words and this piece brings that home like nothing else.

Bode opened Thistle's bedside stand and retrieved her favorite set of playing cards and a small photo of his parents smiling happily at the camera at some northern fishing camp. He slowly picked up her reading glasses. At that moment, Thistle's elegant Chelsea clock chimed seven times. Ship's clocks are used to mark half-hour increments for every four-hour watch on old sailing ships. At 8:00, 12:00, 4:00, and again at 8:00, there are eight chimes, or bells. The next half hour is one chime, until the time runs through the four-hour cycle to eight bells. These soft bells are a unique nautical measure of time.

"Bill and Jonny obviously left that for you," I said softly. "You and your mom shared Woodford Harbor and its ships and all they stand for."

As Bode lifted the clock into his hands, he asked me if there was anything else I wanted.

I stood quietly for a moment and looked over the assorted items hanging in the closet and folded on the shelves. And then I saw it. I smiled and lifted out her blue chambray gardening shirt.

"How about I carry on the tradition of this great old gardening shirt?"

That was it for him. Finally, his tears came. We held each other for what seemed like a long time. Finally we split apart and sank down on the edge of the bed.

"Tell me when you're ready, Bode."

After a bit, he put his hand on my knee and we left the familiar scent of Thistle's vanilla behind us.

FOURTEEEN

WE WERE BOTH on automatic pilot for the short drive back to Bode's. I offered to come in and help pick up the house after his guests' departures, but he assured me that Beth and Spicy had loaded the dishwasher and changed and remade all the beds before they left. Again, I reflected on the blessings of a functional family, all looking out for each other.

"I can't describe how tired I am," said Bode. "I understand that life goes on, but just how that's going to happen is beyond me right now."

"I can't imagine how you feel. I'm dog tired myself, but we have to eat. Why don't you take some time here, then order a pizza and come over? Charlie should be home from soccer practice, and I think this is one of those nights when politically correct foods be damned—let's eat pizza! And lots of it! Washed down with all the beer and wine our bodies will tolerate."

Bode gave me a weak smile, but at least it was a smile.

"See you about six," he replied.

I was soon off in my Jeep, but even depressing the accelerator seemed to require effort. Once home, I parked, then dragged my-self up the railroad-tie steps and through the front door. I could hear country music emanating from the third floor and had a sudden burst of energy when I contemplated seeing Charlie. How can a mop of curly hair surrounded by piles of clothes, hairbrushes, and scattered papers seem so exciting? When I reached the top of the steps and called out over Blake Shelton, I was rewarded with a smile that made it all worthwhile.

"Hi, Mom! Soccer was so much fun! I played goalie for a half! I have never even played defense, but I loved it! You just throw yourself in front of that ball and go for it!"

"Do you ever consider the three years of orthodontia we went through?"

She sent me a blank stare, followed by, "What's for dinner?"

"Pizza. Bode's picking it up."

"Will he get mushroom, cheese, and bacon?"

"Yes, Charlie. He knows just what we like. When he walks into the Woodford Harbor House of Pizza they already know his order."

"Oh, good. I love you, Mom."

I don't know where that came from, but the spontaneity was unquestionably marvelous. It's amazing how life gives you anti-dotes for grief at the most unexpected times.

I went down a level and replaced my good clothes with periwin-kle sweatpants and a long-sleeved Captiva tee shirt from Jensen's Marina. Combined with the endearment I'd just received, it picked my spirits up considerably.

I unloaded the dishwasher, uncorked a nice bottle of red wine, set napkins and plates out on the coffee table, added two little candles, and felt the mood was perfect for eating too much pizza. I puttered around doing whatever one does with the half hour in the kitchen before someone arrives, then turned and saw Bob's massive head leading the way through the door. I'm pretty sure he smiles when he sees me. Could be me, or maybe the dog biscuits I keep for him on the counter. His gentle mouth accepted several, then he plopped down right in front of the refrigerator, making it impossible to open.

Bode entered with two large, slightly greasy square boxes and put them in the warm oven I had waiting. A whack on the butt and a quick peck on the cheek, and our evening had begun. Well, not quite. First Bode had to get Bob away from the refrigerator so he could grab himself a cold beer.

"A bottle of wine tonight?" he asked then, suddenly noticing the bottle of merlot on the table. "It's not a box! What's the occasion?"

I usually drink my wine from a cardboard box. It tastes great, is made at a very good vineyard, and is packed in a vacuum bag so it doesn't go bad. Makes all those incriminating wine bottles disappear from the trash as well. Best of all, though, you really can't measure how much you're consuming because it's all hidden behind cardboard.

"I just feel like we deserve to do everything we can to get through all this. You have been a champ, Bode. Your house was descended on for four days, you arranged all the meals, and you organized the service. It's time to just take a breath and really relax."

"You're a good one, Z. So where's Li'l Chuck?" he asked, referring to Charlie.

"I'm sure she will be down the minute she gets a whiff of that pizza!"

Bode popped the bottle cap off his beer and poured me a generous glass of the divine red liquid. We toasted, then stood sipping our preferred beverages. Actually his was more than a sip, and perhaps mine was, too. The moment stood as a testament to our return to a normal life, and we both sucked it up.

We heard, before we saw, Charlie's entrance. Her stocking feet were rather heavy on the stairs coming down. She's not a big girl, but neither is she a delicate flower. Thank goodness for that. She whooshed into the room with arms swinging, her perpetual monologue flowing.

"Hey, you guys! That pizza smells unbelievable! You know, I don't think we have it nearly enough. Cheese, tomato, mushrooms, a bit of pork; plenty of dairy and veggies—two important food groups. With a pop of protein. Milk tastes pretty asgusting (her version of disgusting since she was little), so maybe a Diet Coke wouldn't kill me? How 'ya doing, Bode? You sure have a lot of relatives. They're gone? Just us?"

We waited while Charlie poured her Diet Coke over ice, then clinked the glasses together for our customary toast. It's interesting how each person in a group fills their unique spot. Our assemblage wouldn't be complete without Bode, and it wouldn't be complete without Charlie. And I like to think it would be lacking without me.

"You know, Bode, I really am sorry about your mother. It seems pretty bad to have your mother die," offered Charlie.

Pretty bad? Where were devastating, heart wrenching, and tragic? I thought.

"But you're lucky you have your brothers. That helps, right?"

"Well, it certainly is nice to have them. But they don't make up for not having my mom here. Not at all. We have memories of growing up together and are feeling similar grief, but our lives have turned out pretty differently. Jonny's out in Washington practicing medicine, Bill's in Boston being a big-time lawyer, and here I am. Having lived in Boston and worked in an investment firm, I know I can do the work. But it wasn't the life I wanted. I always had a different focus than they did. I love being on the water and using my body as well as my mind. I think they were more driven mentally, and were never really athletes. Sportsmen maybe, but not heavy lifting."

"I know!" added Charlie. "You don't even look like them as much as they look like each other! Isn't that funny?"

Just hysterical. Oh, dear.

"Let's talk about something other than my mother. Or my childhood. Or anything to do with the old days. Enough. Have the police found poor Ollie? They were ubiquitous around town this morning, but they seem to have disappeared already. Not as tenacious as they are on TV."

"Maybe they think he's left town by now," I said, having no idea what they thought.

A silence started to envelope the room, so I asked Charlie about her soccer practice. This, of course, brought on a breathless, one-sentence stream of consciousness description of playing goalie vs. forward for a good ten minutes. When that topic was exhausted I asked about her quotation project.

"The quotation is supposed to deal with family," she replied. "Your Abraham Lincoln one is very good, but I found some others online. I read some writings from Buddha, and I really liked this one: 'Family is not about blood. It's about who is willing to hold your hand when you need it most.'"

With that, we all got up, had a spontaneous group hug, and headed to the kitchen for pizza. I felt a contentment I hadn't thought possible when the day began.

CHAPTER
FIFTEEN

B ODE GRABBED ANOTHER beer, I refilled my wine glass, and Charlie brought in the pizza. Bob was a bit too interested in the boxes to relegate them to the floor after we had served ourselves, so we set them on a bar stool.

Those first glorious minutes that begin a meal, filled with lots of munching and very little chitchat, are wonderful. Contented silence filled the room. I finished my entire first slice without a murmur. When I sat back to wipe my fingers, I realized I had not shared an important part of my day with these two.

"I went over to Ty's gatehouse with Uncle Henry this morning. What a place! It's really an elegant mini-mansion, with everything reduced in scale. The stone fireplace goes the height of the room, and the stones defining it—though only half the size of the boulders used in the mansion—give it the same magnificent look. The trim is all polished mahogany with built-in shelves and drawers everywhere. And of course Ty didn't have a thing out of place. I didn't look, but I'm sure his socks were organized by color. There was nothing personal around the room anywhere. Not a photo to be seen, although he did have his tennis trophies prominently displayed.

"Uncle Henry found an interesting little box on his closet floor. It had a black-and-white photo of a rock formation, and a Ziplock baggie that contained some kind of red dust or sand. I'm not certain where the photo was taken, but it kind of looked like the rock formation around Darling Park. Uncle Henry is sending the red material out to be tested."

Bode suddenly leaned forward with excitement. "I bet I know what it is! I remember Joey, the old lobsterman, talking about the Red Paint People who colonized Maine 2,000 to 6,000 years ago. Think about that!

"They lived off the land and, of course, the sea. Stone and bone tools have been discovered, along with spears they may have used to kill swordfish from rudimentary boats. No pottery or metal tools have turned up, though.

"Their gravesites were the first clue of their existence. They apparently spread red ochre over the bodies and goods they buried as a sign of honor. It could be that those red particles in the baggie Henry found are really ochre.

"I wonder if the black-and-white photo was taken at a burial site where the ochre was found," Bode continued. "What did the rock formation look like again?"

"Well," I replied, "it actually looks like the long wall with the two little indentations right by Darling Park. Remember the wall we used as a backstop when we played softball? It's right by the Abenaki Tennis Club."

"Imagine people walking along our very shores 2,000 years ago! Now *that* is mind boggling," Charlie speculated. "It must have been hard in the cold winter. I wonder what their boats looked like? Maybe I could do a research paper on them someday."

"Good idea, Li'l Chuck. I'll help out however I can when the time comes," offered Bode. "I love local history like that."

The conversation lulled as the pizza was slowly devoured.

"So who do you think killed Ty Waters?" piped up Charlie, looking over at me.

In a way I wished she would stop obsessing over it, but then, admittedly, it was an unusual event.

"It seems like a slew of bad feelings are being stirred up about Ty. He wasn't someone to whom I gave a lot of thought or attention, but there are a lot of folks in town who didn't much care for him. Believe it or not, there are actually women coming to the funeral home with tennis balls they want to have put in his casket. Even Bonnie at The Driftwood was bemoaning his death.

"He always had a flock of folks around him at The Old Port, although I can't imagine any of them inviting him for Thanksgiving. He appeared so superficial. But it seems a bit extreme to want him dead—and to want it so badly you would wallop him with a shovel. It's likely someone from town, though, which means it's someone we probably know. That is the awful part.

"I'm going to have to meet with Ollie and Alice at some point, after Ollie is back," I went on. "I don't believe for one minute Ollie is capable of doing Ty any harm, but it will be interesting to see how his twin brother feels about dealing with his remains and funeral. Poor Ollie, how unfortunate it must have been to have Ty as your twin brother. Alice, though, is a trooper. She seems to be the large-and-in-charge one of the two."

"I know," added Charlie. "Whenever you see them he always has kind of a hang dog look, with his too-long hair hanging around his downcast face. And he always looks tired. But she and her little fire hydrant body just blast forward, daring anyone to get in her way!"

"Where did that come from Charlie? I didn't know you were such an observer of mankind," I said.

"Guess that apple didn't fall far from the tree," laughed Bode. "Little girl has been hearing such talk her entire life.

"But really," he went on, "I don't trust any guy who blow dries his hair and wears immaculate starched shirts and pristine white sneakers day in and day out."

"Now, now," I teased, "don't be so judgmental. My new mantra, when I occasionally find myself being overly critical, is to give people the benefit of the doubt and try to believe they are 'doing their best.' Maybe Ty *was* doing his best!"

"Oh, Mom," groaned Charlie, "is this the sequel to the *One-Step Guide to Overall Improvement?* I thought you were just going to be nicer to people? Now you're adding another step?"

"Z, you just have that nasty little streak of cutting to the chase four seconds after you meet someone. It's in your DNA!" added Bode.

"Oh, no," howled Charlie. "Could this really happen to me? Am I going to suddenly be snarky every time I see Miss Gordon in science because she's such a stiff? Or will I suddenly be filled with the milk of human kindness and cut her some slack for 'doing her best'?"

The intimate, lighthearted laughter felt wonderful.

"What is the subject for your quotation tomorrow, Charlie?" I asked.

"Death."

"Well, in my business I've seen a lot of it. One of my favorite quotations is the Bertolt Brecht, 'Do not fear death so much, but rather the inadequate life.'"

"That seems a bit much to me," said Charlie.

"How about George Burns?" I replied. "He said 'If you live to be one hundred, you've got it made. Very few people die past that age.'"

"I think right now the quotation that comes to my mind is Cicero's, 'The life of the dead is placed in the memory of the living'," said Bode quietly.

Charlie came over and sat on the other side of Bode, and the three of us remained that way for some time.

CHAPTER
SIXTEEN

I KNEW SOMETHING WAS wrong the moment my head cleared the next morning. Two things, actually. I felt woozy from a bit too much wine—and the other side of the bed was empty.

My fourth glass of wine the previous evening had obviously taken a toll. And the empty bed? I suddenly remembered that Bode had gone back to his own house last night. All the events of the past week had left him wanting peace and quiet in his family home.

I closed my eyes against the coming day until I heard the shower running in Charlie's bathroom. Since she is not one to rise any earlier than necessary, I knew I had better get moving.

I arose slowly from bed and padded to the bathroom, where I took the act of brushing my teeth as a start to my recovery. I fought the urge to put on jeans and a sweatshirt, instead pulling on washable, but presentable, black pants and a white permanent press shirt. The nip in the early morning air necessitated a light sweater vest for warmth.

Charlie was downstairs before me. She gave me a suspicious

look, but said nothing. It wasn't exactly a prize parenting moment knowing your daughter was cutting you some slack for overindulging, but we made it to the car and pulled out on time.

As we drove past Redmond Island, Charlie spoke up. "The quotation assignment for tomorrow is about friendship. I was Googling it and found a nice one: 'No man is an island, entire of itself; every man is a piece of the continent.' John Donne wrote that over four hundred years ago."

"That's nice Charlie." My sudden surge of pride pulled together all the loose wires in my head. "Very nice."

As we drove the lovely route to the high school my mind was focused on Redmond Island. At times I worried that Charlie wasn't even aware the island was there; that she took for granted all the beauty around her. Today she had proven me blessedly wrong.

My mind wandered to connections on land and with the human spirit—then back to the land. The separation between the mainland and Redmond Island was indeed tenuous. At low tide it was an easy walk to the island, and yet not everyone was aware of this. I doubted the state police who had been searching so diligently for Ollie were aware. No, almost certainly not. I suddenly had a wonderful idea. I needed to cogitate on it for a bit, but already it was rapidly percolating in my brain.

Charlie brought me back to the present. "I have a soccer dinner after practice tonight," she said. "I'll get a ride home." Arriving at the high school, we exchanged farewell smiles and a quick hug.

The next step in my day was to give my body some protein, so I headed for The Driftwood. Going in there almost felt like putting on a pair of old slippers; you know that comfort is coming.

Carly was at the front table waiting on none other than Daniel Dunkirk. I blocked the knee-jerk thought that came to me of what a skinny little brittle-boned numb-nut he is and merely nodded. Luckily, Carly was the perfect antidote. Her cheerful smile worked its magic, and I was happy as a monkey in a banana factory when I sat down at a nearby table for two.

Carly and her brother Tommy had inherited The Driftwood

and ran it just as it had been run for decades. The red-and-white-checked tablecloths, black metal chairs, and uneven floor were unchanged. Carly's daughters worked there now, so I could only hope that in the future that Charlie and her kids would enjoy these wonderful times as well. Oh, stop! I thought. You're not even forty, and you're already going down memory lane.

I pulled myself back to the present and now faced the daily challenge of deciding what to have for breakfast. I used to have a half order of blueberry French toast every morning, but as I neared that awful birthday that loomed before me I had changed to my single-egg omelet with cheese and salsa. Neither held much appeal this morning, so I decided on poached eggs on wheat toast. Hopefully they would settle the turmoil within me. Carly took my order, and I settled in to wait.

Suddenly, a loud voice boomed into the restaurant from the pass-through to the kitchen. "Hey, Lizzie! What's with the poached eggs? What have you been up to?" It was Tommy, who rules the kitchen. Nothing gets by him. I was less than thrilled to have last evening's overindulgence made public, but Tommy is not one to be silenced.

"Thanks, Tommy," I replied. "Yup, help me here."

Just then the front door opened. In walked Bode. Our smiles met in mutual delight, and he joined me.

"How are you doing?"

"Oh, I'll be fine. It all just takes some getting used to," said Bode. "Has Charlie hit quotations on change yet? 'Nothing endures but change?' 'The more things change, the more they stay the same?' Some of that stuff drives me nuts—or maybe I'm just a bit fragile this morning."

"Whatever. What are you up to today?" I said, moving on.

"I have some parts to order for the boat, and I think maybe I'll take Bob for a walk down on the beach. I'm still not ready to head out and haul traps. How about you?"

"If I have a minute I'm going to go down to the Woodford Reporter office to see Pepper. I can't get that photo of the rock formation out of my mind. It looks so much like the one by Darling Park. Maybe she'll remember if there was any controversy surrounding the tennis club when it was built. She could probably look it up in an old issue."

"She's a walking encyclopedia of knowledge. If anyone knows, she will," said Bode.

"I have some paperwork I have to get out of the way, and then I'm going to head down to The Old Port at lunchtime to see if I can find some of Cam's buddies. They might have some ideas for his service. That sister of his was so bad." I decided not to expound on the subject. It would be beating a dead horse to re-enact that miserable scene.

"And I guess I'll also stay tuned to receive more tennis balls."

Bode ordered his breakfast, and Carly reminded us of the big concert The Driftwood was hosting the next night at Darling Park. The working pier that the lobstermen use is not town-owned, but rather the responsibility of the lobstermen themselves. Recently, a storm had inflicted damage on some of the rotted pilings, and the expense for the repair was pretty steep. The Driftwood had stepped in and decided to host a benefit concert with Livingston Taylor to help defray the cost. It appeared the entire town was coming—but then again it's not often we have a celebrity come to town.

"Jennie is balking at making the introduction tomorrow night," said Carly, nodding Jennie's way.

"Just because I know Livingston Taylor doesn't mean I can stand up and introduce him to all those people! It's not what I do!" protested poor Jennie.

"Oh, come on," I said with some humor. "You've never backed down from anything in your whole life! And you know him. You're just talking about an old friend. What do you remember about him?"

"Ha," said Jennie, with a smile. "He and his brothers and sisters, Alex, Kate, Hugh and James were always singing together. My mother told me that she sat next to their mother, Trudy, at one school concert. The five of them had just sung together, and

Trudy turned to my mother and said 'They're really quite good, aren't they?'"

"That's perfect, Jennie, go for it!" I encouraged her. She looked less than convinced, but seemed more ready to take it on now.

"You guys are welcome to come back here after the concert. Our little rock star has invited Livingston here for a post-party get-together," said Carly.

"Ha! Great! Count us in!" I instantly replied.

Our breakfast arrived and I dove in, hoping for relief. The day was moving forward, and I was having a little difficulty keeping up with it.

CHAPTER
SEVENTEEN

BODE AND I left the comfort of The Driftwood and stepped out into a sunny, crisp fall day. We walked to the railing at the town landing and quietly soaked in some of the sun's warmth; before the long, winter would settle in. I think I appreciate the sun most in these later months because I know it won't be around much longer. Neither would the boats, which were already being taken from the water and transported to winter storage; it's always a sad sign for me. Although not a big fan of the heat and humidity of summer, I am always happy when there is an opportunity to be out on the water.

The brilliant idea that had come to me as I took Charlie to school was starting to lose some of its original aura, but I decided to offer it up for Bode's judgment.

"I had a peculiar thought as I drove by Redmond Island this morning," I began. "I've been feeling terrible for poor Ollie, and worrying about where he is. I'm sure he's fine and has easily out-smarted the state police by virtue of having home field advantage, but it looks worse and worse for him the longer he remains on the loose. It occurred to me that he may have scurried out to the island at just the right tide and is hiding out there. Redmond Island is only accessible by foot at low tide, something only a local like Ollie would know. The police wouldn't know enough to even look there.

"It's low tide now. Want to take a walk?"

Bode turned to me with a smile. "That sounds like a great idea! We don't walk out there nearly as much as we should. Quite honestly, I haven't had the extra energy to be concerned with Ollie, but if it gets us out to that beautiful spot I'm all for it!"

His truck was right behind us, so we immediately jumped in and were off.

Redmond Island is a beautiful outcropping of land about a hundred yards offshore. I always think of it as a perfect microcosm of New England: There's a sandy beach, a grassy field, a rocky ledge, and a pine forest, all in scale to fit on its five acres. Someone even hung a boat bumper from a tree with heavy rope to create a small swing. It is a living jigsaw puzzle.

We parked along the road and walked out to the path to the island that is exposed only at low tide. I could tell this entire outing had lifted Bode's spirits, and I was enjoying the salt air and sunshine myself. We arrived at the beach, walked over the muddy flats, hiked across the field, and started climbing up the rocky lookout that plunges thirty feet into the sea on the other side. It was exhilarating just to feel its minimalist majesty. Bode's arm around my shoulder made the moment sublime.

Finally breaking apart, we started hopping rock to rock to the western shore, where there was a mini forest of pine trees. A rugged little path took us through the trees and back onto the beach. Luckily Bode was in the lead, because if I had come across Ollie first I might have had a heart attack. Quite honestly, I was enjoying the adventure so much I had totally forgotten our original purpose. But there he was, crouching under a tall pine.

I squelched my initial instinct to say, "Dr. Livingston, I presume?"—but I would have liked to.

Bode spoke first. "Hi, Ollie. Are you all right?"

Ollie's frightened eyes held the answer. He was scared to death and hungry, but healthy and in need of a shower.

"It's okay, Ollie," I eventually got out. "Everyone is so worried about you. I'm sure if you just come back with us Uncle Henry can straighten this whole thing out. We know you would never do something like that. We do."

Ollie's eyes filled with tears, and he quietly stammered, "Really, I don't hate Ty the way people seem to think I do. He's not always kind to me, but I understand him and know why he does what he does and says what he says. I have the same feelings he does, I just act on them differently. I feel terrible and very, very sad that Ty is gone. He was my brother—my twin brother.

"Alice so often speaks for me that people assume everything she says and feels are *my* thoughts and feelings. She does—did— dislike Ty. She may even have hated him. It doesn't matter. But that people think I could do such a thing is just..."

"It's all right, Ollie. It really is. People don't think you did any- thing of the kind. It's important that you come back and explain it.

"We'll help you get to Uncle Henry, and he'll stay with you until the state police come. He'll protect you as best he can—and he can be a pretty ferocious bull dog when it comes to protection." A little humor can go a long way in alleviating fear.

Ollie sighed, wiped his nose, and, with Bode's help, stood up. Together we trudged back down the path and began our trip across the broken clam shells and rocks to land. Squeezing into the truck cab together was less than pleasant, but knowing how uncomfort- able Ollie was put my discomfort into perspective.

We parked at the Town House and walked together into Uncle Henry's office. I knew Ollie was in good hands the moment I saw Uncle Henry pop into gear. There was no anger or suspicion and no accusations. He gave Ollie a glass of water and offered him the sta- tion bathroom. We explained where we had found him, and Uncle Henry touched my arm as a gesture of thanks. This is equivalent to a bone crushing bear hug from most people. I was pleased for myself, and for Ollie as well.

While he was out of the room, I quickly told Uncle Henry about Bode's recounting of the Red Paint People.

"You know, now that you mention it, that does ring a bell. I didn't connect it to the red substance we found in Ty's box, but it's an interesting theory. I've sent the bag into Portland for analysis, which usually takes a week or so. I'll let you know when I hear. Thanks, kids, for everything."

Ollie reappeared looking considerably better. We reassured him again, then escaped back into the dazzling sunshine. Bode drove me to The Driftwood, where I picked up my car.

"Wish me luck. I'm on my way to a Pepper encounter," I teased. "I'll let you know how it goes. By the way, Charlie has a soccer dinner tonight. Should we hit The Old Port?"

"Great idea," was his perfect response.

CHAPTER

EIGHTEEN

I MADE THE EASY walk from the Town House to the *Woodford Reporter* office. Pepper's desk was the first thing you saw upon entering, so it was best to prepare yourself for the encounter before opening the door. I collected myself and pushed the door open. Pepper was unusually silent, probably because she was glued to her computer monitor. Her raised index finger spoke volumes about not interrupting her and being patient. I wasn't offended.

I was reasonably certain she wasn't fixed on an important news flash, but rather in the middle of an online cribbage game. When she finally did deign to address me, it was with a disapproving look.

"Good morning, Pepper," I began. And then I realized I had a news tip, having just come from Uncle Henry's office. "I have a deal. I have some breaking news that I can share with you right now, but I need some research done."

Deals didn't sit well with Pepper. She looked at me calmly and said, "Just give me the news, dearie."

Obediently, I related that Ollie had been discovered on

Redmond Island and was being escorted to the state police offices in Portland. I didn't mention my own involvement in the story.

Pepper perked right up and was about to call Uncle Henry's cell phone, one of the perks of living in a small town where everyone knew everyone's personal numbers, when she caught herself short and asked me what information I needed.

I spoke quickly as I knew I had a limited amount of time. "Do you remember if there was any controversy when the Abenaki Tennis Club was built? There are some strange things going on, and I'm wondering if you remember anything unusual. If not, perhaps you could look it up. I think it was about ten years ago."

"Sure, sure, dearie," she said dismissively, madly dialing her cell phone.

As I was closing the door behind me, I heard her accosting poor Uncle Henry on the phone. I'm sure he was not pleased with me.

I started the Jeep and drove straight to Bainbridge Funeral Home. How many times have I driven that route? And how many more times I will do it? Way too many to contemplate. Following my usual routine, I greeted Mr. Stanley, who was busy arranging fresh flowers in the entryway.

"Those are lovely, Mr. Stanley," I said. "Did I miss anything this morning?" I decided not to mention my dramatic rescue earlier.

"Not much—unless you count the four additional women who came in with tennis balls. Two of them overlapped, and it was quite awkward."

"They don't cover these situations in mortuary school," I replied with a wink.

"I'm going to work on some billing and then head over to The Old Port for lunch."

"That's a bit rare," he said. "You're usually a dinner person there."

"Believe me, I'm not going for a Bloody Mary. I want to chat with the folks there and get some ideas for Cam's service. I imagine those he served and spent time with know him best. I'm a bit apprehensive, but I'm sure it'll be fine. Girl's gotta do what a girl's gotta do."

I received a less than approving look, but must admit it was fun to have a good time with Mr. Stanley every once in awhile.

I took my tarty little self down to my office and dutifully went through the bills. Before I knew it, I was good and ready for my 'wild and crazy' lunch.

CHAPTER

NINETEEN

I MADE THE QUICK walk to The Old Port feeling almost intoxicated by the sunshine. The trees were turning glorious shades of yellow, orange, and rust. The air was crisp and the sky azure. But with this came unpleasant thoughts of what was to come. I want to tell myself to just enjoy the day, but thoughts of the looming winter invariably color my mood.

Trying to give my attitude a mental 'slap upside the head', I breathed in the last of the fresh air and opened the heavy door that marked the entrance to The Old Port. The portal in the entryway might seem cheesy in some honky-tonk town, but here in Woodford Harbor it rang of authenticity.

Part of the charm of this place is that when you enter you don't know if it is night or day, summer or winter. It has an identity independent of the world outside. For starters, it's dark, with a unique scent of stale beer, cigarettes, and old grease from the fryolator. That, and the waxed mahogany bar and mix of bar stools and tables, give it an ambiance that *is* The Old Port. As unnatural or perverted as it might seem to revel in this atmosphere rather than the glorious outdoors, I had known The Old Port my entire life, and I loved it.

As my eyes adjusted to the dark, I spotted a group of six gathered in front of the beer taps. A solitary figure was hunched over at the far end of the bar. I looked closer and recognized it as Dexter. My compassionate side kicked in, and I approached him to see how he was doing. He had obviously been there awhile and was a bit the worse for wear.

"How are you doing, Dexter?"

He turned to me with the eyes of a sad bloodhound. "Oh, Lizzie, I don't know. I just can't believe that Ty was here yesterday and that today he's gone. Like really gone. I'll never see him again. Seems so unfair. He was just the best guy." It was refreshing to see someone genuinely upset by his death. I guess you never know about relationships.

"I'm so sorry, Dexter. Do you think you'll still drive to Florida to work for Mr. Chillingsworth this winter?"

He nodded his head in the affirmative, but without much enthusiasm.

I left Dexter to his beer and moved toward the assembled group of customers and their beers.

My awkwardness evaporated quickly. I marched into the thick of it, ordered a beer, and joined the conversation about the Patriots. There was a big game with Miami coming up on Sunday; luckily I was up to date on the strengths and weaknesses of both teams.

"No way are they going to stop Tom Brady," said one.

"Are you kidding me? Their defensive line not only can't stop him, but their defensive backs are putty in the hands of our wide receivers," offered another.

"We might have enough interceptions on Fiedler to beat his receptions to his own team!" I added gaily. They got a charge out of this, and I seamlessly entered the conversation.

"Is Rocky around, guys?" I asked. "He offered to take care of Cam's things on his boat and in his little studio. He rented it furnished so I guess there's not much of Cam's there. Rocky is just the nicest guy—and treats you all like family."

I was greeted with an overlapping chorus of, "You're not kidding!" and "He's the best".

I went on. "I'm trying to plan a memorial service for Cam. You guys knew him pretty well from being here so often for lunch. Do you have any suggestions? I want it to be about him and to be a reflection of his personality and what he cared about. What do you think about when you think of him?"

"Well, he knew I liked Bud Lite," offered one fellow I recognized as Luke, a local plumber.

"He knew what everyone liked. And he was great at getting us to calm down if we got our tails in an uproar," added another.

"He made a mean Bloody Mary," said one more.

"Can you think of anything else?"

"Oh, yeah! Remember when he won The Great Race?" asked Sam, an off-duty bartender.

"He was off-the-wall furious!" they all roared in response.

"Why?" I asked innocently.

They howled at that, too. "Because if you won it was assumed you cheated, and the next guy was declared the winner!"

"I've heard about The Great Race, but I was in Michigan when all that was going on," I replied. "What was the deal?"

"About twenty years ago two guys placed a bet. One said he could get from Portland to Woodford Harbor by water faster than the other fellow could by land. The bet was on, and they tried it one year. I don't remember who won, but they had such a good time doing it that the next year some more guys joined in. Before you knew it, it was an organized event; I use the term 'organized' loosely. The race grew in numbers every year after that until it became more like a circus!" explained Sam.

Luke enthusiastically stepped up to the plate with his recollections. "Of course the best part was that the finish line was on State Street in front of The Old Port. The guys that came overland—runners and bicyclists—would race down State Street while the guys who came via the water, in canoes and kayaks, would pull their boats out by the fishermen's dock and carry them *up* State Street. There was always a beer truck there to greet them. If you had a tee shirt to prove you had paid the entrance fee, you could drink all the beer you wanted."

"Yeah!" added another. "And it wasn't like you hadn't been drinking the whole way here. All the modes of transportation were well stocked with six packs."

"The start in Portland was at four in the morning, so of course everyone had been up all night the night before drinking."

"Remember the twelve-man bicycle? They made it all the way! And some of those watercraft were outrageous. No wind power allowed, only manpower."

"I was only about eleven the year three guys decided to sky dive in. One got caught in a tree, and one broke his leg; I think they ended it after that. It was getting too dangerous, there were too many drunks causing damage, and it just got out of hand.

"But I clearly remember all the beer-filled canoes and boats in the field behind The Old Port. My underage friends and I went on a rampage back there and had plenty ourselves."

"One year a woman who lived next door got fed up and came out with a hose, squirting all the guys who were peeing through her fence into the garden."

"I remember seeing—oh, what was his name? He was a tight end for the Patriots, an enormous guy. He passed out in his canoe before he even got up State Street."

"Cam did that race at least five or six years, but that was before he started working here. I don't think he even drank back then. It's the only way to be a bartender, I guess."

The group was thoroughly enjoying their recollections of a unique time in Woodford Harbor's past. I instinctively joined in the raucous revelry and found myself guffawing as well. It may not have been Woodford Harbor's finest moment, but it was something that would live in town lore long after all of us were gone.

It took a moment for everyone to settle down. Realizing I had come dangerously close to missing a meal, I took the opportunity to order a "puckburger", as the skinny little hamburgers are called here. I added Swiss cheese and sautéed mushrooms to give it a punch.

"Luckily, I think we have all settled down quite a bit since those crazy days. Cam certainly did," continued Sam. "He worked here for the past twenty years and was one of the nicest guys in town. He loved being on the *Jolly Mon* and making his music."

"His guitar was an extension of his left arm, I think. It seems inconceivable, I know, but sometimes I think he sounded even better than Jimmy Buffet on some of Buffet's own songs," said Luke.

"Maybe it's because he was singing from a place we were all familiar with. We shared his space and experiences and could relate to his take on the lyrics," continued Sam.

"Beyond that, he was also quietly generous. He loaned me five hundred bucks one time when I was in trouble, and he would occasionally take high school kids from the football team out for a sail if the coach gave him a heads up that one of them needed 'fresh air'. Every summer he hosted excursions for wounded veterans on the *Jolly Mon*. They just loved it!" added Luke.

"He had his own share of tragedy, too. His parents died when he was pretty young, and then he had that gorgeous girlfriend sometime ago. Supposedly she and Cam and the boat were perfect together," continued Luke.

"Didn't she drown off Martha's Vineyard?"

"Yeah," said Luke. "He never really wanted to talk about it. I met him when he first came to town, and I had the feeling this was a fresh start for him. The past was past, and he was ready to immerse himself in Woodford Harbor."

"He did kind of open up to me on the *Jolly Mon* late one night," offered Sam. "His father was in the navy, and the family was stationed around the Caribbean and then in Key West for a time. He was in Boston for college and ended up on Martha's Vineyard, but I don't know much about his time there. It was a subject he didn't like to talk about."

An uncomfortable silence followed this, as remembered sympathy filled the room.

"What kind of boat is the *Jolly Mon?*" I asked, trying to keep the mood upbeat. "He donated it to the United States Naval Academy, so it must be special in some way."

"It's a fabulous boat! It's a Cherubini," answered several in unison.

I scooped up the last mushroom with the squishy bun, drained the last of my beer, and pushed my stool back. I left a ten-dollar bill on the bar, which I knew was good for everyone, and prepared to say my goodbyes.

"Thank you so much. Cam was obviously a special guy, and I think we should have an equally special memorial service for him. Can I count on all of you to help me with some of the logistics? I want it to be especially nice for everyone, but mostly for Cam," I said.

The synchronized nods spoke to the strong bonds within my little town.

ABERNAKI
TENNIS CLUB

CHAPTER
TWENTY

EXITING THE OLD Port, I was blinded by the brilliant sunshine, and simultaneously discombobulated by my ringing phone. Fumbling, I managed to answer the intrusive little thing. I was met with the jarring voice of Pepper, who launched into her message without even the hint of a greeting.

"So," she announced, "I did find one person who filed an objection to Mr. Chillingsworth's fancy tennis club about twelve years ago when it was proposed. It was retracted about three weeks later. And guess who it was, my little friend?"

I sometimes wondered how much my affection for Pepper can take before her sense of drama does me in. "Who?"

"Ty Waters!" came her delighted reply. "Yup, our old tennis pro objected to the tennis club, but it is not clear on what grounds. Rather interesting, though, that when the thing was finally built he became the head tennis pro. And if you think about it, he also lived in Chillingsworth's gatehouse! *Mighty* interesting!" she gleefully continued.

I hated acknowledging how intriguing I found this information, but I knew she could sense the excitement in my voice. Discordant circumstances seemed suddenly to come into focus. I'd liken it to when the optometrist puts that crazy machine in front of your eyes and suddenly you can read an entire line.

Ty Waters and Arthur Chillingsworth—now *there* was an odd couple. Perhaps tennis, like politics, creates strange bedfellows.

I thanked Pepper, but before I could disconnect she was asking me what kind of mustard I would prefer in our deviled eggs on Friday night. Her obsession with food was never-ending! I suggested Grey Poupon, mostly because it sounds so sophisticated.

"Can you deal with a bit of paprika on top?"

"Yes," I told her, trying hard not to sound like I was in a rush, which I was. "Gotta run, Pepper. I'm sure we'll be in touch." I hung up.

I immediately put in a call to Uncle Henry, but was disappointed to hear he was still in Portland with Ollie.

I needed someone to share Pepper's information with. Instinctively I hit Bode's number; in a moment I was greeted by his welcome voice, the affection evident.

"It's really good to hear from you, Z," he said. "I'm having kind of a rough time here at the house. I'm not sure what you want, but I was just about to call you. Are you up for coffee? Or iced tea? I'll even get you a big sugar cookie from The Cake Whisperer! Meet me over at Darling Park in a bit?"

"That's beyond perfect, Bode," I responded enthusiastically. "I just came across something I'd like to discuss with you. I'll drive over and meet you there!"

As badly as I felt for Bode, I had to admit it was kind of nice to be needed. Acknowledging vulnerability shows strong character to my way of thinking.

The sun was getting low in the sky as I approached the granite bench overlooking the harbor at Darling Park. The golden light it reflected was magic against the colored hulls of the boats.

I was pulled from my reverie by familiar footsteps behind me. It was Bode, carrying a small cardboard tray that held a paper cup of tea and a larger plastic cup filled with a brown liquid and a lemon floating on top. A small white paper bag held the promised cookies.

"Here you go, Z," said Bode. "I got two. A sugar cookie for me, and I took the liberty of getting you an M&M cookie."

"Good call." I smiled and leaned over, giving him a quick kiss. "Chocolate will always be rewarded with a kiss, for future reference."

"Like this is news to me?" he laughed.

The first bite of that cookie was superlative, as the first bite always is. The combination of the buttery sugar and chocolate M&Ms lit up my soul.

"Talk to me about something, Z," said Bode. "I'm having the hardest time thinking about Mom not being here. Good grief, I'm forty years old and want my mother. It's making me nuts!"

"Sorry, my friend," I told him. "That biological love you have for your mother *never* ends. When we experience the physical loss of a loved one, we're left with a very primal feeling of bereavement."

"But here's something to distract you for a bit. Pepper called to say that there was dissension when the Abenaki Tennis Club was built—and Ty Waters was the one to object! Within three weeks of his objection, though, he withdrew his challenge, and the rest is history.

"Interestingly, despite his grievance about the club being built, it was he who was given the tennis pro position when it opened. Curious. If you turn around, by the way, you can see that our old backstop is now a part of the tennis club. It was built on land outside the boundary of Darling Park, against that rock. If the red substance found at Ty's place is indeed remnants of red ochre, finding it along with the photo is really wild. Perhaps that spot was a burying ground for the Red Paint People. I should think folks might frown on a tennis club being constructed over a graveyard."

"Are you saying Ty had this information and used it to blackmail Chillingsworth?" asked Bode incredulously.

"The thought had occurred to me. It would certainly explain

his position at the club, his deluxe accommodations in the gate-house, and that very fancy little car of his."

"Z, this is a lot to swallow. Ty was such a foolish little mole. Could he possibly have had the gumption to stand up to Arthur Chillingsworth?"

"You know what I say, Bode," I replied. "Never underestimate the impudence of an impudent man."

I continued. "And Chillingsworth might well have wanted to be done with the power this little fool had over him. It works as a motive for me."

"With that paunchy belly of his, I'm not sure Chillingsworth could even pick up a shovel, let alone do the deed," said Bode.

"Yes, but he has a little manservant who does everything for him now, doesn't he?" I said coyly.

"Z, you're not implying Daniel Dunkirk . . ."

I smiled my answer.

CHAPTER
TWENTY-ONE

BODE PICKED HIS jaw up from the grass beneath the granite bench, and we went our separate ways.

I stopped at Stowaway Sweets, Woodford Harbor's local chocolatier, on the way home. I know everyone thinks they know the best chocolate, but really, there is no competition for these delicious, delectable delights.

The establishment boasts quite a clientele. Eleanor Roosevelt used to visit the shop four or five times a year, complete with a Secret Service entourage. Gifting them to Winston Churchill, Queen Elizabeth, and Prince Philip, Mrs. Roosevelt helped expand their audience overseas—and the queen remains a loyal customer to this day. Katharine Hepburn and Robert Frost were devotees, and every president since Calvin Coolidge has ordered Stowaway Sweets for the White House.

My mother has her favorites registered on a little index card filed behind the counter. She is in the all-dark-chocolate camp and favors cashews, caramel, and almonds as accoutrements. As her daughter, I tried to improve on her choices, but couldn't. My only addition was adding dark chocolate-covered potato chips. On this day, I spent a bit more than I wanted to, grabbed a free sample, and was happily on my way.

I called Mr. Stanley on the drive home and cleared up a few details. Once home, I changed into jeans and a light sweatshirt for my date. It was a bit on the slovenly side of the dress code, but I was feeling victorious and almost imperious with my newfound hypothesis. Truth be told, I loved the idea of throwing Daniel Dunkirk under the bus.

I was waiting in the driveway and jumped into Bode's truck the moment he stopped. It was a speedy trip into town, as I think Bode wanted a beer as much as I wanted a glass of wine.

Not much had changed at The Old Port since my earlier visit. The cast of characters around the beer spigot had broken up, but I was sorry to see Dexter still on his stool. Bode stepped forward to order a Dark 'n Stormy and my house merlot. I ducked behind him and went over to see Dexter. Hunched over, he was staring at his beer. His sorrowful, red-rimmed eyes looked up when I gave him a nudge. "Are you all right?" I asked quietly.

He looked searchingly at me, gathered his strength to focus, and murmured, "Thanks, Lizzie. I feel terrible. Rocky just came by and asked Sam to give me a ride home. So nice. I feel terrible." I gave his shoulder an awkward squeeze, and watched as Sam made his way toward us.

"Nice, Sam," I said.

"Rocky's the deal," he said. "He's here for everyone."

Bode found me, and as he handed me my wine, a hand grabbed me. I turned around to find Carly, Jennie, and Tommy, all standing at the end of the bar.

"You can't get blueberry French toast *here*!" chortled Carly, laughing at her own joke. It didn't take much to know they had been here awhile.

"We might have a lot more fun at the Driftwood if we served beer instead of all that coffee!" howled Jennie. Oh my.

Tommy was fixated on the television, watching the statistics on the Thursday night football game. Not only did he know everything there is to know about every player and coach on the Patriots, he also knew how every player on every team might impact his boys. His wife was an incredibly good sport about the Patriots logo emblazoned in the middle of her living room rug, the dog named Brady, and the children named after the offensive line, but she put her foot down when Tommy learned that Tom Brady didn't eat tomatoes and tried to ban them from the house. Tommy is so . . .Tommy!

I took my glass from Bode, took a gulp of red wine, and dove headlong into the raucous conversations surrounding me. Everyone seemed to be aware that Ollie had turned himself in to Uncle Henry; fortunately we were not a part of the story.

"Did you hear Ollie turned himself in?"

"Really? Ollie wouldn't hurt a flea!"

"Yeah, but Ty was pretty awful to him!"

"Remember when they were in high school, and Ty made Ollie trip when he was going up to receive his diploma?"

"I remember when he tried to frame Ollie for all the graffiti at the high school. It was so obviously a Ty move!"

"Hey, who knows! Maybe Ollie is a closet serial killer!"

And so went the local gossip.

I had just ordered my second glass of wine when Bode gave a nod, indicating our favorite table was open. I followed him over and sank wearily into the seat. My burst of energy was evaporating, and I could tell he was having a hard time holding up his end of all the chatter. We each took two deep breaths, looked at each other, smiled, and picked up the menus. I knew I was having fried shrimp, and he knew he was having a lobster BLT, but picking up a menu at a restaurant seems required somehow.

We placed our order, and Rocky exited the kitchen to join us. He's a caricature of a kind old man, and I felt his warmth immediately as he sat down. His craggy features, white hair, and deep-set blue eyes are set off by a comfortable smile. Although he has never married, and has no direct offspring, his generosity has afforded him a multitude of grateful 'children'.

"I heard you were in to see me this afternoon," he said. "I assume you were not in for the beer, but rather to discuss Cam."

I smiled. "You're right—although that beer tasted pretty good! Sam, Arthur, and Luke were all enthusiastic about putting together a memorial celebration for Cam. What good guys. And what a dear Cam was. So sad, so young."

"I know," said Rocky. "Some people just have a knack for living life, doing what makes them comfortable, and enjoying it. His was a seemingly simple life, but who really knows. He certainly understood the fact that giving is the best gift.

"I went through his studio," he continued. "He had minimal possessions, as you might expect—just the bare essentials of clothing, his guitar, and some sheet music. I think his lack of interest in possessions is particularly interesting in contrast to the attention he lavished on the *Jolly Mon*. She is in pristine shape, every piece of brass polished and every line secured. That was his love. I'm going to give her a final cleaning later this afternoon."

We all sat in silence for a bit, ruminating on the short life of Cam. It was so rich in its simple way, but a bit mysterious as well.

Our meal arrived, Rocky returned to the kitchen, and we happily imbibed. Comfort food is so...comforting. Bode finished up my fries, we paid up, and headed for the door.

The crisp night air enveloped us. It was lovely, and the silence was so soft. Like hitting yourself on the head with a hammer so you can feel good when you stop, that's the way I feel about going into a crazy, loud spot for dinner. It's so nice to leave.

CHAPTER
TWENTY-TWO

I FELT BODE'S ARM against me before I even opened my eyes. Sometimes I think it's the minutiae of life that centers our universe and grounds us. I let myself revel in the moment and kept my eyes closed. I felt Bode stir against me, and before long we had connected in a more carnal fashion. And then it was back to sleep.

Last night had been tough, although it had begun well enough. After a pleasant night out, we found Charlie at home, happy and full of soccer. We watched part of the Thursday night football game, then crawled into bed—and that's when something just let go.

Maybe it was the ordinariness of things that got to him, for it was a scene that had played out innumerable times before. Part of that scene had always included Thistle, though. She was always a presence, a consideration, in his mind. Now that she wasn't a part of it any more, the reality hit—and hurt.

I held him, but there's really nothing to be done for a person in primal pain. Who doesn't know the feeling of wanting their mother? Regardless of one's age, finality is excruciating. It was a long night.

The inevitable sound of Charlie's shower caught us both by surprise.

"Either she's up early, or we shouldn't be in this bed," I said. "And it's pretty clearly not the former."

"Z, how about we take a little time together this morning? Get a couple of bacon-egg-and-cheese sandwiches to go and head out on the *Lizzie G?*" When Bode had painted this moniker on the stern of his boat, it was—to me—better than any engagement ring.

He found no hesitation from me. My priorities were clear.

"Absolutely! I'll get Charlie to school and grab the sandwiches at The Driftwood. Pick me up at the town landing?"

"You got it," he smiled in reply.

I happily threw on my jeans and *Catch and Fillet* sweatshirt and was downstairs in a heartbeat. In no time I had Charlie's English muffin and orange juice in hand. She slathered on some peanut butter, raised the glass to her lips, and drank the juice in a haze. We were in the Jeep before she knew it.

As we rolled past Redmond Island, I thought of the last time I had thought about it and hoped Ollie was faring well. I also remembered Charlie's quotation, the one that had started it all.

"What's your next quotation, honey?"

That seemed to perk her up.

"It's about our decisions and how they affect us. How about this quotation from Aristotle: 'We are what we repeatedly do. Excellence then, is not an act, but a habit.' In 300 BC he knew that 'Actions speak louder than words.'"

"The timelessness of basic wisdom is fascinating," I commented, enjoying this intellectual moment with my "little girl."

We were nearing our drop-off spot when I realized we didn't have a plan for the Livingston Taylor concert yet.

"What time will you be home from school?" I asked. "We have to figure out our plans for Livingston Taylor."

"Oh, Mom, I made plans to go with some friends from the

soccer team. We're going to get sandwiches from the Blue Canoe and sit together."

"Will you need a ride?"

"We can just walk. It will be fun," was her answer, and she was out of the car.

My mind was whirling. My little Charlie always went to events with Bode and me. We were a threesome. But she was sixteen now, and I guess things change. "The only constant is change." These quotations were becoming annoying.

CHAPTER
TWENTY-THREE

I DROVE DOWN TO The Driftwood and entered the general hubbub with a festive attitude. Knowing Bode and I were going to steal a few hours on the water together almost felt like skipping school. And I loved it!

I walked to the back and ordered two bacon-egg-and-cheese sandwiches on grilled English muffins. Jennie noticed I had forgotten the iced tea and coffee with cream and two sugars. And right she was!

I looked behind me and saw Uncle Henry sitting alone at a table. I went over to join him while I waited. "Good morning, dear," he said, looking over his glasses. "You're looking mighty chipper this morning."

"Bode and I are going out on the *Lizzie G* to pull a few traps. He's having a rough patch with Thistle gone."

"Lucky to have you, that boy is." It was an uncharacteristically sweet thing for him to say. I think the loss of Thistle was affecting quite a few people.

"We checked for fingerprints on the shovel that was near Ty's body and, of course, it was wiped clean. I'm no coroner, but I noticed at the time that the back of Ty's head, where he was hit by the shovel, didn't look as bloody as his forehead, which had hit the gravestone. There was so much blood around his face that it gave the appearance of blood everywhere. But that's not how it was; there was no blood on the shovel."

"That seems strange," I mused. "Why wouldn't the shovel be covered in blood as well?"

"I looked more closely at the photos taken of that indent in the grass behind the headstone. It seems pretty clear that Ty turned around in surprise, and when his body twisted he lost his footing. His left foot slipped backwards, leaving a deep hole.

"As for fingerprints, obviously whoever lifted the shovel did not want his or her fingerprints on it. If Ollie had been the culprit, he would have had no need to wipe his prints, as they belong there. But at that moment there may not have been a lot of analytical thinking going on; he may have just instinctively wiped them off.

"It *is* curious," Uncle Henry continued. "Lt. Daniels finally released Ollie from state police headquarters after questioning him for almost 24 hours. Poor guy. It's so hard to watch an officious oaf like Daniels take one of my people away. I guess bureaucracy is a necessary annoyance, but annoying really isn't an adequate word.

"Any word on the body, yet?"

"No."

"Hey, Lizzie, I have your order," called Jennie

I walked over and noticed her fidgeting and twisting the check she was about to hand me.

"Jennie, are you still worried about the concert tonight?"

"Lizzie," she told me, eyes wide, "I'm absolutely terrified. I hate getting up in front of people and speaking, and I don't even know what to say."

"Look at it this way, Jennie. You're speaking to a number of people, yes, but they're *your* people." In my mind, I quickly credited Uncle Henry. "I'm sure you know at least one out of five and probably more. Just get up, look at all the familiar faces, and tell the story of your classmates—the Taylor kids—performing at your grammar school. It's interesting, but also endearing. Trust that 'your people' love you, which they do. Do your best, that's all."

Thankfully, her farewell smile was bigger and more relaxed.

I grabbed the bag of sandwiches and the tray of drinks and was happily on my way.

The swells of fall had arrived in the harbor, and the float rose up and down with them. Bode was just coming in, Bob hanging out on the starboard side. I set down my stash, took the line, and secured the bow. Bode jumped off, tied up the stern, we loaded up, and pushed off. Sometimes I think I'm happiest riding in my Jeep with the top down, but that doesn't hold a candle to riding in a boat skimming across the water.

The *Lizzie G* is a working lobster boat, complete with the smell of bait in her hold. Bode hoses her down and scrubs her thoroughly every day, which mitigates the odor somewhat. Combined with the sense of order he keeps, she's a shipshape little craft. Each lobsterman has his own color-coded buoys to identify his traps below the surface. Bode's design is the ubiquitous Dartmouth green with white stripes.

The buoys bob on the water with a line attached to a trap on the ocean floor. The traps themselves have two compartments, the kitchen and the parlor. The kitchen holds a bait bag full of smelly, disgusting fish, tantalizing to a lobster. A funnel-shaped net leads him from the outside to his dinner, and a second funnel-shaped net then leads him into the parlor. Easy as it is to crawl *into* funnels, it is nearly impossible for the lobster to wriggle his way out. Ideally, the lobster remains in the parlor until he is hauled out.

Lobsters do have some recourse, however. A gauge measures the carapace, which is the distance from the back of their eyes to the beginning of their tail. Each lobster is measured, and if the carapace is less than 3 1/4" the lobster is too small, and is immediately returned to its home. Females are protected as well, so that they can continue to populate the species. Hundreds of little black eggs on the underside identify the ladies, and they go right back in.

The starboard side of the *Lizzie G* holds a sturdy pot hauler to pull up the lines on the traps. Bode just recently added a hydraulic engine so he doesn't use his own manpower to pull each one up. I think it was a fortieth birthday present to himself.

I love to go out with Bode and just haul ten or twenty pots at a time. That's recreational lobstering. Lobstering is one of those professions that has a glorious ring to it, but entails hours of physically demanding work. The real thing involves pulling, grabbing, and hauling lobster traps in all kinds of weather. A love, as well as knowledge, of the sea is imperative.

Bode shut down the engine and lowered the anchor out by Children's Island. Suddenly seagulls ruled the sound waves. This island is home to a YMCA summer camp. A small ferry carries the little guys out each morning, and returns them home in the afternoon. Sailboats, arts and crafts, and even archery keep the small fry active, happy, and blessedly worn down by four o'clock. At this time of year the deserted little cove on the northern end provides perfect protection from the wind.

With Bob inches from our laps, we nestled in, and opened our steamy little sandwiches, wiping the grease from the bottom of the wrappers on our pants. Sometimes bacon, eggs, cheese and buttery muffins fill the bill. We munched in silence, interrupted intermittently by having to shoo Bob's enormous nose away.

Bode seemed to eat his sandwich in two bites and was ready to go before I had even finished my first half. Each bite of this decadence should be deliberately savored. I surrendered to Bob's enormous brown eyes and sacrificed my last bite.

"That was some detective work yesterday Z," said Bode. "How did you ever even think Ollie would be out on Redmond Island? Quite the little mind you have cranking in that pretty little head of yours.

"So what's next? Who whacked Ty?" he went on. "My brain is feeling kind of numb. I haven't really given it much thought. Aggie has planted that annoying seed of doubt in my head involving Ty, that is irritating even to consider. And while I know it doesn't really matter, of course it really does matter. I don't much care that Ty is gone, but it is quite something to have him murdered right here. And seemingly by someone we know!"

"Of course, I love to speculate about Daniel Dunkirk being put away forever for this, but I do have one other person in mind who seems kind of suspicious. Motive, proximity, and no alibi," I ventured.

Bode looked at me quickly to see if I was joking, and saw at once that I was serious.

"Z, what are you talking about?" he asked quickly.

"I hope no one else puts this together, but doesn't Alice seem like a prime candidate? She hated Ty, for so many reasons. One of them being that he constantly humiliated her beloved husband. That's a bitter pill to swallow for twenty years. And she was in the cottage right next to the murder scene. Her alibi? That she was with Ollie as he slept. If indeed he was sleeping, that leaves her free to roam and cause all kinds of havoc."

I waited, hoping Bode would blast a hole through my theory, but his shocked, mute posture did nothing of the kind.

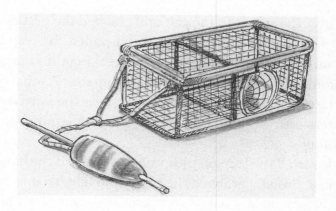

TWENTY-FOUR

T HE THOUGHTFUL SILENCE followed us out of the harbor. "I thought we would pull the five off Halfway Rock, the five off Tinkers, the five off Tom Moore's, and then come back for the five at Children's Island," Bode suggested. "I'm not going to use the hydraulic hauler for these few traps. I think the exercise will be good medicine for me."

"Fine by me," I answered, and let the boat and Atlantic Ocean work their magic.

We headed out towards Halfway Rock, which originally marked the halfway point between Kennebunkport and Portland. Now its significance lay in its abundance of lobsters.

We slowed down and put on our lobster gloves and rubber aprons. It's a messy business, hauling line and traps up from the bottom of the ocean, and you need all the protection you can get. Bode and I have our own system for pulling traps, although I think I am more of a distraction than a help. Bob and Bode easily pull over a hundred traps a day without me. As Bode slowed the boat, I leaned over the side with the gaff and grabbed the first buoy. Bode quickly snatched the line from me and pulled the trap up hand over hand. I love the sound of the trap breaking through the water and coming aboard. No other sound compares. As that first trap broke the surface, we could immediately hear the satisfying sound of lobsters scurrying around inside, tangled around each other and flailing.

Bode rested the trap on the gunnel and undid the bungee cord that held it closed. I grabbed the gauge and handed it to him as he pulled the first lobster out. He flipped it over on its back and found it covered in little black eggs.

"Back she goes," he said.

He then proceeded to flip the next one over. When he saw no eggs, he positioned the gauge at the back edge of the eye socket. Discovering that it didn't stretch over the length of the carapace, he gave a little whoop.

"Nice going, Bode!" I said. "You've got a keeper!"

I quickly slipped a dark green rubber band on the end of the banding tool, handed it to him, and watched as he squeezed the handles, opening the band and slipping it seamlessly over the lobster's claw. One by one, he banded the remaining two keepers, which followed the first into the aerated barrel on board.

This is where Bob jumped into action. Somehow the two of them have worked out a routine. While Bode disconnected the bait bag from the trap, Bob grabbed a small fish from the bait barrel in his mouth and handed it to Bode. Bode then put it in the bag and replaced the bag in the empty trap. I have often thought of videotaping the procedure because I am sure it would win an award somewhere.

Bode motored us back to our original location and I slid the newly-stocked trap back into the water, letting the line play out through my fingers, and then threw the buoy back in. Before doing so, though, I gave it a quick kiss. I don't think many lobstermen know this trick.

We grabbed the remaining four traps and motored over to

Tinker's Island. Tinkers is only about a hundred yards offshore, but it is home to a dozen or so adorable summer cottages. It's an easy row from the mainland; according to the few who live there in the summer, though, it's a world away. With no electricity or running water, it's only for the hearty. Because the water is deep around the island, Bode had five lines to retrieve. His efforts afforded us five more lobsters.

We repeated this same operation off Tom Moore's Rock and at Children's Island. Two hours later we had twelve beauties for Bode's keeper, the metal cage that ties off the stern of his boat on the mooring and sits on the bottom of the harbor. When he goes into The Lobster Company to sell them, all he has to do is retrieve them from the keeper.

We hosed down the boat on the way in and decided to cook up a few to make lobster rolls for dinner. The sun overhead afforded a comfortable warmth and took the chill out of the autumn air. The spray from the *Lizzie G*'s wake made rainbows above each crest. I could sit at the stern and watch that forever; it is mesmerizing.

"I'll bring in four nice ones, cook them, shuck them, and then bring the meat over for you to make lobster rolls, okay?" asked Bode. "Get some really good potato chips, Z. If we are going to have lobster rolls we need designer chips! What are you thinking of for dessert?" he added.

"Not to worry. I am a connoisseur of potato chips, and the dessert will be chocolate. We'll have the finest picnic at the concert! Did I mention, by the way, that Charlie is going with her friends instead of us? Oh, dear, she's growing up so fast!"

"It's taken her sixteen years," smiled Bode. "Guess it just happens!"

I gave him a jab in the side and sat back for the ride in. Suddenly, I remembered our cookies. Bode and I always have a few Pepperidge Farm Brussels at the end of a lobstering run—or sometimes in the car—or sometimes even after breakfast. Bode appreciates the thin layer of dark chocolate and the minimal wafer. Not too rich, it's the ideal chocolate treat for both of us.

As Bode approached the dock, I jumped off with a cookie clenched in my teeth, and gave him a wave good bye. He managed to find my butt for his traditional whack before I was out of reach.

I was walking happily up State Street towards home when I noticed it was close to noon. Uncle Henry and I have a standing lunch date at the Blue Canoe every Friday. I had been so absorbed in my morning on the water that it had almost slipped my mind. Fortunately, I didn't have to go home and dress up, but could remain in my jeans and tee shirt. Life was getting better and better.

CHAPTER

TWENTY-FIVE

I WALKED UP STATE Street to Washington, then headed across town past the bakery and savings bank. I eyed one of those M&M cookies, and considered buying it, but postponed the purchase until my walk home later.

The sun, combined with the cool autumn air, was wonderful. I turned the final corner and saw Uncle Henry seated at one of the outdoor tables. His girth filled his chair nicely. People had sometimes mistaken his size for weakness, but Uncle Henry is as strong as anyone I know, and as fleet of foot as a twenty-year old. It is just an overzealous appetite that gives him that pleasantly round appearance.

"Hello, dear! How was the lobstering?" he called.

"Not bad. We got twelve and brought four in for lobster rolls. Do you want me to make you one? Are you going to the concert?"

"Sure thing on both counts," was his reply. "Tell Bode I have a six-pack of that new micro-brewery beer from Kennebunkport. I'll bring one for him. Are you sure you have enough meat for me, though?" The rhetorical nature of his question was evident when, without missing a beat, he continued, "I'm sitting with the town officials tonight. I get so tired of entertaining that librarian at all these functions, but at least the fire department is full of live wires!" An odd choice of words. I let it go.

"There's plenty. Charlie is going with her friends and is going to pick up something from here."

"She's not going with you?" He raised an eyebrow.

"No, I have already been accused of over-mothering her, so please don't start."

"Well, I highly doubt the child will end up in a cell down in the Town House! When are you leaving for Captiva by the way? I envy you; it's a beautiful spot. I miss your mom and dad too. That little sister of mine is quite the cook! I need her!"

"Uncle Henry," I said, directing a glance at his round tummy. "I think you're doing just fine without her."

"I'm not talking about any life threatening malnutrition. I'm just happier when she's cooking for me," he tried to explain.

"Enough of that. Let's concentrate on our next meal here. What are you having?" I asked him. "Actually, let's go in and take a look at the menu. I probably know it by heart but it helps to see things spelled out to make a selection. I feel like I get the meatloaf sub with cheese more than I should, but oh, my, it *is* tasty!"

"That sounds good to me," said Uncle Henry.

"Or maybe I'll have egg salad with bacon on a wrap. Then I'll have enough room for an M&M cookie," I mused.

"Oh, yes, you don't want to fill up on lunch when you'll be walking home past The Cake Whisperer," kidded my dear uncle.

We greeted the line of people inside; between us, we knew almost all of them. We reached the front and ordered. It's always a mini-drama for me to get a sandwich at the Blue Canoe, as the sandwiches are all so good. Usually they include little sides of pasta salad or fruit, but they give me a little gingerbread man cookie instead. Makes me very happy. It's the little victories that really define a good life.

On this day, I had gone wild and crazy and ordered the meatloaf sandwich, feeling fairly certain that I would have room for that M&M cookie.

We sat back down outside and checked out our meals. Yes, mine included the petite confection.

"We've done well, Uncle Henry," I said, admiring our choices.

I had just finished my first half when I noticed Uncle Henry sopping up the last of his meatloaf. He settled back, took a final drink of his coffee, and said, "I have some rather distressing news."

No, no, no, I thought. I am having the most wonderful day and am anticipating a spectacular evening. Distressing news does not fit in.

When I said nothing, he began, "Lt. Daniels and his band of merry men have it in their heads that they have uncovered another suspect in Ty's murder. Of course, their speculations come solely from the objective evidence at hand. They have none of the insight we have. Their latest target is poor Alice."

"Uncle Henry, that's dreadful. Alice works so hard and is such a down-to-earth human being. She's angry, yes, but if ever anger was justified this would be the time. She's worked hard her whole life taking care of Ollie and their son, not to mention keeping the town cemetery up and running. Putting up with Ty and his arrogant ways was a full-time job in and of itself. It seems so unfair to add this burden to her already taxing life."

"I know, Lizzie," Uncle Henry agreed. "I'm doing everything I can for her. But if you're putting together an objective jigsaw puzzle, her pieces fit uncomfortably well. She had the motive, no denying that, and logistically she was within a hundred feet of the murder scene. And her alibi? That she was watching her sleeping husband? Weak, weak, weak."

I concurred. "In a two-dimensional world, perhaps. But Alice? Alice just would not do that. Would not, could not. Oh, dear, I feel awful. What can we do?"

"I think at this point all Daniels can do is take her in for questioning and generally try to harass her. Hopefully, he'll soon realize he's barking up the wrong tree. All he cares about is solving the case; it doesn't bother him a bit to run slipshod all over peoples' lives in the process. Frankly, he gives police a bad name."

"A lot like Dunkirk giving lawyers a bad name!" I snapped.

"Well, aren't we a couple of naysayers," smiled Uncle Henry.

I took a breath and smiled back at him. "But what can we do for Alice? Should I have Bode call his brother Bill down in Boston to represent her?" I asked.

"No, not yet. Daniels really has no case at this point, just superficial accusations. Let's give him time to get down off his high horse. I doubt he'll keep her overnight."

"Here's what we can do," I said. "Let's figure out who *did* whack old Ty. Trouble is, it's not so much who *would* have, but who *wouldn't* have! It's amazing that troublesome people like Ty Waters continue to cause trouble even after they're gone."

"You're right, Lizzie. Who knew this little girl of mine would grow up to be so wise?" said Uncle Henry affectionately. I needed that little bit of tenderness to calm down, but it did not diminish my need to clear this mess up. Too many people were being adversely affected, many of them unfairly.

I realized too, that I was one of those people being touched by this loser. The coroner wasn't going to keep that body forever, and everyone seemed to assume it was coming to Bainbridge Funeral Home next. I needed someone to foot the bill. So many tennis balls, so little money. Yes, even in death he was an annoyance.

CHAPTER
TWENTY-SIX

UNCLE HENRY AND I shared goodbyes, and I started off down the street and back to reality. The day on the water followed by lunch with Uncle Henry had been stellar, and I hated to have the magic end.

I eyed The Cake Whisperer up ahead and knew I could ward off my disappointment for at least a few more minutes by going in and treating myself to the biggest M&M cookie they had. I munched it slowly, savoring each bite, as I headed home to change into respectable clothes.

And then the proverbial lightening bolt hit me. I suddenly realized that I work for myself, so no one can tell me what to do. To heck with respectability, I was going to walk straight to Bainbridge Funeral home in the very clothes I had on! After checking in with Mr. Stanley, I was not going to my desk, either, but to the side yard. My father always preached that the success of our business was closely related to its overall appearance, so I decided to clean up those nasty leaves that had collected on the south side of the building. And if I did that I could keep these jeans on. Decision made.

As I rounded the corner, I saw Mr. Stanley out on the front porch shining the brass doorknocker. No one wanted to be indoors on one of the final warm, sunny days of fall.

"That looks wonderful, Mr. Stanley," I exclaimed.

He turned and smiled. "I was just thinking what an important part of the business this antique knocker is. A beautiful piece of brass, welcoming generations through these doors. I remember when your grandfather bought it. Your grandmother thought it was exorbitant, but he insisted that a simple, dignified ornament represents so much. He was a remarkable man."

I felt a bit inconsequential standing there in my less-than-dignified jeans, getting ready to rake leaves. Was I really adequate to fill my grandfather's shoes?

"And you, Miss G," he continued. "Carrying on all the wonderful traditions and moving forward at the same time. It is still such a pleasure to be a part of all this."

I could not have been more pleased. Hearing such kind words, and feeling so genuinely loved and respected, made me promise myself to play it forward. Offer kindness whenever the situation presented itself. I don't believe there's anything more important than that.

"Thank you so much, Mr. Stanley," I beamed. "I was just remembering my father's words about how important every detail is in the appearance of a business, and I came to rake up all the leaves that have gathered on the side of the building."

"Between the two of us, dear, we'll soon have everything ship-shape," replied Mr. Stanley.

"When you finish that why don't you head home for the weekend? I'm off to Captiva tomorrow morning and will be back Monday morning. I hope you don't mind coming in for at least half a day on Monday, and then first thing Tuesday morning we'll put together Cam's service. If you need anything in the meantime just give me a call."

"Lovely, Miss G," he said in his soft voice. "I'll finish up inside." With a final swipe of the polishing cloth, he was off.

I grabbed a rake and gloves from the small storage shed in the back corner of the lot and happily began my task. I had three neat piles of leaves lined up along the sidewalk when I sensed, rather than heard, someone behind me. A glance over my shoulder revealed Dexter standing awkwardly a few feet away, shifting his weight from one foot to the other.

"Hello, Dexter! Nice to see you. What can I do for you?" I inquired, wanting to get to the point rather than chat about who knows what. I was so enjoying my perfect day.

"Yes, Lizzie, yes," he began. "I guess I have always seen you as a very responsible lady and a pillar of the community."

I squelched my desire to run.

"So I thought you were someone I could talk to about a problem I'm not sure how to deal with. Yeah . . ."

I clenched my hands around the rake's shaft to keep myself from throwing it up before me to ward off whatever was coming.

"You see," he meekly continued, "there are a few things going on that I think further complicate Ty's death."

Oh, brother, what more could there be?

"You see, Ty and I have been together—you know, together—for over ten years. I can't tell you how much I adored the man, and grieving him in this cloak of secrecy is very difficult for me. Oh, dear..."

I think surprised would be a gross understatement of my reaction. I was flipping dumbfounded. At the same time, I felt a great rush of sympathy.

"This is further complicated because of the dealings the two of us had with Mr. Chillingsworth. On my own, I don't feel capable of dealing with them."

"Does it have anything to do with the Red Paint People?" I asked, pretty much knowing the answer.

"Yes, Lizzie, yes," he squeaked out. "I saw Henry take that box with the extra red sand in it away, and I was pretty well certain you would put the pieces together. There was no rational reason for Chillingsworth to be so generous to Ty. But Ty concocted this plan and, I must say, it has worked perfectly.

"The threats were not purely one-sided, as Chillingsworth knew that Ty and I were lovers. Had people known that Ty was gay, his constant charade of flirting with all the ladies would be exposed and much of his appeal would disappear. Chillingsworth lived in fear that the burial grounds of the Red Paint People would be exposed. And with the Abenaki Tennis Club built over it, he panicked that there would be hell to pay.

"There's another important detail that I also fear will come to light. I assume Henry took that sand sample in for testing. Well, there is no mystery or anything sacred about that sand. Ty made the whole thing up, and we bought the sand at a craft store. I'm terrified that it will be discovered that the Red Paint People story—and the red sand—are a scam. Who knows how Chillingsworth will react?"

My snarky side was seeing some dark humor in all this, but one look into the terrified eyes of Dexter made me tamp it down. The poor guy was in a terrible situation.

"Dexter, let me first say how truly sorry I am for your loss. It's devastating enough to lose a loved one, especially one so close to you. To be unable to share your pain with others makes it that much harder. To carry that secret all these years had to be difficult—and painful as well. I am so sorry for both of you."

"I couldn't agree more," said Dexter, hanging his head. "It was the one issue that Ty and I could not resolve. We had just had another go round the night before Thistle's funeral. I wanted so badly to live the life we shared together for all to see, but Ty had a streak of insecurity that he kept deeply buried beneath his glamorous tennis pro persona. I liken it to the way important men want their wives to remain loyal—and silent. In our situation, I was not even afforded the role of partner.

"All this anger and turmoil inside of me makes Ty's death even harder to deal with. To think that our last time together was so contentious!"

"Dexter," I said, leaning in to him. "You and Ty had many years of happy memories and good times. Don't let this one incident discolor so much good. I'm sure Ty loved you in his own way, and as best he could."

His thankful eyes gave me hope that if he didn't understand this right now he would see it more clearly in the future. Dexter's news, however, did make me dislike Ty even more, knowing he had treated this good man so poorly.

"It's certainly your decision as to how you want to proceed with Arthur Chillingsworth," I went on. "As it stands, Uncle Henry has not mentioned the Red Paint People story to anyone, so the report on his findings need not be made public. I know you do beautiful work for the Chillingsworth's, and you have a good relationship, so it doesn't seem to me that anything drastic need happen between you and Arthur Chillingsworth. Difficult as it may seem to go on, your life is stable in many respects. Time is the only healer in cases like this."

I decided not to mention the fact that Pepper was privy to much of this information, as it would only serve to worry poor Dexter further. I felt certain I could elicit a code of silence from her.

"You just go about your business, keep your head down, and see how it all plays out. Hopefully, we can find whoever raised that shovel against Ty and get some justice."

"I would like that very much," said Dexter, as he slowly backed up in a retreat to the street. "Yes, thank you..." he mumbled.

I made quick work of collecting my leaves in a barrel and storing it in the back, all the while bursting with this new information. It certainly cast a bright light on many mysterious shadows.

CHAPTER
TWENTY-SEVEN

I TIDIED UP AS quickly as I could, as I was dying to get home to talk with Bode. Just as I was rounding the corner with my tools, I saw Mr. Stanley locking up.

He turned. "Have a lovely trip, Miss G, and do give my best to your parents."

"Will do, Mr. Stanley. I'm going to try to have a chat with Arthur Chillingsworth while I'm there; I want to see if he's willing to contribute toward Ty's service. I doubt the coroner's office is going to keep his body much longer. The widespread assumption is that we're handling his service and burial, and that makes me feel responsible somehow."

"That's not entirely true, Miss G. But he was a well-known person in town, and it seems wrong somehow for him not to be shown the proper respect. Forgive me for saying this, but what would we do with all those tennis balls if he were to go to another funeral home?"

I had never heard Mr. Stanley be even remotely sarcastic. It struck me that Ty was so outrageously arrogant that he had even rubbed Mr. Stanley the wrong way. That's going some.

"Well, there's that," I smiled. "You know how to reach me, and I can hop a plane at a moment's notice if need be."

I locked up, set the alarm, and started to walk home. There was almost a skip in my step. Sometimes a little change of scenery is a very good thing.

I made the walk in just a few minutes. Charlie didn't appear to be home yet, so I hopped in the Jeep and headed to Brown's for picnic supplies.

The store was very busy, with most of the customers huddled around the sandwich counter. I assumed most of them were waiting for sandwiches for the concert. I waded through them, with an occasional wave and greeting, and headed to the bread counter. I found my favorite hot dog buns, the kind that are sliced open on the top and allow for the sides to be richly buttered and browned. In my opinion, these are the only rolls adequate to hold big hunks of lobster meat.

As this was a special night, I bought two different kinds of chips, plain for Bode, and Maui Onion for me. I surveyed the chocolate confections in the bakery section, but nothing really grabbed me. I still had part of my M&M cookie, but was planning to finish it on the flight to Fort Myers. There had to be something here that would be special enough for tonight! And that's when I saw it. I was pretty sure that Bode, like me, had not had a Hostess CupCake since childhood. I grabbed a package and considered getting two, but in the end reigned myself in.

As I rounded the corner to the checkout line, I ran into Rocky holding a basket full of sandwiches.

"Look at you, Rocky! Are you feeding an army? I thought you owned a restaurant!" I kidded him.

"You know, Lizzie, I actually considered closing The Old Port tonight. I love Livingston Taylor so much I wasn't sure I wanted to serve a beer to anyone not going to his concert! I got over it, and the place will be open, but I'm taking a bunch of the off-duty bartenders to the big event. I'm afraid they'll bring an inordinate amount of beer, so I want plenty of sub sandwiches to sop up the alcohol."

I smiled as he went on, "I was actually going to give you a call. I was cleaning out the last of the things on Cam's boat and came across an envelope with *Geoff* written on the outside. I wasn't sure what to do, so I opened it. There is a substantial amount of cash and a letter written to someone named Geoff. I felt bad reading it, but I figured someone would have to do it. I haven't mentioned it to anyone yet because it seems best to wait for this fellow Geoff to claim it—the letter as well as the cash.

"It's an incredible note and makes me want to know this fellow."

"That's fascinating, Rocky. Hopefully this person will surface. It's curious, isn't it, that we know so l little about Cam. He was out there and very much a part of the community, but he kept his past to himself. Sam mentioned something about a girlfriend drowning off of Martha's Vineyard some time ago. I wonder if it has anything to do with that?"

Rocky sighed. "We've all been thinking about what to do to honor Cam, and the boys came up with the idea of having a celebration of sorts down by the harbormaster's office on Tuesday, which would have been Cam's birthday. They want to bring the *Jolly Mon* up to the dock and, after a short service, have a reception there with beer and steamers around noon. I am more than happy to supply both. In keeping with Cam's quiet, low-key personality, I think we should keep it simple, but meaningful."

"How would you feel about my setting up a small sound system and adding some Jimmy Buffett music—only if you think it would be appropriate. I think he embodied that music," I offered. "It might also be nice if a few people spoke; not random, extemporaneous speeches, though; those don't usually work very well. In fact, I'd be happy to run the program. Would you be up for saying a few words? And maybe Sam?"

"That would be great, Lizzie. It's something I know I can trust you with—and it's very nice of you.

"It seems too bad, doesn't it, to gather all the people who are most important to Cam, tie up his beloved boat, and play the music that filled his soul, and not have him there to enjoy it," said Rocky.

"Let's hope this brings him pretty close," I said.

We each headed out to begin our evenings. The shared excitement of the concert almost reminded me of Christmas Eve. Everyone would be celebrating it in their own way, but everyone would be celebrating the same event.

CHAPTER

TWENTY-EIGHT

COMING INTO THE house, I ran into Charlie swinging her duffel for Captiva down the last flight of stairs.

"Is that it?"

"Yeah. Really, what do I need besides a few bathing suits, shorts, my Mucky Duck tee shirt, and a sundress if we go out?"

It would be the pot calling the kettle black to question her choices, as mine were practically identical. I might substitute a polo shirt for her Mucky Duck tee shirt, though. There is something so comforting about going to a familiar spot, where you know just what to expect. It's even better knowing that everything you expect will make you supremely happy.

My parents began going to Captiva when I was in junior high school. Geographically, it's located in Florida, but it doesn't feel that way. It feels more like an island in the middle of the Caribbean. No building can be higher than a palm tree, and there is just one main street. Street is actually a bit of a stretch, as it is not much longer than a couple of football fields. A general store and two funky outdoor cafes stand at one end, and The Mucky Duck anchors the other. Inside the Duck is a lovely bar and restaurant, but its real claim to fame is the seaside patio, where live music accompanies spectacular sunsets nearly every night.

I was encouraged to bring a friend on the week-long vacations we spent down there at Christmas and in March. My having a traveling companion was a win/win for everyone. It kept me out of my parents' hair, and although I had free rein with whomever my friend du jour was, we couldn't get into much trouble on Captiva, as there was no place to go. It was just an idyllic little spot on the end of a long, skinny sand bar.

My parents started spending longer and longer stretches of time there when I went away to college in Ann Arbor. About three years ago they took the big leap and bought a decrepit little cottage there on what is really just a sandy lane. They spent the first winter they were there replacing rotted wood, scraping, and painting. Under my mother's supervision, they redid the interior the next season. All the while they were making friends and getting involved with local projects. The transition to spending half the year down there was seamless. The house comfortably accommodates Charlie and me and an occasional guest.

We have a fairly predictable routine when we visit. Breakfast at RC Otters is a must, time on the beach is a ritual and, time permitting, a bit of fishing. Throw in a few dinners at outdoor bistros and a dinner at home with steaks from Bailey's market, and you have a complete package.

We were leaving at the crack of dawn, and I was impressed by Charlie's organization. When I realized she was about to leave the house to go to the concert, though—without me—I admit to being a bit flummoxed.

"Are you leaving right now? Where are you going? Who are you going with? What time will you be home?" I flung question after question at her.

"I'm on my way to Darling Park to see Livingston Taylor, just like you. Five of us from the lacrosse team are getting sandwiches from the Blue Canoe on the way. I'll be home when it's over."

Put like that, it didn't seem so outrageous. I guess I just felt I was losing a bit of control, that she was slipping through my fingers.

"Good, then. Maybe we'll see you over there."

I'm not sure if she rolled her eyes, but it was a mighty quick kiss on the cheek that marked her departure.

Feeling oddly empty, I put the groceries away in the kitchen and went upstairs to pack. I made quick work of throwing in my predictable choices and was downstairs buttering the hot dog buns when Bode arrived. It was a quiet entrance, as he had left Bob behind. No Bob, no Charlie. The little sting on my butt and the smooch on my cheek lifted my spirits quickly and brought me back where I belonged.

"Let me see the lobster meat!" I said. "Wow, that's a lot! You squeeze every last morsel out of those bright red shells, don't you?"

He smiled. "Yup! Never saw a lobster leg that didn't have enough meat to keep. This is going to be good!"

He grabbed me, and we started dancing around the kitchen to his rendition of "Carolina Day."

"You know what I say? We don't dance nearly enough!" I sputtered between twirls. So many of life's problems can disappear with just a little fun.

"Okay, let me go now!" I told him. "We need big fat lobster rolls to go with all the beer, wine, and potato chips. And look what I bought for dessert!"

Bode looked over at the Hostess CupCakes and gave me another bear hug. It's amazing what a simple memory conjures up. He packed the drinks in a small cooler, and I put the sandwiches, chips, napkins, and cupcakes in a canvas bag.

"I have an extra lobster roll in case Pepper wants compensation for her deviled eggs, and I have one for Uncle Henry, too," I said. "He's bringing some kind of new craft beer for you to taste. I wonder if we'll see Charlie and her friends there. I think there are a couple hundred people going."

"Turn off your mother brain," Bode chided me, "and hurry up! I'm ready for a beer." Grabbing my hand, he led me out the door.

It was then that I finally turned off that mother brain and regressed to a carefree girl jumping into a truck with her boyfriend.

CHAPTER

TWENTY-NINE

O N THE DRIVE over I tried to explain to Bode all that Dexter
had told me. I was having a hard time focusing on it as the
festive mood of the evening and upcoming weekend had me a bit
frazzled. Although Bode listened, he didn't seem really engaged
either. We did, however, agree that Ty and Dexter had been treated
horribly by Chillingsworth, and I think we both saluted their black
mailing scheme with some guilty satisfaction.

We parked some distance away from the venue, believing that
a pleasant walk is preferable to being stuck in traffic. Bode pulled
over by the Town House, and we gathered our two chairs, the
cooler, and the canvas tote, and were off. I tried to picture what this
scene might look like from an airplane. Undoubtedly, like a flotilla
of many little ants heading in a slow progression to the same hilly
spot at harbor's edge.

We arrived at the top of the hill ourselves and took a look
around. People were grabbing spots close to the improvised stage,
hoping, I guess, to see what color Livingston Taylor's eyes were. As

for myself, I have always preferred to be as close as possible without being jammed in with other people. This usually means stage left or stage right; either location affords me good visibility with little competition. Taylor's stool was on a stage at the top of the rocky outcrop and about twenty feet from the water. We found a place fairly close and were perfectly happy.

I glanced around and saw a group that included Gus and Aggie at one of the picnic tables that lined the back of the park. I waved and headed over.

"Good evening, Lizzie!" offered Gus. "What a night to be under the stars!"

"Lizzie, dear!" chimed in Aggie. "Join us for a little glass of wine, will you?"

I saw Bode off to the left, claiming his beer from Uncle Henry, so decided to join the group.

"You're a jolly group," I said. "Do you have a little red wine you could spare?"

Gus was the first up and gallantly presented me with a little red Solo cup filled to the brim.

"Is Alice back yet?" I asked the group. "It's awful that they took her into Portland, and put her through all those questions. It's obvious those police don't know what they're doing, or they wouldn't do that to such a good woman."

"Well, police work has to be done objectively," said Gus. "Hopefully, a more subjective evaluation of the situation will get her home.

"And how foolish is all this fuss about the demise of a worthless human being?" Gus went on. "Ty Waters was nothing but trouble his entire life. He was trouble for Ollie and trouble for Alice. She has every right to want him dead."

"Now, Gus," I interrupted.

"You men never much liked Ty the way we girls did," chimed in Aggie. "He treated us so nicely and was so generous with praise about our shabby swings and clumsy ball placement. But I do think he had a special place in his heart for Thistle. She was the only one he would play with in the club doubles matches. And they always seemed to win, remember?"

"I saw the trophy at Ty's yesterday," I commented.

"Such foolishness," grumbled Gus. "Obviously, *she* didn't want the damn fool thing."

"Enough, Augustus," said Aggie. That seemed to get his attention, and he quieted down.

"I'd better head over and say hello to Uncle Henry and the town bigwigs," I told them. "You guys certainly got the better table! *They're* out in the bushes!" As I left, everyone was laughing.

At the "town table," Bode was holding court. I wondered if every small town in America had a similar bunch at its helm. I wondered, too, if every small town's head librarian always had a crush on its local sheriff. Our own Miss Whatever Her Name Was seemed to be laughing hysterically at everything that came out of Uncle Henry's mouth and had plunked herself right down beside him. He seemed oblivious, so at least she wasn't bothering him. But she wasn't exactly ingratiating herself to him either. I chose not to concern myself with it.

"Hey, young lady! You forgot my lobster roll! Bode got his designer beer, now it's your turn. You owe me!" teased Uncle Henry.

"Come over to our spot with me and we'll get it," I replied. "We haven't found Pepper yet, so haven't gotten our deviled eggs. Maybe you'll get lucky and get one of those, too. Let's go!"

As we snaked our way through the crowd, I gave Uncle Henry a Cliff Note version of all Dexter had told me. Even told with no drama, it was an amazing set of tales. I could almost see his computer-like brain analyzing each detail as he absorbed it.

"That's an amazing amount of new information," he admitted, "and so enlightening. I guess I'll start by calling off the tests on the red sand. There's so much happening just now and frankly I'm dumbfounded. It somewhat undermines my confidence that I always know what's going on in this little town. Apparently I don't, and that leaves me feeling a bit disillusioned."

"Oh, Uncle Henry, stop!" I chided him. "By the way, have you heard anything more about Alice?"

"In fact, I have. It seems she's not making things easy for them. I don't think she realizes what a vulnerable position she's in. She has no alibi, was practically on top of the murder scene, and has a motive she keeps replaying for anyone who will listen. Maybe we should have sent a lawyer with her to minimize the damage."

"Poor thing," I said. "Although she's probably felt a great deal of rage for Ty all these years, she's done a pretty good job of keeping it to herself. Given an opportunity like this to speak up, she just can't shut it off."

"Maybe so, Lizzie, maybe so, but it almost has me wondering, with this torrent of animosity, if she might have been capable of wielding that shovel."

"The shovel didn't really hit him all that hard, did it Uncle Henry?" I countered. "In fact, did it really hit him at all? It wasn't necessarily a colossal blow that caused Ty to smash into the grave marker in front of him, was it?"

"Let's just keep our thinking caps on, Lizzie." Uncle Henry reassured me somewhat when he said, "They really can't keep her down there for too much longer. They have nothing but circumstantial evidence. No word on the body, yet?"

"No, Uncle Henry," I answered, seemingly for the fiftieth time.

We continued on our way and bumped into Pepper and the newspaper staff huddled together.

She caught sight of us and before I could even say hello a platter bearing little half eggs nestled in oval indentations was thrust under my nose. She looked tickled pink when my delight showed plainly on my face. For all her pseudo grumbling about sharing these little delicacies, she couldn't contain her joy when someone praised them.

I had just taken a second and was about to move on when I caught a look from Pepper. I could read her face like a book, and I knew just what she was angling for.

"Want a lobster roll, Pepper?"

"You betcha'! Can you bring it over? These old knees aren't what they used to be."

"Sure thing," I smiled.

Uncle Henry and I retraced our steps. I picked out two of the beautifully wrapped treasures and handed them to Uncle Henry. "One for Pepper on the way back, please," I told him.

Bode and I plopped down in our chairs and started to get organized. He pulled a beer out of the cooler, and I handed him my bottle of wine and the corkscrew. There are things that I am perfectly capable of doing, but there is something nice about having a man open the wine.

He performed that gallant act and poured a healthy portion of the red liquid into my big plastic wine goblet. We clinked glasses and gave each other happy, contented looks. The accompanying course of lobster rolls and fancy chips only heightened our mood. Coupled with anticipation of the upcoming concert, we felt we were living high on the hog. I concentrated on enjoying this very moment, the now moment we were in, with no distractions. It didn't seem anything could possibly dampen our spirits.

The sun set then, leaving only a golden light in its place. We sat back as Jennie stepped up to the mike to introduce her friend. Two different voices called out in unison to tease her; it was just what she needed to finally relax and enjoy the moment.

"Hi, everybody!" Her cheery voice was loud and clear, and the water echoed it back over the assembled crowd in festive mode. "Isn't this just great!"

CHAPTER
THIRTY

I LEANED CONTENTEDLY INTO Bode. I think I smelled it before I heard or saw it. It was something bad. Very bad. I looked sideways and saw Uncle Henry half leading, half dragging, Charlie. She was disheveled, to say the least, and her eyes weren't focusing properly. The combined stench of vomit and Seagram's Seven probably has a place in most everyone's memory, and it's not an odor anyone cares to revisit. Bode jumped to attention immediately. And me? For a brief moment I just wished it could be a minute ago when life was good, and we were all entranced by the magic of the music.

Unfortunately, that was no longer possible. The mess was here and now and unavoidable. The men lowered Charlie into the chair previously occupied by Bode, and took over. Bode left to get the truck so he could pick us up at the bottom of the hill. Uncle Henry helped me with all the paraphernalia. I was so shell-shocked I wasn't feeling much of anything. I wasn't so much angry at Charlie, as I just wished it hadn't happened. But then, like all mothers, I kicked into gear, helped her up, and in not a terribly maternal manner steered her toward the street. Uncle Henry followed behind us, toting the gear.

"I found her in the bushes not far from where we were sitting," he told me. "There were four other girls, but they weren't in such tough shape. They were all pretty scared. When I suggested they go straight home, they nodded at me like four little deer in the headlights and scampered off."

The three of us wobbled down the path together, blessedly invisible. Livingston Taylor was the one who had everyone's attention as he sang "Heart and Soul". Despite our predicament I found myself quietly humming along. When we reached the street, Charlie was sick again. I put my hand on her forehead and offered her a tissue I found in my pocket. Bode arrived with the truck, and we prepared to load up. I had but one resolute thought in that moment. I turned Charlie's head toward me, looked her directly in the eye, and said, "Do NOT get sick in Bode's truck."

We made the trip home with no dire consequences. Bode helped me get Charlie into the kitchen, gave me a peck on the cheek, assured me he would be there to pick us up in the morning, and disappeared.

"Charlie," I began. As she groaned and laid her head on the counter I thought better of all I had in mind. "Honey, eat some of these Saltines and drink this ginger ale. It's pretty much all we can do until your system works the alcohol through."

"Mom, I can't close my eyes. Everything is whirling around and around. I don't know what to do," she whimpered.

"Put one foot solidly on the floor, and try to keep your eyes open. This will pass. Do I need to tell you the consequences of drinking too much? Maybe not. I think you are living that lesson in spades.

"I'm not going to talk too much about this as I think the punishment is fitting the crime; my scolding would only be redundant. But I'd like to remind you of your quotation: 'We are what we repeatedly do. Excellence then, is not an act, but a habit.'

"It will be awhile, Charlie, before you and your friends gain my trust again. You blew it tonight. I'm going to help you upstairs now, but I expect you to be up and dressed and ready for our flight at six a.m. sharp."

With that, we got up and the poor little thing actually crawled up the steep stairs to her room. I left her equipped with more Saltines, a bottle of ginger ale, and a plastic bucket.

Once she was upstairs I was left hanging, as they say, high and dry. I rectified this somewhat by pouring myself a healthy glass of red wine. I curled up in Charlie's big chair, put on my "cozy" playlist, and hoped that Alison Krauss would calm me down.

Suddenly my subconscious fairly jumped out of my skull. It sent me flying from the chair. I hit autodial on my phone and immediately heard Bode's voice in my ear.

"Can you come back over real quick, Bode?"

"Wow, that was quick! Need me, huh?" he laughed.

"No, seriously. Get your sweet self over here pronto!"

I quickly turned off the lights, lit some candles, popped a beer for Bode, and waited. My heart was pounding. It seemed like forever until he arrived, but it couldn't have been much more than ten minutes.

I sat still as he came through the kitchen door.

"Well, well, I know we won't be seeing each other for a couple of days, but this seems . . ." he started.

"Come here, Bode. I have just had the most amazing thought. Listen to me. I was sitting here letting my mind wander a bit and suddenly it occurred to me! You *are* your father's son! Ty was gay! He did nothing but flirt with all the ladies. He and Thistle had, at the most, a totally innocent relationship. He probably did love her; so many people did! But he is definitely not your father!"

"Z, you are genius. I was so distracted when you were talking about it before that I didn't really listen. But of course you're right. You're right! Well, then, how does one celebrate knowing who one's father is?"

He jumped up, blew out the candles, and up we went. It was the most wonderful celebration.

CHAPTER
THIRTY-ONE

I OPENED MY EYES around 5:15, right before my alarm went off. Bode was already gone. I assumed he had left to go home to Bob, but those details diminished in light of the ordeal before me: getting Charlie on that airplane.

I heard nothing from upstairs. I dreaded this whole thing. I love my little girl, and I hate to see her suffer. And I knew she was going to suffer getting her poor, whiskey soaked body down the stairs, in the truck, through the airport, and on the plane. I hoped for a respite by the time we arrived in Fort Myers.

It was a great relief when I heard her shower running. I didn't want to add insult to injury by having to physically haul her around.

I relived last night in my mind. What a wonderful, wonderful realization it had been, and what a wonderful gift it was for Bode. I still felt a warm reel of happiness and relief spinning inside me.

I went downstairs to pack Saltines and M&Ms for the airplane ride; Saltines for what might be an ugly situation for Charlie, and M&Ms for me. I have a fear of being at 30,000 feet with no chocolate. My little bag and Charlie's duffle were right by the front door. I felt like Bode was picking up a couple of Girl Scouts; we certainly were prepared. What came dragging down the stairs a few moments later was no Girl Scout, however. It was a beleaguered sixteen year old with a headache I could almost feel and a body having a tough time with the upright position. I had the good taste not to ask if she was hungry and kind of led her outdoors to sit on the porch.

When I heard the truck tires coming up the lane, I grabbed both bags, closed the front door, and scampered down the front steps. Charlie navigated the same path behind me with a bit more care, and we were soon on our way to the airport.

Bode gave me a quick kiss and Charlie a nod brimming with sympathy.

We chatted in the front seat in muted voices so as not to intrude further on the hurting puppy in the back seat.

"Great night, Z" Bode said. "Who knew I would ever be so happy just to know that Dad is my father? It's like hitting yourself on the head with a hammer. I wish the whole thing had never come up, but it sure feels good to stop the whacking and have this whole thing resolved.

"And I must say," continued Bode, "the whole idea of Chillingsworth having Dunkirk do something like that doesn't sound as outrageous as it should. If I thought more of either man it might seem totally farfetched. But Dunkirk and Chillingsworth? Maybe not so much. And from what I have experienced, when Chillingsworth tells Dunkirk to jump, his only response is 'How high?'"

"Are we awful?" I responded. "I don't know, but I do know that Dexter is a devastated fellow with a huge loss to deal with. I want to help him however I can. Maybe his hypothesis is somewhat outrageous, but life can be crazy."

We spent the rest of the ride bemoaning all the things Bode would miss while we were away on our two-day trip.

It wasn't long before Charlie and I were in the security line. She was being a trooper, putting one foot in front of the other, but I felt terrible for her. Your little girl is your little girl. Even when she's not so little, and the trouble is self inflicted. I just wanted to get on the plane so she could sleep.

Having performed all the contortions one is expected to execute to be safe on the plane, we were through security and at our gate. I offered to get Charlie anything she might want, but she had spotted the Saltines and declared a bottle of water to be her choice. I headed to Dunkin' Donuts and grabbed an iced tea, a chocolate croissant, and a big bottle of cold water. It cost three times what it should have, but when you are trapped in an airline terminal it's worth it.

I was feeling pretty darn good about myself when I looked up and caught the gaze of the man across from us. I almost jumped out of my seat. It was none other than Daniel Dunkirk. I had the immediate impression that he knew all I had said about him in the last eighteen hours and almost ran. But with steel composure I merely smiled and grunted something akin to "good morning."

His response mirrored my enthusiasm "Going to see your mommy and daddy?"

"Yes, my parents are down for the season," I responded civilly. "And you?"

"I have a meeting with Arthur Chillingsworth," he replied. "Business."

Ha! I thought. Who would ever want to see him socially? Stop, I told myself.

"I'm hoping to see him down there too," I said.

"Why would you have occasion to see Mr. Chillingsworth?" was his boorish reply.

"Business," I said.

Luckily we were not seated anywhere near him. Charlie fell into her seat and was asleep before we took off. It made me feel better just knowing she felt better, or was at least blessedly unaware of how badly she did feel. I watched the ground sink down below us and marveled at how organized the world appeared from up here—people moving from place to place with a purpose, roads organized to take them where they needed to go, and all arranged so perfectly. It didn't always feel that way when you were in the middle of it, I thought. I waited until I was served my Diet Coke and cookies, ate them with gusto, then fell into a contented sleep next to Charlie.

THIRTY-TWO

AS THE WHEELS of the plane hit the tarmac, I had a moment of complete discombobulation. Where was I? One look out the window at the swarm of luggage handlers racing around in shorts and tee shirts reassured me instantly. Yes, we were indeed in a land of warmth and, perhaps more importantly, color. In northern climes, where winter colors become so muted, it can be like living in a world of black and white and gray. Landing in Captiva, I felt like Dorothy landing in Oz. It felt so good.

Looking left I saw Charlie going through a similar metamorphosis. I saw her eyes suddenly focus when she realized where we were; luckily, those eyes were clearer and more alert than the previous evening. My girl was back.

I had spotted Daniel Dunkirk on the plane when we boarded. Deplaning, I counted my blessings that I had been in the tail; he would be gone by the time we exited. Tanned people in shorts waited on the tarmac for arriving friends and family. I love watching folks come together on these occasions for regardless of what awkwardness might lie ahead, the initial moments are almost always good.

Charlie and I made our way down the escalator to the car rental desk. I always need the independence of my own wheels, regardless of the situation. Even when staying with my parents, I have to know I can hop in my car and go and do as I please.

Because we had a premium membership, we skipped the line and went straight to the garage. I was a bit surprised to see Dunkirk leaving the garage in a sensible, nondescript white sedan. We, on the other hand, hopped into a bright red Mustang convertible. The added cost gave me the pleasure of riding with nothing between me and the sunshine.

While Charlie set all the buttons on the radio to her favorite country stations, I maneuvered my way out of the airport. The sun was bright, but we were ready, having had the foresight to grab our baseball hats from our luggage. Just seeing palm trees was enough to fill my soul. Someday, before I die, I want to own one.

I watched as Dunkirk's tin can on wheels went up the I-75 ramp. I knew a short cut that made that route archaic, so we booked a right onto Alico and began the journey to our final destination. For all the natural beauty of Captiva, the road trip through Fort Myers is quite the opposite. The roads are all ten lanes wide, with left- and right-hand turn lanes that come up too quickly for one to anticipate. One wrong move can take unwary drivers a good five miles out of their way before there's an opportunity to turn around. It is lunacy to even think of crossing these roads on foot.

And then we saw it.

"Mom, it's still there!" exclaimed Charlie. "It's so bad!"

I looked up and sure enough, there was the billboard that asked the question, 'Are you paying too much for childcare?' Florida seems utterly preoccupied with discounts: Eat before 5:30 and get half off. Buy ten gallons of gas and get a box of animal crackers. But discount child care? Charlie and I had laughed at the lunacy of this sign for years.

We had jockeyed around crazed drivers for close to half an hour when the toll booths marking the entrance to the causeway—and the islands—appeared. Frankly, I consider the six-dollar toll the best-spent money on earth.

Cruising down Sanibel's Periwinkle Way, we were welcomed by all our familiar spots. Not a single chain restaurant or chain store disrupted the ambience of this place. There wasn't even a stoplight. We soon turned onto the San Cap Road for the final seven miles to Captiva. Long and straight, it is ideal for bicyclists. Pedestrians, however, are well advised to heed the 'beware of alligator' signs; they are authentic, and not just a Disney touch. When I at last spied the beautiful pink sign announcing The Lazy Flamingo on the right, and we had crossed the little bridge over Blind Pass, I let out a long sigh of contentment; we had at last reached our precious island.

The first few miles of road has lovely homes on either side, all with island names: Pelican's Roost, Hakuna Matata, and Seas the Day.

"Orange You Glad! Wine Down! Happy Ours!" shouted Charlie gleefully, reading the whimsical names of others we passed. "Barefoot Way! We're really here, Mom!"

The road bent in a crazy S-curve, then took a sharp left. We passed our favorite duplex, Pair-A-Dice, and continued on past Jensen's Marina. We crossed Andy Rosse Lane to Egret Avenue and there we found the sandy trail that leads to my parents' little cottage—and our ultimate destination—Final Nest.

The front door banged open before the car had come to a full stop, and my parents rushed out to pull us from the vehicle and into their waiting arms. Before long we and our luggage were comfortably settled inside.

I always marvel at how such a little structure can be so grand. It was already old when my parents bought it. Although ninety percent of the island's homes are perched on stilts, the better to weather hurricanes, ours is not. Ken and Mildred figured that if a hundred years of hurricanes and floods had left Final Nest unscathed, it was best to leave it be.

French blue shutters and a shiny coral door provided the cottage's front with a bold and colorful accent to the bright white clapboards. A bright crushed-shell walkway snaked through the lush, dark-green foliage of dwarf boxwoods, and carissa bushes bookended both sides of the small front porch. Their lovely white flowers were in bloom when we arrived, and I looked forward to the sweet fragrance that would fill our night air and waft through the open windows. Palm trees at the perimeter of the small lot afforded all the shade we needed to survive the sometimes unbearable tropical sun.

We entered the house together arm in arm, almost as a single unit. Charlie and I had previously decided to let last night's misadventure remain unmentioned and put it in the past. Keeping up the chatter, Charlie and I went to our room and put on shorts, tee shirts, and flipflops. We emerged still in mid-conversation. Everyone jumped on the golf cart for a trip to the Mucky Duck, where Dad and I went in with our order: four burgers, three beers, and a Diet Coke. The camaraderie both inside and out was festive on this Saturday afternoon in October. It is, indeed, a magical place.

We carried the drinks out and joined Charlie and her grandmother in the warm, salty air. I straddled the bench at the table and raised my glass. Four happy faces exchanged "Cheers!"

CHAPTER

THIRTY-THREE

THE FESTIVE, MEANINGLESS jabber continued throughout the meal. Charlie kept getting up and running down to the beach to test the water. I was in awe of the recuperative powers of youth.

Because of Charlie's impatience to get to the beach, our meal was a bit rushed. Nonetheless, we happily jumped back on the golf cart for the trip back to Egret Avenue. There was a mad dash to the bedroom when we arrived, this time to don bathing suits. We snatched up a few of the beach chairs, umbrellas, and towels my parents always have at the ready and in no time at all I was reclining in a Tommy Bahama beach chair under a rainbow-colored umbrella on a white sandy beach.

I noticed Charlie kept giving me a look, clearly implying that I was behaving like an old fart. If only to prove her wrong, I pulled myself out of the chair and ran toward the water. There is nothing better than that first dip into the sea after being held captive by harsh weather for weeks. I felt every problem, every sad and bad thought, and every concern melt away. Nothing existed except the invigorating water and me. Flipping onto my back, I watched my painted toenails float on the surface, framed by a backdrop of blue sky and green palm trees. Nirvana.

Reality returned in due course. As Charlie headed off for a walk down the beach, I took that time to fill my parents in on all the goings-on at home.

I began with the discovery of Ty Waters slumped against the headstone, cut to Ollie's flight and Alice's questioning, and closed with my meeting with Dexter. It would not be hyperbole to say they were almost speechless.

"That's a lot to happen in just two days in our peaceful little community. Uncle Henry must be up to his ears with the state police," said my dad.

"Why, it's just terrible," exclaimed my mom. "Who would think such goings on could happen in Woodford Harbor? It does seem that the murderer is local. Gracious. Ollie and Alice? And really, Daniel Dunkirk? I've always felt Arthur Chillingsworth was a bit infatuated with himself, but a murderer?"

I gave my mom a reassuring pat on the knee and addressed my dad. "You're right about Uncle Henry; he *is* fit to be tied. I'm trying to help him—and everyone involved—which is why I'm going to see Arthur Chillingsworth tomorrow. Ostensibly, it's to see if he'll help out with Ty's funeral expenses, but it's also to ascertain his take on all this. By the way, Dunkirk was on our flight down."

"Maybe to collect his loot for knocking off old Ty," my father said, grinning. Somehow the humor was lost on me. Maybe I was too close to the whole thing and had lost my objectivity. Or perhaps my father didn't grasp the seriousness of all that had transpired.

"Maybe it's not a good idea for you to go over there," my mom added in a worried tone.

"Mildred, please!" huffed my dad.

She cocked her head and rolled her eyes at him as she had done nearly every day for over forty years.

Charlie eventually returned from her walk. "Mom, help me

collect some shells, will you? I promised Bode I would find a perfect horse conch for him, and I want some colorful shells to put around the mirror in my bedroom."

"If we come down early in the morning, we'll find so many more," my mother told her. "Let's wait until then." As much as Mom might know about shells, she's a bit out of touch when it comes to the sleep cycles of sixteen-year olds. There aren't many things that will get Charlie out of bed at the crack of dawn, and I'd put money on the fact that getting the best shells was not one of them.

Charlie wouldn't be put off, another teenage trait, and insisted we try our luck now. The two of us spent the better part of the next hour in the Sanibel stoop, the posture one presents while bent over searching the sand for prize shells. We were not disappointed and returned with pockets full of beauties. Our haul just reinforced the barrier islands' worldwide reputation as 'shell heaven.' Frankly, this is but one of many reasons we love Sanibel and Captiva.

We had no sooner plopped down in our chairs again when my dad announced, "Folks, I think it's time we take that golf cart home, clean up, and bring some cocktails down here in time for the sunset."

There was not a hesitant bone in this group. We folded towels, flattened beach chairs, and collapsed the big umbrella into a manageable shaft for transport. My parents used the indoor shower while Charlie and I took turns in the al fresco shower at the back of the cottage. The outside shower runs a close second to the feeling of a first dip in the ocean. Crazy as it may sound, I always feel cleaner when I shower outdoors.

Inside, my dad had opened a lovely bottle of red wine for me and had limes floating in sparkling gin and tonics for my mother and him. Charlie reveled in her Diet Coke. Before long we were all back in the golf cart for a return trip to the beach.

Every sunset on Captiva is an event, and the enthusiasm for the nightly ritual is unparalleled. Groups of people were gathered the length of the beach to witness the end of another day.

"Think you'll see it, sweet Charlie?" asked my father, giving his granddaughter a playful shove towards the water.

"I don't know, Papa, but at least I'll tell the truth about whether I do or not. You say you see the green flash all the time, but there's no way you can prove if you really do or not!" was her lengthy retort.

A green flash is a phenomenon of sunsets everywhere but they are most visible on Captiva, where the flat horizon over the ocean offers a clean, unobstructed view of the sun setting. Under the right conditions, a flash of green light appears for a second or two at the top tip of the setting sun just as it dips below the horizon. Ideal conditions require the night to be clear, with no clouds on the horizon, and the wind to be minimal so as to produce a calm sea.

Captiva sunsets also often coincide with dolphins cavorting along the water's edge in the golden glow. Sunsets here are, for me, a truly magical experience.

I sipped my wine, counting my blessings, and held Charlie's drink while she went in search of more shells. It felt good to be a thousand miles away from the craziness that was Ty Waters. But there was a definite hole without dear Bode standing next to me. Guess you can't have it all.

CHAPTER
THIRTY-FOUR

T HE HAPPY CHATTER continued all the way back to the cottage.

"I saw it, Papa," said Charlie, addressing her grandfather. "That makes two times. The first was when I was little and wasn't sure if I saw it or imagined it. This time, though, I definitely saw it! I saw the green flash!" she exclaimed.

"Charlie, I always knew you were a bright one. It's a sign of intelligence to see that light," teased my dad.

"Papa, I think you're making fun of me, I really do."

"No, my dear," said my dad, enveloping her in a bear hug. "I think you're bright, brilliant, and observant all put together." I smiled. There was so much love encapsulated in that small moment.

We tumbled into Final Nest and my mom pulled a steak worthy of a still life from the refrigerator.

"A steak from Bailey's is truly a thing of beauty," I observed.

"I know," said my dad. "I take my time when I'm picking one out and peruse them all. Never seen any meat market like it. I'll light up the grill, and we'll transform this beauty into another form of art—the culinary kind!"

I flopped down on the old sofa and felt the comfort of being cared for. It was a wonderful feeling.

My mother's expertise in shells translates into a bit of a problem in this tiny little cottage, as she has to do something with all the shells she collects. There are mirrors framed in shells, smiling faces in picture frames lined with shells, and collages of shells in shell frames. Her toilet seat is the ultimate, though. We were all aghast when we heard she had poured a layer of epoxy over shells she'd lined up along the seat, but were charmed by the result. Hers was a harmless obsession, and she took such pleasure from it. How could we begrudge her this happiness?

The little cottage suited my parents to a T. The worn couch I was on and a large old farmer's table more or less dominated the living space. The kitchen was in a little extension at the back so the cook was a part of the action. Two lamps with shell shades sat at either end of the couch, and a shell chandelier hung over the table. Its six mismatched chairs were painted in tropical colors that gave their disparity a somewhat united look. All the photos in the shell frames were of family.

Charlie had gone to our room, and Dad was preparing the steak outside on the grill. That left just my mom and me in the little room.

"How is Bode doing with Thistle gone?" she asked quietly.

"Oh, Mom, it's so hard to watch. He's devastated. She had been getting physically weaker and weaker, but it was so gradual you hardly noticed. Her soul, by contrast, was as strong and wonderful as ever. We had a nice service for her, and—as you might expect—half the town showed up, which was nice for Bode and Jonny and Bill. I hope that being on his own this weekend will help him deal with his grief."

"She was a dear lady; so much fun and so kind. They were a wonderful family. I like thinking of you as part of it," she said.

Just then the door flew open, and the tantalizing aroma of perfectly grilled steak filled the room. We quickly set the table, poured more wine, and placed salad and baked potatoes at each place setting. The commotion—or perhaps the smells!—roused Charlie and soon we were all seated around the feast.

After a quick toast, we attacked our plates as one.

"Ken, I was just talking with Lizzie about Thistle. Weren't she and James and the three boys a wonderful family?"

"Yes, they were," he replied, wiping his mouth. "I knew James from the hospital before his untimely death. He was very well respected, a good physician, and a gentleman. Thistle gave him a real run for his money, but it was just innocent good fun, I think.

"It always seemed a bit much to me that those four couples did so much together," he went on. "They obviously enjoyed each other's company, but it seemed suffocating to me. Gus and Emma were wonderful people. Bright and curious, they were always eager to learn something new. Aggie and her husband, on the other hand, seemed to be the followers in the group. They were nice as nice can be, but never really instigated anything. As for the Chillingsworths, I never did understand their place in that crowd. They made an odd addition to my way of thinking, but I suppose the group welcomed the accoutrements they were able to add. Who wouldn't enjoy the tennis club they had in Woodford Harbor and the giant yacht they moor down here. In truth, though, I always thought Thistle and James sat at the top of the pack."

"How did Ty Waters fit in to all that?" I asked.

"The women seemed to worship him," my mom chimed in. "Frankly, I could never see the allure. It could be because I don't play tennis, but what in the world could those four mature ladies see in that caricature of a tennis pro? They actually giggled when they were talking about him in a group. Of course, Thistle and Aggie could giggle about anything, but even Emma, with all her intellect and sophistication, seemed to want his attention!

"And then there's Gloria, for heaven's sake! Even she worshipped Ty. Had he bothered to notice, I'm sure Arthur would have been annoyed. Poor Gloria, he pays her absolutely no mind. He never has, and he probably never will."

"The men of the group didn't think much of him at all," my father remarked. "I think they saw him as an annoying little bug that just wouldn't go away. I couldn't believe it when Ty got the job down here in the winters. It was actually rather comical from a distance."

"Well, it's not so funny for Ty, now," I said.

That quieted things down for a bit. After cleaning up, we all hopped back on the golf cart to go to Latte Da for some of Queenie's famous ice cream.

I ordered first. "I'd like a single scoop of double espresso chocolate chip, please!"

"A double scoop of mint chocolate chip for me, please," added Charlie.

It was my mom's turn next. "Oh my, two scoops of red raspberry sorbet for me."

Fishing in his wallet for money, my dad stepped up to the counter. "Two scoops of Pine Island mango for me, please." There is something wonderful about having your father buy you an ice cream cone regardless of your age.

We headed back to the cottage and sat peacefully on the four little porch chairs, happily consuming every frozen morsel. It was then I remembered the Stowaway Sweets for my mom.

"Mom! I almost forgot," I exclaimed. "I have a pound of your personal chocolates from Stowaway Sweets! Just a minute!" I jumped up and rushed to my room, returning to present her the gold foil box with a flourish.

"Thanks so much, dear," my mom said with a smile. "I'll take good care of them."

This selfish teasing didn't last long; it was less than a minute before she tore the foil off the box and opened it to share. She did, however, extract the biggest cashew turtle before anyone else had a chance to dive in.

The chocolate treats were the finale of our first day on Captiva. Soon, four very happy, very tired people fell into their respective beds for what each hoped would be a night full of pleasant dreams.

CHAPTER
THIRTY-FIVE

I WOKE UP EARLY the next morning and took my phone down to the beach to give Bode a call. It was glorious. Tiny waves lapped at the ocean's edge, nudged landward by the gentlest of breezes. I could already anticipate the heat the sun would provide later. For now, however, it was just a soft, enveloping warmth.

I grabbed an abandoned beach chair and dialed the familiar number.

As soon as I heard his voice, I felt Bode right next to me, could almost feel his breath.

"Morning, Bode. Oh, I so wish you were right here. It's lovely, but not complete without you."

"Thanks, Z. It's a bit rough up here without you. They say there are five stages of grief, but they also say root canals can be necessary. I understand the concept, but it doesn't mean I have to like it," he told me.

"I know. I know exactly what you mean. We'll be home tomorrow. I promise you, too, that you'll begin feeling better with every

day that passes. Is Bob keeping you good company?" I asked, trying to lighten the moment.

"He certainly is," responded Bode, already a bit more upbeat. "He knows there's something wrong, though. He senses it. He stays right next to me all the time. He even slept on the bed with me last night."

"That better not become a habit," I retorted. "If it does, where will I go?"

Bode changed gears. "Here's some good news, Z," he went on. "I saw Henry at Brown's last night, and he said they've released Alice, and she's home. He said Ollie is still pretty angry about the whole thing, but that everything else had pretty much settled down.

"Have you seen Chillingsworth yet? It would be really nice if he'd chip in for Ty's funeral. Judging from what Dexter said, though, it might not be much."

"Could be," I said, "but don't forget that Chillinsworth also likes to keep up appearances. By the way, Dunkirk was on our flight coming down. He's such a nasty little puke. He may not be a murderer—but then again who knows? Stranger things have happened!"

"Take it easy, Z." I could hear the smile on Bode's face.

"What are you up to today?"

"I was going to start going through the house, beginning with the kitchen, but I just don't feel like it. Instead I think I'll take Bob out to Redmond Island for a good long walk at low tide. The fresh air will be good for both of us."

"Good idea, Bode. You're taking care of yourself first, which is just what you need. When we're back tomorrow morning," I teased, "I'll give you something to smile about." I so hoped he could hear the seductive smile in my voice.

"Thanks, Z. I'll be looking good and forward to it," came his cheery reply.

I decided to tie up the one loose end back home and called Mr. Stanley. He agreed to set up a meeting for me with Ollie and Alice on Monday afternoon. I couldn't go forward with a plan for

Ty Waters' funeral until I had checked in with them. Hopefully, I'd have good news for them by then on financing the service.

I strolled the length of the beach at water's edge, my toes enjoying the warm water that lapped the shore. I watched my favorite birds, big old pelicans, dive into the ocean in search of breakfast. I've read that a pelican's death can most often be attributed to this behavior. Apparently, the repetitive impact of hitting the water leads to blindness, which in turn prevents them from finding their prey. Ultimately, of course, they starve. I guess that's why I get a little sad every time I see them doing this.

But enough of sad thoughts! I rebooted my brain and sought a more positive place. I began thinking of dolphins, those smart and playful creatures of the sea, when I noticed a great blue heron standing about twenty-five feet away at water's edge. His beady little eye stared at me, daring me to get any closer. Deciding this was *his* domain, I turned around to return home. The sun was getting higher, and I could already feel its increasing intensity. That and a marked grumbling in my stomach quickened my pace.

When I turned up Egret Avenue I could see activity around the cottage. My dad was just coming back from The Island Store with his newspaper, and my mom was sweeping sand off the front porch. We exchanged "good mornings," and I went in to check on Charlie. She was asleep, but easily aroused with the offer of breakfast at RC Otters.

Charlie opted to drive the golf cart, a first for her. She may be sixteen years old, but she's still a little girl to me. Just the thought of her behind the wheel of a real car made my head spin. Other than running the cart's fat wheels over the curb as she turned onto Andy Rosse Lane, she did a fine job.

We chose a table on the patio, under a large faded umbrella adorned with an island beer logo. Angie, our favorite waitress, was on duty so there was a raucous round of smiles and hugs. Years ago, Angie had teased me about the Patriots illegally deflating footballs, and I had surprised even myself at the way I snapped at her. The Patriots are, of course, an important part of my life, but my reaction had been a bit harsh. I couldn't quite bring myself to apologize, so we went down the street, bought a toy football, deflated it, and went back and presented it to her. It is still behind the bar.

She arrived with two coffees, an iced tea, and an orange juice for Charlie without being asked. Orders slid off our lips like the habits they were.

"Egg on a Roll, please," I said.

"Happy Otter, please," said Charlie.

"Granola, please," added my mom.

"And I'll have a Crabby Times," finished up my dad.

With that, we raised our mugs and glasses and smiled.

I always find it a shame when breakfast ends. It's so comfortable sitting there in the sunshine, and the food is so good you just want to keep eating, regardless of your bulging tummy. But finish we did, so it was back home on a Charlie-driven golf cart.

"Charlie, I'm going to go down to Red Fish Pass and do a little fishing off the breakwater. Do you want to join me?" asked my dad.

"Oh, yeah," smiled Charlie.

"Put some sunscreen on and remember to wear a hat," I said, intercepting her on the way out the door.

"Looks like I'm off to pay a visit to Arthur Chillingsworth," I announced to the rest of the room. "It's only about a twenty-minute walk, and I think the exercise will clear my head. I don't think I'll be there any too long. Wish me luck."

"I'll call the authorities if you're not back by noon," quipped my dad.

"Ken, it's not funny," snorted my mom.

On that note, I was off.

CHAPTER
THIRTY-SIX

T HE CONSTITUTIONAL DID, indeed, clear my mind. Walking down a road surrounded by palm trees and bougainvillea, combined with fresh salt air, puts a lot of things into perspective.

The loss of Thistle still stung, of course, but I realized how thankful I was to have known and loved her. I also recognized her importance to our community and vowed to incorporate her indomitable spirit and life of good works into my own life.

Conversely, I recognized what little impact Ty Waters' death was having on the world. Even as they lined up to stuff his casket with tennis balls, no one had any interest in taking care of his funeral arrangements. Poor Dexter, who had been treated so badly, couldn't help, and Ty's own flesh and blood, his twin brother, wasn't in a position to do so either.

I considered my upcoming meeting with Arthur Chillingsworth. His age, stature, and—quite honestly—his wealth, intimidated me. But I needed information from him and would have to put those fears aside. I had to be clever, too, and find a way to obtain the information I wanted without asking directly. If I referenced the Red Paint People, would it make him nervous? How would he react to my request for funds for Ty's funeral expenses? I had to be subtle, no doubt about it—and devious and somewhat disingenuous. None of these were my strong points.

Half an hour later I approached the Chillingsworth mansion. Its size was impressive, but the overall style of the house didn't do much for me. I noticed a little white tin can of a car in the driveway and assumed, correctly, that it was not Gloria's. No, it appeared that Dunkirk had preceded me. I gave the big brass conch knocker on the front door a hearty rap and was soon greeted by Gloria herself. Her tennis outfit was so dazzlingly white it made me wish I had worn sunglasses. Fake—and extraordinarily plump—lips held her equally white teeth captive in her mouth. She greeted me with an exuberant air kiss.

"Lovely to see you, dear. The boys are having mimosas out back on the patio. Do join them," she gushed vapidly.

I made my way down the hallway to open French doors that I assumed led to the patio. Not to belabor my judgment of their taste, but the mundane and—dare I say?—tacky accoutrements reminded me that wealth does not always breed good taste.

I could smell Chillingsworth's aftershave before I even reached the door. When he saw me he graciously stepped forward and welcomed me with an odiferous peck on the cheek. I would need to scrub that off as soon as I returned home; otherwise it would annoy me the rest of the day.

Chillingsworth was a caricature of a wealthy man in his early seventies. His freshly pressed khaki shorts were a tasteful length, his light pink polo shirt looked brand new, and portions of a needlepoint belt peeked out from beneath his overhanging paunch. Every so often I'd catch a glimpse of the country club logos that adorned it. The initialed pinky ring told anyone who chanced to look that he was somebody. His balding head sported a rich man's tan and set off a pair of penetrating blue eyes that were impressive. Impressive, yes, but with a side of harsh.

Dunkirk stood off to the side, looking ridiculous in a Hawaiian print shirt. Its muted colors made him look even pastier. His hair-less, fleshy white arms looked as though they had been prisoners in sleeves for a long while. Sometimes I think it's easier to talk with someone when their obvious weaknesses are staring you right in the face; it makes me feel like the powerful one. Dunkirk's fashion statement was screaming tacky, so I knew I had the upper hand in this. Blessedly, he'd forgone sandals for sneakers, so I didn't have to be further repulsed by his exposed toes.

"May I offer you a mimosa, dear?" It was Chillingsworth.

"Thank you, no. I'm not quite ready for that. But thank you for seeing me. I assume you've heard about Ty Waters' untimely end. It's caused quite a stir in Woodford Harbor."

"Yes," he agreed. "It was a bit of a shock—and leaves me without a pro up at Abenaki. I don't anticipate it will be difficult to fill the job, though."

Here it was, yet another not-so-heartfelt reaction to Ty Waters' absence on Earth. Thankfully, it wasn't the tirade of unpleasant-ness I had feared.

"You and Ty worked quite closely together. He was a nearly permanent presence at the Abenaki, and I assume you saw a lot of him down here as well, as he worked at the club where you play. You must have been pretty good friends." I waited for a reaction. I could have sworn Dunkirk twitched, but Chillingsworth was smooth as silk.

"We had a working relationship," he said.

"I've been trying to find any relatives he might have had that could come forward to help with his funeral expenses. Uncle Henry found almost no personal items in the gatehouse when he went through it. No family photos and no letters, only an item that was somewhat out of the ordinary. There was a box that held a small bag of reddish sand. It seems puzzling, but Uncle Henry is inves-tigating," I threw out.

"My dear, there is no need for you to go digging around in Ty's life. I would be more than happy to take care of any expenses you might incur arranging for his burial. Don't you worry about a thing." Then Chillingsworth quickly repeated his initial admonishment. "There's absolutely no need to poke around."

Dunkirk looked just as I had suspected, nervous as a canary around a cat.

"That's very kind of you, sir," I said. "I'll choose a minimal casket and perhaps plan a small graveside service. Many folks seem interested in attending, but no one has stepped up with an offer of payment. This is most generous of you." And saves my hide at the same time, I thought.

"Certainly, dear, certainly. Let's just put this all behind us as quickly as possible."

"By the way, Mr. Dunkirk, it was nice to see you at Thistle's reception. Did you enjoy the service?" I was digging for information.

"No, I was just at the reception."

"That's a shame. The service was lovely. Where were you?" I asked, hoping I sounded casual.

"On the phone with Arthur," he replied quickly, a bit too quickly to my way of thinking.

"That's correct," smiled Chillingsworth. The smile was almost a sneer and borderline chilling. My skin crawled.

I thanked my host profusely and headed out the way I had come in. He graciously followed to show me out.

"Don't you worry your little head about those funeral expenses," he reiterated. "Just let me know what I owe you, Lizzie."

I walked out feeling like a mini Sherlock Holmes. I had put Arthur Chillingsworth sufficiently on edge to offer to pay for Ty's funeral, and I had established Dunkirk's alibi as questionable.

With all this laborious work behind me, I was ready for a beer on the beach!

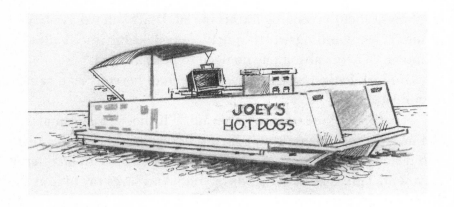

CHAPTER
THIRTY-SEVEN

I WANTED THAT BEER, so made quick work of the return walk. A note at Final Nest relayed that everyone was already at the beach and that lunch would be supplied by Joey's hot dog boat. I tucked the note into my pocket. It made me so happy that I knew rereading it on a snowy, windy day in February would lift my spirits.

I quickly donned my bathing suit, slathered on some sunscreen, shoved my feet into flipflops, and scrambled out the door. The beach is almost deserted at this time of year, so I spotted the three of them immediately. A quick dash across the hot sand and I was back in my familiar beach chair again. I reflected briefly on my conversation with Dunkirk and Chillingsworth, then, deciding I preferred my current reality, I put it to rest and followed Charlie into the water. We splashed around, raced from buoy to buoy, then looked over the horizon and saw Joey's pontoon boat making its way up the shoreline. The gas grill on the back of that boat produces the finest hot dogs in the world. Anywhere. Joey grills them within an inch of their lives, then offers mustard, relish, onions, and sauerkraut. Add to that a few frozen candy bars and you've got the perfect beach lunch.

As he pulled the craft up to the beach, Charlie and I ran from the water to our chairs for money. The frosting on the cake was that Joey always remembered us. I tended to stand a little taller when the nicest guy on the beach—and the king of the hot dogs—recognized me. I felt proud somehow. His tanned face, bright blue eyes, and fabulous smile were all Captiva needed to promote itself as one of the best spots on the planet. Joey never disappointed.

Charlie sipped happily on her Diet Coke while the rest of us popped the tops of our cold, frosty beers. The world's unpleasantness faded far away for a bit. My pleasantly marinated brain and full belly had the proper effect. I closed my eyes and was quickly out.

When I awakened an hour later, I looked left and saw that my mom, too, had found that a nap in the sunshine was a good idea. On my right, my father smiled down at me from his elevated chair.

"Welcome back," he said with a smile. "I guess you don't often have a beer at lunch. You were down and out, and I think your mother has the same affliction."

"Oh, Dad, that felt so good. This all feels good," I replied. "Getting away is so nice. Thistle's death and this whole Ty murder business is exhausting. I love being here with you and Mom."

"Charlie has decided to hike down to the lighthouse, so while she's gone tell me what Arthur had to say for himself? Was his trusty sidekick, Daniel Dunkirk, with him?" my father asked.

"Yes, he had arrived before me," I began. "It's so interesting to watch Dunkirk's reactions to Chillingsworth's emotions. Dunkirk displays the physical reaction you'd expect to see from Chillingsworth, while Chillingsworth himself just sails along without missing a beat.

"I intimated that he and Ty must have been fairly good friends given the time they spent together, but Chillingsworth was quick to distance himself; he described their relationship as strictly professional. Then I dropped the fact that Uncle Henry had found that baggie full of red sand in Ty's closet. I told him we were looking into that at the same time we're trying to locate relatives or old friends to pay for his service. Dunkirk twitched, and Chillingsworth quickly assured me there was no need to look into either. 'I would be more than happy to take care of any expenses you might incur arranging for his burial,' he told me. I could tell he was anxious to end those lines of inquiry, though, when he told me, 'There's absolutely no need to poke around.'

"I then went after Dunkirk and asked him if he had enjoyed Thistle's service. He admitted to being at the reception, but not at the service. When I casually asked him why he hadn't been there, he told me he had been on a call with Chillingsworth. I might be reading too much into this, but he answered my question much too quickly. Wouldn't you have to think about that for a minute?"

"Well . . ." my father began.

"I know, I know. Maybe I'm trying to hang too much on old Dunkirk's head."

"Sounds a bit presumptuous to me," my mother muttered from the left.

"Oh, Mom, quit being so sensible. How often do you get to take out your feelings in such an entertaining manner?"

"Thinking someone is a murderer?" was her reply.

"Stop! Stop, Mom! I'm just having a little thoughtless fun. You know how judgmental I can be, although I'm working on it. I now cut people slack while I'm ravaging them in my mind. I try to imagine that they are 'doing their best.'"

"Doesn't seem to be working too well," she offered. At that, the three of us had a good laugh.

Charlie approached us, back from her hike. Her skin was a somewhat tender shell of pink.

"You feel okay, honey? You look a little charred."

After assuring me she was fine, all four of us took a final dip before heading to the golf cart—and the cottage. This would be my last evening in paradise before returning to all that awaited me in Woodford Harbor.

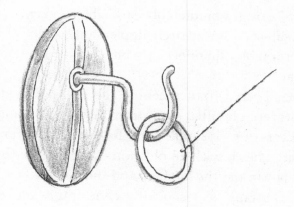

CHAPTER
THIRTY-EIGHT

NO SHOWER COMPARES to the one taken after a day at the beach. There's a lot of bang for the buck in the simple ritual of rinsing off sand, salt, and suntan lotion. Feeling that slight scratchiness on your sun-baked skin when you dry off; well, that's the frosting on the cake.

The four of us gathered our freshly scrubbed selves on the front porch. There had been no discussion about where we would have our last meal because we knew it would be at the Lazy Flamingo. The Lazy F, as we call it, is really the definition of saving the best for last.

It's basically a bar, a pub in the palm trees if you will. The building, as one might expect, is bright pink, and the logo is a stylized flamingo wearing sunglasses. The high stools around the U-shaped bar are so hard they can bruise your butt in less time than it takes to watch a football game, but that doesn't affect its popularity.

Neon beer signs hang from the corrugated metal walls, and the taps themselves are things of beauty, bearing the exquisite graphics of brewery logos. It's predictably dark when you enter, and carries the universal—and not entirely unpleasant —odor of a "good old pub." Several tables line one wall, but the majority of the seating is at the bar.

Tom has been a fixture behind the well-polished mahogany counter forever. A familiar smile from him is always another sweet moment. Everything is simple here. Tom writes your order on a slip of paper, attaches it with an old clothespin to wire that stretches between the bar and the kitchen, and shoots it in.

The cast iron oyster-shucking contraption on the bar is in almost constant use; the resounding *thunk* it makes each time an oyster is opened always makes me salivate. Its rhythm is the bass clef to the Lazy F's melody. However, it's not the only cacophony in the place. Between the shout-outs for order pickups and the occasional clang of the tarnished old bell that announces another big tip for the bartender, the place is definitely not for the shy and retiring.

The heart and soul of the Lazy F, though, is its ring toss game. A large hook is screwed into the corrugated metal about six feet up one wall. Nearby, a ring attached to a string hangs from the ceiling. Patrons score a "ringer" when they're able to swing the ring onto the hook. There's apparently a method to it, and regulars spend inordinate amounts of time attempting to master the skill. Mastering the hook and ring pretty much defines the experience that is the Lazy Flamingo. The occasional clang of the metal ring connecting with the metal hook draws everyone's admiring attention to the hero who threw it.

The four of us grabbed a table, and Dad went up to place our initial order. Three beers and a Diet Coke were a foregone conclusion, and the baker's dozen oysters on the half shell were a fine prelude to the meal to come.

Before long Charlie got up, grabbed the big ring, and gave it a beautiful swing toward the hook. It clanged without landing inside the curve, but it wasn't long before she had her first success and bowed to the crowd that cheered her. She was so pleased with herself that the three of us knew better than to follow her act. Our success would only lessen her achievement, and to what end?

We nestled into our booth and were slurping down a beautiful plate of oysters when I looked up and spotted Daniel Dunkirk walking in. The appendages that emerged from his Hawaiian shirtsleeves didn't look as though they had seen a drop of Florida sunshine since I had last seen him. I told myself he was 'doing his best' and abolished all the snarky comments buzzing around in my brain.

I was chasing down another oyster when I looked up to see Dunkirk step up to the ring toss game. I hated the thought of such a dweeb being part of a game I thought was so cool. Quickly—too quickly, I thought—the sharp clink of metal on metal reverberated through the bar. A "ringer!" As folks cheered, he got two more in a row. Then he did what I have to admit is the ultimate cool move. Standing next to the hook on the wall, he threw a "reverse ringer." He performed a stiff little bow to acknowledge the crowd's enthusiasm and returned to his seat.

I was forced to give him a smile as he walked by our table, but it killed me. The appreciative look I gave him was entirely fake and devoid of any authentic emotion.

"Lizzie, your mouth is hanging open," said my dad.

"This is just too bizarre," I sputtered. "How can Daniel Dunkirk be so good at ring toss?"

"Well, dear, it's not actually an Olympic sport. It doesn't require much endurance, strength, or physical prowess. It's just a certain knack for swinging a ring."

"I don't care. It just doesn't seem right somehow," I continued.

"Lizzie, I've always told you that you can't put people in boxes," offered my mom. "No one is all good or all bad, and you cannot mentally incarcerate them within the confines of a designated area. Trust me, people will always surprise you.

"I think your estimation of Daniel Dunkirk might be overly simplistic. You mustn't let his moment of cool upset you."

While her insight didn't sit well with me, it certainly resonated.

"Mom, you're right, of course. So right. I need to learn how to think outside the box. It's just that it's so easy to assign folks to good and evil boxes. And Daniel Dunkirk..."

"Lizzie, dear," my mom began. I knew better than to pursue it any further.

CHAPTER
THIRTY-NINE

MONDAY MORNING ARRIVED way too early. I threw our bags and Charlie into the rental car and was off before sunrise. Mom staggered out to bid us adieu, but it was a tired and weak wave that sent us on our way. I knew she was snuggled back in bed before we had even hit the S-turn. The trip to the Fort Myers airport is a piece of cake at 5 a.m., but my fear of hidden police officers on the San Cap Road helped me keep my speed below 50 mph. Still, I was on the edge, the speed limit being 35 mph. We made quick work of returning the car and going through security and were both on board and asleep almost before the wheels left the ground.

Boston Harbor was outside my window before I knew it. In no time at all I was looking into the welcoming eyes of Bode, who grabbed both of us in a big bear hug. The cold gray sky couldn't eclipse the warm rush that coursed through me knowing that our circle was once again complete.

"How was it, L'il Chuck?" asked Bode.

"Oh, Bod, I got to drive the golf cart, and I was really good at it. No kidding, I accelerated, braked, and steered. I was amazing!" she bragged unabashedly.

"Good to know," he said. "And what's the "ringer" report?"

"Ha! I got one in about four tries at the Lazy Flamingo! The place went wild!"

"All in all, it sounds like a successful trip."

He turned to me. "And you, my little friend, have a busy day ahead of you if I understand correctly. You're meeting with Ollie and Alice in two hours."

"And you know that how?" I inquired curiously.

"I had dinner with Pepper last night," he told me. "She had run into Mr. Stanley, and he mentioned the meeting and...you know the rest. She knows everything. And, boy, can she cook a leg of lamb with little roasted potatoes. It was out of this world!"

"I know, I know," I smiled. "With a delectable mint jelly. I'm sure she loved having you as an audience.

"And yes, Mr. Stanley did set up a meeting. I want to get their input about Ty's service before I begin putting it together. They'll certainly be relieved to know that Chillingsworth will cover the cost."

"It would only add insult to injury to ask them to pay anything for Ty's last party," observed Bode. "They've suffered with him their entire lives and now they have to defend themselves against allegations that neither deserves."

"I'm not looking forward to the meeting, as I don't know either of them very well. I hope they won't spew vitriolic anger at me. I really don't want to be a target for all they must be feeling. I'm just the messenger. Thank goodness I don't have to ask them to pay for this foolishness. Maybe I should have charged all those ladies a dollar a tennis ball to help fund it," I said jokingly.

"You guys, I'm so glad you're back," Bode reiterated. "Why don't we celebrate your return by going to The Old Port tonight?"

"Are you kidding me? I have so much homework to do, and I have phone calls to make! I need to reconnect with my friends after being away," declared Charlie.

"Two whole days without you! It's positively devastating. How did they manage?" I kidded. "But good for you, at least one of us is being responsible and getting down to work. As for me, I would love to go to The Old Port."

"I know, I know. There are plenty of Stouffer's turkey tetrazinni dinners in the freezer for me," said Charlie. "I'm cool with this."

"Thanks, Bode," I said as we piled into the car for the ride home. "I think she's probably seen enough of me over the last few days. I love the idea of some alone time with you."

Arriving home, I begged one more long hug, then reluctantly pulled away, said good bye, and dragged my suitcase up the steps.

Charlie and I made short work of emptying our suitcases and filling the washing machine with summer clothing that we wouldn't use again for a while. I pulled on my black pants and clean white turtleneck, then added a sweater for my upcoming meeting. Charlie was jabbering to one of her friends on the floor above me, so I let a quick, shouted goodbye herald my departure.

It felt great to hop back in the familiar Jeep, but my toes felt imprisoned in my shoes. I already missed the let-it-all-hang-out freedom of my flipflops. Mr. Stanley greeted me with a warm smile as I entered the back door and offered me a mug of steaming hot chocolate.

"I haven't had this for a few days," I said, "and it tastes just right! Thank you, Mr. Stanley. Thanks also for setting up this meeting. It's one of those things that must be done, but I'm a bit apprehensive. Can you bring in some tea after we've sat down? That seems to lessen anxiety for everyone; just the smell is comforting."

"Be happy to, Miss G. You'll have them relaxed in no time. You're so good with people," he told me. "I don't like to burden you with too much since you've just returned, but Rocky called and asked if you could meet him this afternoon around 3 p.m. to go over the details of Cam's service. He said you'll find him in The Old Port kitchen. I told him you'd call if it was a problem."

"Thank you, that will work fine—and thank you for your encouraging words. I'll take all the help I can get." I smiled appreciatively.

"I've got to go through all this mail on my desk right now. Just give me a heads-up when they arrive."

"Will do."

And with that, I began shuffling letters from one pile to the next, paying absolutely no attention to what went where. My focus was on my upcoming challenge.

CHAPTER
FORTY

BEFORE I KNEW it, Ollie and Alice had arrived. Mr. Stanley had settled them comfortably in straight-backed chairs across from my desk. Again, my affection for him for soared.

The pair looked like salt and pepper shakers. Both were round and dressed in worn jeans and faded flannel shirts. Their hairstyles were similar, too, which is to say there was no style.

"Good morning, Ollie, Alice. I am so sorry for all that is going on around you. This must be a difficult time," I began. I refrained from offering any condolences.

Alice spoke first. "Frankly, I'm not really sure just why we're here. Ty may be dead, but he continues to torture us! I didn't like him when he was alive, and things haven't changed, except that now I have to defend myself against a murder charge. And dear Ollie! To accuse him of such a thing— phooey! Believe me when I tell you—and anyone else willing to listen—that he didn't and couldn't do it. To tell you the truth I'd be some kind of proud had *I* thought of whacking that sculpted blond hair!

"I've always been of the mind that Mrs. Waters must be the only woman in history to have two wombs. Why? Because Ollie and Ty could not possibly have shared such a small space for nine months. Nope. Theirs was not the relationship of brothers, let alone twins. It's a shame Ty didn't stay down in Florida at that resort he thought was so fancy and leave us alone.

"We work hard here in Woodford Harbor. Raised us a nice boy, and we see to the town cemetery. It's a good, honest, simple life, and we bother nobody.

"But here Ty is, still making a mess of things for us. Do shared genes require a person to buy a casket?" Alice finally came to the point. "Because we don't have much in savings, and we're going to need it for *our* future. I have no interest in spending a dime on Ty."

"That's part of the reason I..." I attempted to intercede.

"He never had the time of day for either of us," Alice continued, muting my voice. There was no stopping her now. "He looked down on Ollie because his finger nails were most always dirty. A good honest day's work put that dirt there, which is nothing to be ashamed of. Didn't stop Ty though, he tried to humiliate Ollie whenever he saw him. And me? The disgust in his eyes when he spoke to me was no different; it began when we were kids and never left. What a worthless excuse for a person he was!"

Alice could not be stopped. "And let me just share a recent stunt he pulled. We're not much for lawyers but when we were down to our lawyer's office to organize our wills, he mentioned that Ty had been in recently. Why? I'll tell you why. He was trying to draw on the trust their parents set up for both of them. It may not be much, but he was trying to take more than his rightful half!

"Now, Alice." Ollie gently laid a hand on his wife's wrist.

"Don't 'Now Alice' me!'" she said sharply.

Ollie hung his head and was mute for the remainder of the visit.

I interjected quickly. "I understand that families have different relationships, and I understand your feelings."

At this point, Mr. Stanley knocked softly and entered, enquiring if anyone would like a cup of tea. Alice felt comfortable answering for the four of us. "No, Ollie and I are not tea drinkers, and we really must get on our way."

An unruffled Mr. Stanley excused himself and backed out the door.

I continued. "I was down on Captiva this weekend and met with Arthur Chillingsworth, who has graciously offered to pay for all the expenses surrounding Ty's funeral." I left out the veiled threat that had prompted his offer. There was no need to fuel that flame. "You will not be asked to assume any of the expenses.

"My purpose in asking you here is to find out if there is anything you would like included in Ty's service. You are after all, through no choice of your own, his closest relatives. This is just a respectful inquiry on my part."

"That's very kind of you," said Alice. "We don't mean to be disrespectful, but neither do we feel any respect for his life and how he lived it. I can't thank you enough for contacting Mr. Chillingsworth. We simply must be done with this whole debacle. Seems blood is not always thicker than water."

In my mind I played back Charlie's quotation on family: "The bond that links your true family is not one of blood, but of respect and joy in each other's life." Here was the other end of the spectrum.

I rose and thanked both of them for coming, reassuring them I would take care of everything.

I remained at my desk after they left, pondering the life that was Ty Waters'. It never ceases to amaze me how a death affects so many lives, even someone as plastic as Ty. The "tennis ball ladies" had no real relationship with him, yet each believed his gifts to them of special tennis balls meant something personal. Just how many *special* tennis balls had there been?

He clearly had no family ties; even Arthur Chillingsworth was paying his funeral expenses under duress. At least he had had Dexter, although in life Ty had not acted particularly honorably toward him. I wondered if anyone would even offer to write an obituary. It's a sad state of affairs when that task is unmet. As I began organizing his funeral, it became abundantly clear that he had not lived his life with much respect for those around him. Now that he was dead, many of them seemed to be repaying him in kind.

The introspection soon brought me back to my own circumstances, and I found myself thankful for my own relationships. It brought me full circle back to Ty Waters. I wanted to get this over with and get that monkey off my back.

It was then that my stomach reminded me my next meal was fast approaching. My cell phone rang then, and I saw Pepper's name on caller ID.

"Hi, Pepper," I said gaily. "What's up? I heard you served my man dinner last night!"

"Yes, and you're darned lucky I took care of him," she replied. "You shouldn't let that wonderful fellow fend for himself. I made him a lovely dinner, and we shared more than one glass of Woodford Reserve.

"Do you have time to pop down to the Blue Canoe for a sandwich?"

"Love to," I replied. "Now?"

"Yup."

"See you there," I said, flying by Mr. Stanley with an abbreviated explanation of my plans.

Lunch with Pepper! Always an adventure.

CHAPTER
FORTY-ONE

NOT ONE TO stand on formality, Pepper had already ordered and was waiting for her sandwich when I arrived.

I greeted her warmly and asked what she was having.

"We're both having the meatloaf with melted cheese. I figured why wait for you to arrive and dilly-dally around while you decided what you wanted. I knew it would inevitably be the meatloaf sandwich, so I saved us both a lot of time." Quintessential Pepper!

I have very few hard and fast rules in life, but one of them is to never argue with my old friend. So, although mildly annoyed, I restrained myself and merely smiled.

"And yes," she continued, "you have an iced tea coming." I feared she was looking a little smug, but again, not a word from me.

We settled at a corner table, and I told Pepper all about our family adventures on Captiva. It was all benign background chatter to Pepper, who I knew had invited me to lunch to learn something other than what I had done last weekend.

Sure enough, she cut right to the chase. "I've been giving this

Ty murder case a lot of thought, Lizzie," she started. "Please know, dear, that it is through no affection for Ty that I am doing this, but mostly because I would love to have an exciting headline in the *Woodford Reporter.*" So *this* was it.

"When was the last time we got to cover a murder case in our paper," she asked rhetorically, "much less solve a murder case? We need to liven things up a bit at the old rag."

"And what have you come up with?" I inquired.

"Bear with me, dear, and let me preface this with the source of my deductive abilities. It goes back to my early days in the navy. I was aboard ship for weeks at a time and frankly there wasn't a lot to do. Inactivity, as you well know, always makes me obsess even more about my next meal, so you can imagine how preoccupied I was in *that* situation.

"Every couple of weeks we'd get corn fritters. Man, they were good, those crispy little fried balls bursting with sweet corn! Obsessed with food as I was, I always grabbed a few extra for later and hid them on a counter behind some salt and pepper shakers. I'd sneak back down to the mess hall around 11:30 to grab 'em, but over time they began disappearing before I could get back. Determined to confront the fritter burglar—*my* fritter burglar!— I began staking out the kitchen. One night around 9:30 I caught the little twit and gave him what for.

"Anyway, what I'm getting at is this. I think my past sleuthing success might help us with our little mystery. We need to create a scenario that will help us catch our murderer. We must think of something that might bring them back to the scene of the crime— and I'm not talking salt and pepper shakers! We could stake out the cemetery and then, when the perpetrator returns, I'll jump up and snap a photo!"

This was a stretch, even for Pepper. "Really?" was the only response that came to mind. She deflated quickly, going in an instant from a wildly flapping, gesticulating bird to one dashed on the rocks, lying morosely on the beach. It was sad.

I couldn't let it end like this so I quickly pulled myself together and gave her an encouraging thumbs up, grinning like a fool. "Pepper, what an idea!" I said. It was similar to when you see an ugly baby. Needing to respond somehow to the little creature, all you can say is, "What a baby!"

"You'll talk to Henry about it then? Just let me know what your bait is, and I'll start a rumor about it that will spread through town like wildfire!" I knew she could do it, too. No one had the town's ear like Pepper.

"I'll go down and talk to Uncle Henry about it right now," I said. "I feel so badly for Ollie and Alice, and I'd like to clear their names. Frankly, I wouldn't be disappointed if it was Daniel Dunkirk who showed up! I can't promise you Uncle Henry will let you be there, but he has stretched a few rules in the past. He might actually get excited about this." Crazy as it was, Pepper's whacky idea was starting to grow on me. Granted, it might be an act of desperation for an answer to this mess, but it was taking root in my head.

"You're probably going by the Cake Whisperer to get some monster cookie on the way back to work," said Pepper. "Do you want me to drop you off there?"

I held back a grimace. "No thanks, Pepper. The walk will do me good. I'll let you know what Uncle Henry thinks."

"Okay, dearie, talk soon!"

I thought about walking past the bakery just to show Pepper she didn't know everything, but that seemed counterproductive so I went in and bought a giant M&M cookie. I put it in my bag to save for later, then took it out again, broke off a bite, and marched right over to the Old Town House to see if I could catch Uncle Henry at his office.

I gave a light rap on the door. I can't be sure, but I think the quick jerk of his head as I entered indicated that our local sheriff had been napping. I cut right to the chase.

"Uncle Henry, Pepper just had what might be a great idea to solve this case. We need to think outside the box, and this just might be it!" I related to him, minus the corn fritter part, what Pepper had suggested.

"And I suppose she wants to be behind a tombstone and snap a flash photo when the murderer arrives?" said Uncle Henry, right eyebrow raised.

"Well..." I began.

"Never mind, never mind," said Uncle Henry. "Maybe she has something here, although I can't imagine what would bring a murderer back to the scene of the crime."

"Maybe he—or she—would want to remove fingerprints they had left," I offered.

"A good notion for sure, but you can't lift fingerprints from the rough granite of a tombstone."

"Hmmm," I mused. "Wait! I've got it. Why don't we get the word out that there's a new technique to lift prints from a rough surface, and the state police are coming to do the testing first thing Wednesday morning? If we—and Pepper, who must be chomping at the bit—start the rumor tomorrow, that will leave only Tuesday night for our perp to beat feet to the cemetery to try to remove his or her prints.

Uncle Henry was all in. "We'll hunker down at the cemetery Tuesday night then, and see who arrives with a package of 40-grit sandpaper."

"Pretty much," I grinned.

FORTY-TWO

A GLANCE AT MY watch alerted me that I had better get moving if I was going to see Rocky at 3:00. Between two funerals and a murder, the day was getting away from me.

I walked down State Street at a smart clip and entered The Old Port by the back entrance. I'd never experienced it from this perspective before; it felt a bit like suddenly seeing someone who always wears glasses without them. The kitchen wasn't as large as I had imagined it. The stainless steel countertops were immaculate and the source of much activity. Cooks chopped vegetables at a furious pace while nearby, on the ancient stove, a large and fragrant kettle of corn chowder simmered. I was a tad disappointed as I passed it, for in my mind I always thought the steaming bowl brought to my table had been made especially for me. Another fantasy dashed to the rocks.

Rocky, large and in charge, seemed to be everywhere at once. He smiled when I entered and beckoned me to a swinging door that led us out to a little table at the end of the bar.

Rocky went behind the bar and poured each of us a beer in little juice glasses. It was endearing and almost felt a little naughty. I was having a good time.

"I had a very interesting phone call from our mysterious Geoff," he began. "He called here yesterday because he was concerned about not hearing from Cam. Believe me, it was difficult to break that kind of news over the phone to someone you've never met. I asked him to call me back when he'd had time to absorb it all.

"He rang me back this morning, and we had a wonderful conversation. He told me a great deal about our friend, Cam. His father was in the navy, and the family moved around quite a bit. They were based in Key West during Cam's high school years, and he struck up a friendship there with Jimmy Buffet. Cam was always devoted to his guitar, and Buffet nurtured that passion. Apparently, he was a mentor to Cam in many other respects as well, and they stayed in touch."

"That's so interesting," I said. "No wonder Cam played Jimmy Buffet's music in such a personal way; he obviously understood it well."

"There was so much more to Cam, though," Rocky went on. "He went to college in Boston, and when he graduated he ended up on Martha's Vineyard, where he tended bar. It wasn't long before he began playing gigs in local pubs. Eventually that became his main source of income; bartending just supplemented that.

"He bought an old sailboat on the island and labored with his own two hands to bring it back to life. It was inevitable that he named her *Jolly Mon* in honor of Buffet. He hired a lovely young lady named Sarah to paint the name on the *Jolly Mon's* stern, and that was it. Almost immediately, the two were inseparable. Her primary job was at the Martha's Vineyard Coastal Observatory, recording readings from their tower off the coast; the boat lettering was something she did on the side.

"Geoff really surprised me then by explaining that he was Sarah's brother! He was teaching on the island at the time, and the three of them became quite a team. Cam and Sarah were so happy and full of life; he said it was a delight to be in their company.

"The three of them wanted to give back to the island that was treating them so well, so they organized a sailing program for the island kids. Locals are oftentimes eclipsed by the hordes of tourists that flood the place in the summer, and they wanted these hometown youngsters to have the same opportunities to sail that tourists' kids had. They called the program the Baby Whales and through fundraisers and donations were able to buy six Optimists for the little ones, and six Lasers for the older ones. They loved the interaction with the kids, so it was a win/win for everyone. The cash in the envelope was for this program."

"That's so impressive, Rocky, and it follows that Cam would be involved with a number of the boys from Woodford Harbor High as well, taking them out for a sail if a coach suggested it. What a wonderful guy."

Rocky continued his story. "About seven years ago Sarah tragically drowned. Geoff never offered details, just said it was an overwhelming tragedy for Cam.

"Shortly after her death, he packed up his belongings and sailed the *Jolly Mon* up the coast. He needed a spot to create a new life, and Woodford Harbor apparently had all he wanted. He and Geoff kept in touch sporadically, and Cam sent money once a year to help fund the Baby Whales.

"I told Geoff about the envelope with his name on it and about the life celebration tomorrow. He not only asked to come up, but said he would like to speak if it was appropriate. He's going to be here tomorrow morning, so I suggested we meet at the Driftwood around 9:00 for breakfast. Do you think you and Bode could join us? You can talk to him about the service, but more importantly I'd like him to meet the people who loved Cam in his adopted home. He'll have plenty of time to meet all The Old Port people later."

"What a nice offer, Rocky. I'm sure we can meet you there. This is a lot to take in. It's amazing how you can intuitively sense someone has a big heart and a zest for living, and then you hear this and it affirms what you somehow already knew. Both were so evident in Cam. I'm thrilled to be a part of this but so sorry Cam is gone. We'll make this as heartfelt and inspiring as we can and give a good and generous man the best send-off possible."

We drained our little glasses then and nodded our good-byes.

CHAPTER
FORTY-THREE

I WALKED THE THREE blocks to the funeral home, taking my time and enjoying the fresh air. A conversation like the one I'd just had makes me want to take in all the good life has to offer.

Mr. Stanley was gathering his things to leave for the day, but we gave each other quick updates.

"I have the sound system ready to go for Cam's service tomorrow," he told me, "and we have a podium. The folks at The Old Port are going to set up the refreshments. Apparently there are to be kegs of beer and pots of steamers. These life celebrations are getting more and more curious, wouldn't you say? I remember when Psalm 23 and a few stanzas of 'How Great Thou Art' would do nicely."

"You're right, Mr. Stanley, things are certainly changing. Personally, I find it exciting and love doing all I can for each client. As much as we all have in common, we're also our own unique beings. That should be celebrated."

Mr. Stanley didn't roll his eyes, but I think it had more to do with respect for me than any concession or agreement.

"See you tomorrow morning," he offered. "Have a pleasant evening."

I cleaned off my desk; putting a couple of pens in a holder was actually the extent of it. In a flash, I was driving towards Brown's.

Heading for the eggs and milk, I was surprised to run into Aggie and Gus in the frozen food section.

"And what brings you out here?" I asked.

"Aggie had a need for a Klondike bar and couldn't be dissuaded," said Gus.

"You'll learn soon enough, Lizzie, that when you reach my age a friend with benefits means a friend with a car," interjected Aggie with a smile. "It's fun to be out and about with the real world as they shop for dinner. We've already had our dinner, and sometimes the evening looms large and empty. I thought some Klondike bars would perk it up! I don't know who misses dear Thistle more, Gus or me. These lifetime friendships leave such a hole in your heart."

Gus looked down, and I suddenly felt my chest constrict. I wanted to grab them both.

Aggie suddenly changed the subject. "How is that murder investigation coming along, Lizzie? Imagine something like that happening at Thistle's service! Frankly, I think she would have kind of liked the commotion! She was always one for a little drama.

"What a shame, though, that it happened to Ty; he was so young and full of life."

"Really?" said Gus. "What difference does it make if that low life doesn't come down to breakfast tomorrow? The guy was a waste."

Changing the subject again, I suggested they get their Klondike bars home before they melted. We hugged goodnight, and they were off.

I grabbed a half-gallon of milk, added a dozen eggs, and put English muffins in the basket for good measure. Knowing we had Stowaway Sweets at home guaranteed our coffers were full.

At the end cap full of barbecue sauces I found Dexter, who stood there mesmerized.

"Hey, Dexter," I said, resisting an urge to give him a hug. He looked so lost, and I could almost feel his pain across our carts.

"Hi, Lizzie," came his half-hearted reply.

"Is it hard shopping for just yourself?" I asked, deciding to acknowledge the obvious.

"Well, yes and no," he said. "As you know, Ty went out many nights, either to The Old Port or elsewhere around town. It was hard for me, being the one left behind all the time. When he did stay home, though, I made us wonderful meals. He loved shrimp prepared in any exotic way I concocted.

"There's actually something else I want to share with you, Lizzie, as it affects your friend Bode. I don't know him well, but he seems to mean a great deal to you so he must be a decent fellow.

"All that foolishness about Ty and his mother, Thistle, having an affair is ridiculous on so many levels. The truth is very different. It was her sympathetic character that attracted Ty those many years ago, so much so that he confided to her—and only her—his preference for men. She accepted him for who he was and was extraordinarily kind to him for the rest of her life.

"The three of us actually had a meeting one time, at my request. I had hoped that she could convince him there was no shame in our situation. She tried, but Ty couldn't relinquish his fear. I remained a secret. His grief at her passing was palpable."

"It's all so hard," I said, giving in to my urge to hug him.

"I appreciate you letting me get that off my chest," he told me. Turning abruptly, he went on his way.

After a quick trip through the checkout line, I hopped in the Jeep, turned the key, and found "Margaritaville" playing on the radio. That, of course, took me right back to Cam. I was determined more than ever to give him a service that would capture the essence of his goodness.

As I rounded my corner, I noticed happily that Bode's truck was parked outside. I pushed past Bob's considerable girth at the back door and found Bode and Charlie comparing notes on country music in the living room.

"Getting that homework done, are we?"

"Hey, I'm just trying to entertain our guest. He needs help understanding the subtleties of Old Dominion," laughed Charlie.

"Really? *You* still can't recognize the greatness of Johnny Cash when you hear him! He sings, my little friend, he doesn't just twang a guitar and scream," Bode fired back.

"Enough," I interrupted. "Bode, get yourself a beer and me a little wine. Charlie, I'll make you dinner."

Bode happily pulled a Corona from the drinks fridge and brought me a glass of red wine. As I unpacked the groceries, I took that first delicious sip and listened while my two music critics carried on in the background. I popped a Stouffers turkey tetrazzini in the microwave, poured a glass of milk for Charlie, then interrupted the debate going on in the other room to ask Charlie about her homework assignments.

"Do you have a quotation for tomorrow?" I asked.

"Sort of. It's supposed to be about the power of love."

"That's easy," roared Bode. "Huey Lewis said it all!"

With that, he brought his beer bottle to his mouth as a microphone and started crooning.

> Don't need money, don't take fame
> Don't need no credit card to ride this train
> It's strong and it's sudden and it's cruel sometimes
> But it might just save your life
> That's the power of love
> That's the power of love

We both screamed with laughter until the buzzer on the microwave blessedly put an end to his recital. I scooped the repast onto a plate, set it on a tray, added a napkin and the glass of milk, and Charlie's dinner was served.

She seemed more than content to see us leave. Not for the first time I thought to myself, "Am I really her mother?"

CHAPTER
FORTY-FOUR

I WAS IN A happy place sitting next to Bob, who was in *his* happy place sitting next to Bode. We were in the truck, heading to The Old Port. It's remarkable how simple moments like this can sometimes be so exciting and wonderful. I'm not a girl who needs the Eiffel Tower; a favorite local pub with Bode works for me.

It was the last night of the long weekend, and a good crowd had come to enjoy the tail end of the holiday. We greeted a few folks at the bar, and I glanced quickly at the spot Rocky and I had occupied just a few hours ago; it seemed more like days than hours. We made our way towards the back; Bode and I had a lot to talk about and needed a table with some privacy. Having been away for a few days, I wanted him all to myself. The little back-corner table felt like heaven with just the four of us: Bode, his beer, me, and a glass of wine.

I couldn't hold out much longer and I explained our plot to expose the murderer at the cemetery the next night. I was afraid I sounded like a rerun of *Magnum P.I.*, but the idea piqued Bode's interest. "You have to try *something*," he said. "This seems like the kind of mystery that could become a town legend. Really, how can it hurt? The only person affected will be the murderer. I think it's a great idea!

"The best part, though, is having Pepper sow the rumor. That's right up her alley; she must be thrilled!"

"Actually," I said, "no one has given her any specifics yet. I told Uncle Henry I'd handle it, but I haven't yet. I should have called her before we went out."

"Let's call her now and ask her to come over for a drink! She lives right around the corner, and a cocktail is great bait. Call her," Bode said.

Within a few minutes Pepper came charging through the front door. Peering into the darkness, she searched for us.

"Isn't this a treat!" she exclaimed upon locating us. "I just finished a juicy little steak, roast potatoes, and grilled asparagus. There's no better way to finish that off than with one more tot of Woodford Reserve. I believe you said you were treating?

"So, what's up?"

"We're taking you up on your idea of spreading a rumor. Our entire plan revolves around you getting the word out about the state police coming out here tomorrow night to attempt a new method of identifying fingerprints on rough stone," I offered. "As many people as possible should know about it, especially Alice and Ollie and Daniel Dunkirk."

"This will be a cinch," said Pepper immediately. "There just happens to be a great local petrie dish into which to plant those seeds—Cam's funeral service! Everyone in town will be there. It's a quintessential local event featuring a favorite local bartender. Unless our murderer is in fifth grade, he or she should be in attendance."

I was dubious. "Do you really think it'll spread that quickly, Pepper?"

"You just wait, little girl. I know all about these things."

Sticking to my own rule, I didn't argue.

Downing the last of her drink, Pepper got up and announced her departure. "These old bones need to crawl into bed if they're to be up at five tomorrow. Might be a big day for the *Woodford Reporter.*"

"Listen, Pepper, your idea of popping out of the bushes to take a flash photo of our murderer," I said. "That was never a real consideration. This is a criminal event and should be treated that way—by the police and not any of us."

"I know, dearie, I know."

Over one more wine and another beer, I filled Bode in on all Rocky had shared with me from his conversation with Geoff. When I finished, I could tell Bode was moved.

"It's something, isn't it? To be living a good life, minding your own business, preparing for the next chapter, only to have something so devastating happen. Suddenly you have to start all over again.

"It's remarkable that Cam was able to pick himself up and create another rich and fruitful life, only to be taken too early.

"When I realize how unfair things can be, it makes me feel a bit better about losing Mom. At least she was able to live a long and wonderful life. It doesn't make me miss her any less, but it does soften the sting."

"I know," I replied, taking his hand across the table. "Life is hard, and I am so grateful to have you next to me. I need you as my shock absorber along the way."

After a bit, I continued. "I learned another interesting bit of information from Dexter when I ran into him at Brown's this afternoon, although I'm not sure either of us gave it too much thought. He said that the so-called 'special relationship' your mother and Ty shared sprung from her kind and understanding spirit. She kept his 'secret' and was his confidant. Her generous spirit knew no bounds, Bode."

Next to me, he sighed. "She was remarkable; she took in everything—birds with broken wings, homeless bunnies, and struggling, insecure humans."

We were contemplating all this when our waitress arrived to take our orders.

"I think I'll have a Chicken Parmesan sandwich," I said, switching gears. "Seems like a good companion for this red wine."

"You know, I think I might just have the same," said Bode. We nodded our thanks.

"You know, Lizzie, when I had dinner with Pepper, she was quite forthcoming about her own mother's death and how hard it was for her. I guess she adored her Mum and had a difficult time coming to grips with the finality of it all. I know just what she meant; it's like you relive the loss over and over in small moments every day. When I first opened my eyes in the morning, envisioning the day, there was always a spot for her. Around supper time, I'd drive by every day just to say 'hi.'"

"No one loves us like our mothers," I told him. "Losing your mom is devastating, I know, but as you say, she had a good, long, happy life. You were much more than just a part of it; you created a good bit of her happiness. Hold on to that."

The steaming, just-from-the-oven chicken swimming in a delicious red sauce on thick French bread put an end to any further conversation.

CHAPTER
FORTY-FIVE

W E ARRIVED HOME to find Charlie scooping chocolate chip ice cream into a tall glass of root beer. Watching her wait for the foam to subside, Bode grabbed a glass, too. "What a great idea! A root beer float!" he proclaimed, depositing giant scoops of ice cream into his own glass. They passed the root beer back and forth, each patiently waiting for the bubbles to subside so they could add more. It was a joy to watch them working in tandem. Although not her biological father, Bode was the man who had the greatest influence over Charlie. At moments like this, I loved watching her mirror him.

Both simultaneously determined their creations complete and flopped down on the couch. I grabbed two straws and offered one to each.

Bob, not to be outdone, stretched out in front of them. Watching his head swivel back and forth, his eyes begging a taste, was heartbreaking.

"Bode," I began, "after all that chicken and bread and fries, not to mention three beers, how can you possibly have room for that?"

He looked over his concoction and grinned. "Great isn't it! You're just jealous!"

"So, you guys," began Charlie between sips and spoonfuls, "I really have to find a good quotation about the power of love.

"Seriously, any ideas, Bode?"

"I have always been drawn to the Elbert Hubbard quotation: 'The love we give away is the only love we keep,'" he replied.

"I like Mahatma Gandhi. His thought was equally all-encompassing," I added. "He wrote, 'Where there is love there is life.'"

"How about this one?" said Charlie, picking up a piece of notebook paper on which she had scribbled, "'One word frees us of all the weight and pain of life. That word is love.' Sophocles. That seems pretty comprehensive."

"Well I guess it's 'pretty comprehensive,'" I said with a smile. "Nice to think of you emulating Sophocles."

Charlie shrugged and gave me an appreciative smile, rinsed her glass at the sink, and gave each of us a quick kiss. Bob received a pat on the head.

"'night, you guys," she said softly as she headed upstairs.

"To think that Charlie's research brought her to Helen Keller is so impressive," commented Bode when Charlie was out of earshot. "These daily quotations really get the kids thinking."

"I like to think she is watching us and learning," I said, moving over to sit beside him.

Minutes later, I broke the mood somewhat. "I still have to put the bones of Cam's service together before tomorrow. Do you want to stick around and help?"

"I don't know how much help I'll be, but I am all for watching your computer-like brain create," answered Bode.

"Oh, please, give me a break! I'm not the only one speaking. Rocky, Sam, and Geoff also have parts to play. I'm the one, though, who has to put it all together.

"My role is to welcome everyone and let them know how important their presence is. They need to feel that being at his funeral not only dignifies the importance of his life, but celebrates a man who touched everyone he met.

"Then I want to talk about the significance of the place where we're gathered. For tomorrow, I want guests to think of it as something other than the harbormaster's parking lot. The seagulls squawking overhead, the lapping of the water against the dock, and the sound of the wind are perfect reflections of Cam's life. You don't need a church to be in a sacred place.

"I think I'll have Sam speak first and talk about Cam as a friend. He was the closest friend Cam had here, and they spent a lot of time together on the *Jolly Mon*.

"Rocky can speak next and summarize Cam's life here in Woodford Harbor, then I think it will be only fitting to wrap things up with Geoff. He has the unique advantage of being able to characterize so much of Cam's life.

"I'll end with 'Gone from My Sight,' Henry Van Dyke's famous poem. It's so appropriate."

"That'll be really nice, Z," said Bode, putting his arm around me. "You do a good job of putting these things together. You've somehow found a way to make his lively, salty, kind spirit come alive for all of us."

"Thanks, Bode, that's the idea," I said gratefully. "There's just one more thing. I think we need to incorporate some Jimmy Buffet songs in the service. What do you think?"

"It's perfect, Z, just perfect. I have a whole playlist of his music on my iPhone. Why don't we do the research for that upstairs in bed?"

"Really?" I inquired, raising an eyebrow.

"For sure!" was his answer. "How about, 'Why Don't We Get Drunk and Screw'?"

Even Bob seemed somewhat amused at that, and the three of us headed upstairs.

FORTY-SIX

I AWOKE TO THE warmth of shimmering sunshine on my face. It's always wonderful to know the day before you holds the delights of sunshine, but I was particularly pleased today. The radiance would certainly enhance Cam's service. As I pondered this in bed, I realized that Bode's face was just inches from my own. I instantly put my thoughts about the weather on hold, concentrating instead on the warm body next to me. Bode gratefully got into the spirit, and my day started exquisitely.

I could have snuggled under those covers for hours, but the impending day cleared the cobwebs quickly.

"Can you still meet Rocky and Geoff at the Driftwood around 9:00?" I asked Bode as he rose from the bed.

"Sure can, sounds great," he told me. "I can always check my traps after Cam's service. I've been a bit lax since Mom's…"

There is no easy way to reference your mother's death. It would just take time. The grieving process might differ from person to person, but even at its healthy best it's painful. I arose and held Bode for a moment.

There was pounding over our heads; Charlie was up. I gave Bode and Bob quick kisses, and headed for the bathroom. I made fast work of showering and dressing then headed downstairs. By the time Charlie hit the bottom step, I had set out an English muffin and a glass of juice for her.

"I wish we were going to RC Otters," she grumbled between bites. "Then we could go to the beach and collect more shells for Gram's collection."

"And where would we have dinner?" I asked.

"We would stay home, and Gramps would get one of those beautiful steaks from Bailey's, steam some good Florida corn, and then we would go find some key lime pie!"

"Stop! You're killing me!" I laughed. "Have you got everything you need?"

"Pretty much. We have an away soccer game after school, so I might need a little cash for a snack or two."

"Sure, honey," I said, "but at least supplement it with this apple, okay?"

I loved her even when she was rolling her eyes at me.

"Uncle Henry and Bode will both be here for dinner," I informed her. "Then Uncle Henry and I are going out for a while afterwards."

"Where?" she wanted to know.

"I'm going to help Uncle Henry with a project he's working on," I told her.

"Really? Are you going to follow tracks through the woods, or trap speeding cars, or do a stake-out with him?"

It was my turn to roll my eyes.

We got into the Jeep, pulled out past Redmond Island, and headed toward the high school.

"Hope you girls can hold up the reputation of the Big Blues!" I said as she hopped out. "Good luck, and don't knock any of those beautiful teeth out, please!"

I didn't actually see it, but I assumed that brought more eye rolling.

Stopping at the funeral home, I found Mr. Stanley organizing the sound equipment for Cam's service. Our part-timers were there to help him with the physical lifting, but he was clearly in charge of what went where. I knew I could trust them to set everything up and that the sound would be as professional as could be.

I heard them chatting as they loaded the equipment on the truck,

"Did you hear the state police have found a new way to lift fingerprints from rough stone?" asked one.

"Yeah, they were talking about it down at the Driftwood this morning. They're comin' out here to see if they can identify the guy who whacked Ty Waters. Still can't wrap my brain around the whole thing."

"Please put the speakers in the back so they won't rattle around." Mr. Stanley effectively put an end to their gossip.

I sat at my desk to finalize the details of the service. I knew how I wanted to open the program, and I hoped that my reading at the end would be upbeat and inspiring. I was a bit concerned about my choice of music. It was a bit unconventional but was pivotal to the success of the celebration.

I looked up Jimmy Buffet songs, and the list was overwhelming. His music encompassed so much: sailing ballads, whimsical pieces, and so many drinking songs. I could almost hear the steel drums and taste the margaritas as I flipped through them.

I started reminiscing. I'd been introduced to the early ones by my parents and had followed his music as I grew up. It seemed like "Margaritaville" played constantly on every radio station we listened to at the time. When I was a bit older I began to pay attention to the lyrics as well as the music. His idea of living life to the fullest spoke to me, and I took his lyrics to heart about dealing with the many changes life brings.

Unfortunately, some of my favorite lyrics weren't appropriate for the service. I smiled as "If the phone doesn't ring, it's me," "We are the people our parents warned us about," and "The weather is here, wish you were beautiful" came to mind, but I just as quickly dismissed them.

I eventually made my choices and uploaded them to my iPhone. I left for the Driftwood feeling pretty darn pleased with myself.

CHAPTER
FORTY-SEVEN

I HAD LEFT PLENTY of time for my jaunt to the Driftwood, so my pace was leisurely. I was a bit apprehensive about meeting this fellow, Geoff, and hoped he was a decent fellow who would live up to my expectations. The upcoming service also unnerved me a bit. A funeral at the harbor's edge was somewhat unorthodox and—I thought—fraught with potential pitfalls. I was hardly one to stand on convention but stepping outside the box carries risks. Then I remembered another familiar Jimmy Buffet lyric: "Forget that blind ambition, and learn to trust your intuition." That's exactly what I'm doing, I thought to myself. That's exactly what I'm doing.

The familiar clank and squeak of the Driftwood's front door as I entered went a long way toward calming my jitters. Walking in there was a close second to walking into my own house, and the folks inside were very nearly family.

Before I was fully inside, I heard a voice saying, "...yes, apparently they have a new way to ID prints." It was spreading. Good

I identified Geoff immediately, even before I saw Rocky. The collar of a red plaid shirt peeked from beneath a navy-blue crew-necked sweater. Crisp dress khakis and intellectual-looking tortoiseshell glasses rounded out the look. His persona screamed teacher. His clean-shaven face, curly hair, and big smile marked him as a friend of Cam's.

I walked over to the table. Not waiting for an introduction from Rocky, I gave him a big hug. It was a warm embrace and spoke volumes, taking the place of words we didn't seem to need.

Geoff held out a chair for me as Rocky formally introduced us.

"It's so kind of you to come all this way," I began.

"I cannot tell you how sorry I am to be here for this reason. Cam was one of the finest human beings on earth, and it is tragic that his life has ended so soon," Geoff said in a soft, yet expressive, voice. His words came slowly, and it was obvious that he chose them carefully before speaking.

Jennie arrived then with an iced tea for me. There followed a moment of utter silence as she and Geoff stared at each other. An almost electric current charged the air.

"Geoff!" said she.

"Jennie!" said he.

"Look at you!" she said finally when she gathered her wits. "What are you doing here? How are you? This is unbelievable!"

"And how are *you*?" he tossed back at her, a bemused look suffusing his face. "We were friends back in Oak Park, Illinois, many years ago," he said by way of explanation. "We met in kindergarten, then Jennie left. When *was* that?" he asked her, never taking his eyes from her face.

"Third grade," she told him. "We moved when I was eight." Then, addressing Rocky and me, she continued. "This handsome fellow and I spent a lot of time climbing trees, riding our bikes, and sledding down hills at Taylor Park. Remember, Geoff, when I was selling kisses at the playground for a nickel each, and you told the teacher?"

"I probably saved you a lot of trouble further down the road," he kidded.

"I'm here for Cam's service," he continued. "He was a good friend of mine on the Vineyard."

"Oh, I'm sorry," said Jennie. "I'll be at the service too, so maybe we can catch up afterwards. What can I get for you all now?"

I spoke up first, ordering a child's portion of blueberry French toast.

"What would you guys suggest?" asked Geoff.

"Carly makes some fantastic fish cakes," I answered. "You can't do much better than that."

"Sounds great," said Geoff. "That's what I'll have."

"Me too," said Rocky.

As we sat back in anticipation, Bode arrived and introductions were made once again. The handshake exchanged between Bode and Geoff was strong, and the chemistry between them was instantly evident to me.

"I spent last night at the Mariner Inn," said Geoff. "What a charming spot this is. No wonder Cam was so content here. He had most everything I think he wanted: a beautiful harbor, a rocky coastline, beautiful colonial architecture, and seemingly friendly people. And he was a bartender at The Old Port?"

"Yes, at my place," said Rocky. "He was always punctual, professional, and hardworking, yet easy-going and personable at the same time. He was as nice as nice could be. I think if I were to cut him in half you'd find he'd be nice all the way through.

"He spent a lot of time on his boat, the *Jolly Mon*. Lived on it almost year-round. It took a lot to get him to sleep indoors," Rocky chuckled.

"He would sit aboard her for hours, playing that guitar of his. The music would waft across the water on warm summer nights, and it was magical. Occasionally, he'd play for the lobstermen if they were having a powwow of some sort, but he never played at a club or restaurant. He was a very private fellow. For all his outgoing demeanor, which The Old Port customers loved, he did a lot more listening than talking. There was nothing not to love about him.

"He followed Woodford High School sports pretty regularly and was close to many of the coaches. And if the football coach, for example, noticed a player struggling emotionally or not behaving quite right, he'd ask Cam to take the boy out, usually on his boat. The fresh air and quiet helped Cam get to the bottom of many a teenage problem. He listened and heard the boys, respected them, and understood them as well. He was a natural."

Our breakfasts arrived just then, and we quieted down as we began the meal.

After a bit, Geoff looked at the three of us and somewhat hesitantly inquired, "Did Cam have any girlfriends? Was there any woman he saw regularly?"

I looked at Rocky, who was looking down and shaking his head. "No," I said, "I never saw him with a woman. Actually, I never really thought about it. As much as he was always alone, though, he was also very much a part of the community. It never seemed to me that anything was lacking."

Geoff let out a sigh. "He and my sister, Sarah, were so close— absolute soulmates. They never did the bar scene, even in their early twenties, preferring to stay close to home on the *Jolly Mon*. Sarah's marine biology career was ramping up on the Vineyard, and Cam was gaining more and more of a reputation for his music.

"They were definitely in it for the long haul. They even used to joke that they would name their first daughter 'Little Miss Magic,' something that came straight from a Jimmy Buffett song.

"I was entrenched with my teaching job out there, but I enjoyed my role as the older brother in the trio; it was such fun being with two people who were so connected. When Sarah drowned Cam felt an irrational sense of responsibility. Being suddenly on his own in the world they had traveled together so closely was just more than Cam could handle. One day he came to say good-bye to me, explaining he was going to weigh anchor and see where the *Jolly*

Mon took him. It seems almost serendipitous that he found this town and community.

"I didn't hear from him often. I think I reminded him too much of Sarah. Now, of course, I wish I had been more assertive and come up to visit him. But really, it was his call, and I think he was quite content with his full and rich new life here. Frankly, I can see why."

I resisted the urge to get up and give him a full-blown hug, knowing that sometimes my knee-jerk hugs were a bit much. I gave him the warmest look I could muster across the table.

Carly approached us with a welcoming smile, and we introduced the two. "It's a real pleasure to meet a friend of Cam's," she told him. "He was an asset to this town in so many ways. We are all going to miss him terribly."

As I reached for my wallet, her smile stopped me. "In honor of Cam, I insist on taking care of breakfast. I look forward to being at the service later, where I know you will all do him justice."

As we emerged into the sunlight, I reminded Geoff that the service would begin around the corner in the harbormaster's parking lot in about two hours.

"Hey, man, can I show you some sights?" Bode asked Geoff. "I can take you out on the *Lizzie G* for a little toot around the harbor."

"That would be great. I want to soak up as much of this town as I possibly can."

As I left, I saw Bode introducing Geoff to Bob, who seemed delighted to welcome a new boat mate.

CHAPTER
FORTY-EIGHT

WITH A COUPLE of hours to kill before Cam's service, I decided to focus on dinner. I felt responsible for encouraging Uncle Henry's involvement in my little fingerprint scheme, so I felt the least I could do was feed him a good meal.

I jumped happily into my Jeep and left to fetch food from Brown's. There were no cars in the parking lot at that hour so I had Phil all to myself.

"Good morning!" I greeted him. "I'm having Bode and Uncle Henry over for dinner tonight. What's a good manly meal for those guys?"

Phil smiled. "Beef stew. There's not much that makes a man happier than a hearty beef stew."

"Great!" I said. "Talk to me. What do I need and how do I make it?"

Leading me to the meat counter, he explained. "I'd suggest using half regular stew meat and half beef tenderloin tails. The combination will give your stew a great taste."

203

"That's quite a chunk of change, though, for those little tender-loin pieces," I objected.

"Trust me, it's important."

We walked over to the produce counter next, where he added new potatoes, carrots, an onion, and a head of garlic to my cart.

"I don't think I want the garlic, " I protested again. "It will smell up the entire house."

"You need it," he reassured me. "You're not sautéeing it, so it won't be too bad. Believe me, you absolutely have to have it for proper taste."

Proper taste, proper taste. This was getting serious. Our next stop was the frozen food section, where I grabbed a box of baby peas. "You can use reduced-sodium beef broth if you want," Phil told me as we strolled the canned goods aisle, "but then you'll have to add more salt," he said, smiling. "If I were you I'd just start with the full-strength stuff! While you're over there," he added, "pick up a small tin of tomato paste."

At the conclusion of our culinary tour he took me to the beer cooler and pulled out a can of Guinness.

"If I need a drink while I'm cooking I usually have a glass of red wine," I said.

"You got it all wrong, Lizzie. This is for the stew!"

"Oh, brother," I sighed. "This is nuts. Am I finished now?"

"Well, let me suggest that you might want to serve some of those frozen cream cheese biscuits."

"Really, now? *That* will keep the caloric intake to a minimum," I joked.

We grabbed a package and walked back to the register. As I put my groceries on the counter, Phil leaned over somewhat con-spiratorially. "Have you heard that the state police have some new-fangled way of identifying fingerprints left on stone? I hear they're coming out tomorrow to see what gives with the tombstone where Ty Waters bit it. Not to speak ill of the dead, but..."

I cut him off. "Really? Where did you hear that?"

"I was down at the gas station, and everyone was talking about it," he told me. "Seems we don't have much excitement around here, and this is big. Wonder what they'll find? It'll be nice if the murder is solved. It just doesn't seem right."

"I agree," was my only response.

Plunking down more money than I had intended, I left Brown's and made my way home. Once there I cubed the meat, chopped the onion and carrots, sliced the garlic, and quartered the potatoes. All of it went in the crockpot, followed by the tomato paste and beef broth. I obediently opened the beer and poured it in, though it still seemed a bit marginal to me. I felt a real swell of pride as I plugged the crockpot into the outlet. For me, this was gourmet cooking. I was darn proud of myself.

A glance at the clock reminded me I should be heading to the service soon, so I went upstairs and changed into better black pants and a white shirt that had just come from the dry-cleaner. I added a black sweater vest as a precaution against the light breezes that might blow in off the water and was done. I took a few moments to sit quietly on the porch swing outside, gathering my thoughts.

I feel a nervous responsibility before every funeral and celebration of life. They're the final gatherings of people who wish to acknowledge a deceased person's life, and it's important to me that each ceremony be as rich and personal as I can make it. I want those in attendance to leave on an upbeat note.

I went over the order of events again and reviewed the music selections. All the songs were downloaded on my phone and just needed to be plugged into the sound system.

I went back in the house, grabbed the Jeep keys, put on a layer of lipstick that I knew would last about 45 seconds, grabbed a Stowaway Sweets cashew turtle, and was out the door. Chocolate gives me both courage and confidence. Shallow as it may seem, it works for me.

CHAPTER

FORTY-NINE

I DROVE DOWN STATE Street to the harbor and parked by Darling Park. From there it was a quick walk to the harbormaster's office, a beautiful old white clapboard building with navy blue shutters and a forest green door. It sat on a small knoll behind a flagpole from which fluttered both the American and Woodford Harbor flags.

Mr. Stanley and his group of merry men were busy setting things up in front of the building. A podium stood at the base of the office steps, and three rows of chairs were set directly in front of it for the few who would need to sit.

The town's lobstermen were busy at the back of the parking lot setting up grills; buckets of steamers weren't far away. Beer kegs cooled in ice tubs and filled the beds of three nearby pickup trucks, just waiting to be tapped.

Luke and Sam had secured the *Jolly Mon* to the dock at the base of the gangway. She looked proud and freshly scrubbed, but an important part of her was obviously missing. The brightly varnished box that held Cam's ashes was already in place in front of the podium. Following the service Luke, Sam, Rocky, and probably Geoff, would sail it into open water on the *Jolly Mon* and scatter Cam's ashes. From a distance the activity below looked joyous and celebratory. Up close, though, I was certain there was an air of sadness.

"Miss G, I think we have everything pretty much in place," Mr. Stanley said contentedly as I approached. "Would you like me to play the music?"

"No, Mr. Stanley. Bode and I went over the different songs, and he knows when to play them. He'll take care of it." Wonderful as Mr. Stanley is, I thought it best to cut him some slack in the technical department. He looked relieved; playing songs off an iPhone was not something he'd been hired to do thirty years ago.

I approached the podium and saw that everything was in place, including names on the front row of chairs. Sam, Rocky, Geoff, and I each had a spot. I turned then to see Gus and Aggie heading my way with a group of five; they had come early to stake their claim on the remaining available seats.

"Good morning, Lizzie," said Gus in his wonderful baritone. He gave me a hug, and I reached out and gave each one of them a squeeze.

"It's so nice you're all here," I told them.

"We made the pilgrimage to The Old Port quite often for lunch, dear, and that lovely Cam always took such good care of us," said Aggie. "He never treated us like senior citizens, but rather like one of the crowd. It's terrible to have such a young, healthy man taken from us."

Waves of guests were now walking down the driveway and entering the parking lot. Pepper, of course, was in the middle of it all, flitting from group to group. I was pretty sure I knew what story she was planting here and there as she did so. Uncle Henry stood off to the side, leaning against the railing next to the water. When Uncle Henry was on duty he always seemed slightly set apart from everyone else. A quick wink from him, though, confirmed to me that he was still my Uncle Henry.

Carly, Jennie, Tommy, and the rest of the Driftwood crew were gathered on one side. They must have closed the restaurant for the service, I thought. To my mind, this is exactly how a small, close-knit town behaves. From the corner of my eye I noticed Dexter, who had placed himself near the water's edge, somewhat distant from everyone else.

Bode had arrived and was tying up the *Lizzie G* at the town dock. Once she was secure, he and Geoff jumped off and approached us. Geoff looked a bit windblown and had better color than he had had at the Driftwood earlier. Sometimes salt air can reboot a mind and set it back on course. I could only imagine how difficult it must be for Geoff to acclimate himself to a new town and eulogize his old friend in a sea of unfamiliar faces. I gave him a warm and encouraging smile and pointed to his assigned seat. Bode gave me a sweet smile, took my iPhone, and walked over to the sound system to do his part.

Suddenly I felt Pepper's breath in my ear as she whispered, "I've got this covered, honey. There's not a fish in the harbor that doesn't know the state police are coming tomorrow. Good grief, this is so much fun I could do it everyday. Like bees to honey, they're all entranced." I took this proclamation with a grain of salt, but I was, admittedly, impressed with her prowess.

I had chosen three gentle Jimmy Buffet songs to set the mood as people gathered. I gave Bode a nod, and soon the soft guitar music of "A Captain and the Kid" floated over the parking lot, settling the crowd down for what was to come. The wistful lyrics and soft drums of "A Pirate Looks at Forty" followed. The crowd was quiet and focused when the strains of "Tin Cup Chalice" stole over them.

I waited a short moment, taking in the gulls, the sunshine, and the metallic clank of the *Jolly* Mon's halyards. It was time, and I slowly walked toward the podium.

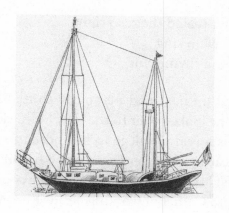

CHAPTER
FIFTY

I SPOKE SLOWLY AND tried to get comfortable with the unfamiliarity of the sound system. After a sentence or two I had mastered it and focused intently on my message. My words of welcome were always fairly standard, but at their conclusion it was always unique territory going forward. It was a pleasure to recognize all the many people who had shown up, I began, for diverse though we all are, we are bound together as one today by Cam. Our location at harbor's edge, I continued, was essential to memorializing the friend we all loved, a man whose love of the ocean was so great. As I finished my remarks, Bode began playing "Jolly Mon Sings." The lilting tune celebrated Cam's boat brilliantly.

> There is a tale that the island people tell
> Don't care if it is true
> Because I love so well
> Jolly Mon sing for his supper every night
> The people fed him well

'Cause he treated them so right
Oh, Jolly Mon sing
Oh, make a rhyme ring

Sam stepped up next and nervously shifted his papers for a moment. Then he looked over to the Jolly Mon, cleared his throat, and began. "It is a real privilege to be chosen to say a few words about Cam, because it implies that I was a friend of Cam's. That's an honor. At first I thought that I wasn't such a good choice because I just worked with Cam. But working beside him every day actually gave me a real appreciation for him. To work with another man in such small quarters, so smoothly and effortlessly, is pretty great. If I was drawing a draft beer, Cam would get ice for a customer's glass from the left side, seamlessly allowing both of us to continue smoothly and without interruption. If he was grabbing a glass and heard someone order a drink from me that used that glass, he would hand it to me in one motion. When we occasionally tripped up, his quick smile erased it all in a flash.

"Cam was a man who kept to himself in a lot of ways. The few times I was invited aboard the Jolly Mon were magic. He would have good cold beer at the ready, usually some great designer pretzels, and a welcoming spot for me in the cockpit. He inevitably pulled out his guitar and would softly sing a few tunes, usually Jimmy Buffet music, and the whole night went from there.

"I'm almost ashamed to say how surprised I am at how much I miss him. He was so easy-going and so readily available for anything that I think I almost took him for granted. But now with him gone, I wish so much I could have had more time with him. He was a gentleman and a friend and will not be duplicated any time soon."

As Sam walked back to his seat, Bode cued the familiar ""Changes in Latitudes, Changes Attitudes." The message of resiliency that Cam showed throughout his life was clear.

These changes in latitudes, changes in attitudes
Nothing remains quite the same

> Through all of the islands and all of the highlands
> If we couldn't laugh we would all go insane

Rocky got up next and took a moment before he spoke. I never thought of Rocky as emotional, but that was clearly a mistake. I watched him pause to collect himself.

"I see quite a few young men come and go in my business. There are a lot of good ones, a few rotten apples, and occasionally a special one. Cam was the latter. At first glance he was just like all the others—clean-cut, blond hair, good build, and a nice smile. I wasn't sure he had what it takes to be a good bartender as he didn't jabber the way many of the successful ones do.

"He didn't jabber because he was listening, listening and caring about what you said. This young man was not just a good bartender, but a stellar human being. He was punctual, professional, and valued everyone, even the poor guys who spent a little too much time at the bar and occasionally needed some help. Cam not only helped them out, he respected them. It was a rare combination.

"He also was great with kids. I think it takes a hell of an honest person to win the confidence of a teenage boy. Kids smell 'fake' in an instant. But when a coach had concerns about a player and brought him to see Cam, nearly always a light would go on in that boy's eyes, and he would start back on the right path. They believed Cam. He had nothing to gain from their success, but they knew he cared.

"Of course, I would love to have had Cam behind my bar for the next fifty years. But really, as I watched him, I knew he had so much more to offer society. I would ponder the question of what he would do next. Whatever it was I knew it would better the world and be worthwhile. This is why I'm particularly sorry to see Cam's life end so terribly early. It simply isn't fair. Maybe that's why I appreciate what William Giraldi had to say on the subject: 'I looked up fairness in the dictionary and it was not there.'

"It's hard not to be disillusioned by this kind of tragedy, but perhaps the more important thing is to celebrate having known such a man. Thank you, Cam. Godspeed."

After giving Rocky's words time to sink in, Bode queued up "Breathe In, Breathe Out, Move On." The lyrics drifted across the water, sounding magnificent. I think the fact that Jimmy Buffet is an exceptionally accomplished poet is sometimes overlooked amid all the Parrot Head shenanigans. His lyrics are timeless.

> According to my watch the time is now
> Past is dead and gone
> Don't try to shake it just nod your head
> Breathe In, Breathe Out, Move on

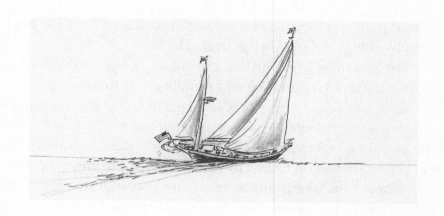

CHAPTER
FIFTY-ONE

IT SUDDENLY OCCURRED to me that Geoff should have a proper introduction before he got up to speak. The word might have spread about his connection to Cam, but it seemed proper to make it clear. I put a hand on Geoff's knee to stop him from getting up and moved toward the podium.

"Friends, our next speaker is very special. We had Cam as part of Woodford Harbor for a relatively short period of time, but Geoff Taylor was his friend for many years and can tell us much more about him. It is a real honor to welcome you, Geoff."

As I smiled at him and then across the crowd, something, or someone, caught my eye at the corner of the driveway. A man was leaning against the building, casually looking us over. There was nothing special about him, dressed as he was in jeans, a long-sleeved yellow tee shirt, and an orange baseball cap. It was the aviator sunglasses, though, that caught my attention. There was something about him, but I couldn't quite put my finger on it. It was odd, but his image seemed to me to be brighter than anything around it, like a charisma of some sort. It bothered me a bit, but I quickly let it go as Geoff began to speak.

"I'm glad to be here," he told the guests, "but I would be even happier if my old friend Cam was standing next to me.

"Cam was raised a navy brat and lived in lots of different spots growing up. In his late teens he was living in Key West, and actually got to know Jimmy Buffet. I think it's evident how much an impact Buffet had on Cam. I'm sure it worked the other way too, and Jimmy benefited from the relationship as well. He and Cam kept in touch, and I know they corresponded sporadically.

"Cam came to Martha's Vineyard after graduating from college in Boston. Like so many, he was a good student but didn't have a clue as to what he was going to do next. He found a home on the Vineyard, which is where I met him, started tending bar, and eventually bought and refurbished the *Jolly Mon*."

Geoff went on to describe the romance between his sister and Cam, and told the story of the Baby Whales. Hearing the tale again made it even sweeter, I thought.

"This is truly a lovely spot," Geoff continued, "and I can see why Cam stopped here for his next port of call. I sense what he saw in this town and in all of you. The water, the rocks, and your community apparently brought him great peace and much joy. I'm so glad he found a place where people appreciated and cared for him, and I want to thank all of you." Geoff welled up then and could not go on. He stood with brimming eyes, looking out over all of us. I rose from my seat, walked to the podium, and gave him a big hug—a hug from all of Woodford Harbor.

Bode then cued up the last of the Jimmy Buffet songs, "It's Been a Lovely Cruise."

> Drink it up, this one's for you
> It's been a lovely cruise
> I'm sorry it's ending, oh it's sad, but it's true
> Honey, it's been a lovely cruise
> There's wind in our hair and there's water in our shoes

Honey, it's been a lovely cruise

Geoff and I returned to our seats as the music started. I could feel myself being overwhelmed by the music and kept my head down so no one could see my tears. Geoff sat quietly with his head bowed.

After composing myself, I walked back to the podium and nodded at Rocky and Sam and Geoff. It was time for the final part of the service. Geoff arose and picked up the small varnished box. Followed by Sam, Luke, and Rocky, he headed down the gangway and stepped aboard the Jolly Mon. All eyes were on the four as they prepared for Cam's final passage. As they loosened the lines, I stepped to the microphone and read "Gone From My Sight," a poem attributed to Rev. Luther Beecher and popularized by Henry Van Dyke:

I am standing upon the seashore. A ship, at my side,
spreads her white sails to the moving breeze and starts
for the blue ocean. She is an object of beauty and strength.
I stand and watch her until, at length, she hangs like a speck
of white cloud just where the sea and sky
come to mingle with each other.

Then, someone at my side says, "There, she is gone."

Gone where?
Gone from my sight. That is all. She is just as large in mast,
hull and spar as she was when she left my side
And, she is just as able to bear her load of
living freight to her destined port.
Her diminished size is in me—not in her.

And, just at the moment when someone says, "There, she is gone,"
there are other eyes watching her coming, and other voices
ready to take up the glad shout, "Here she comes!"

And that is dying...

We all stood silent as Geoff took the helm and Luke and Sam unfurled the *Jolly Mon's* sails. A southwest breeze pushed her on a broad reach out of the harbor. As she grew smaller in the distance, I leaned into the microphone and said all I could think of to say. "Amen."

I looked over at Bode. He nodded and began playing more upbeat Jimmy Buffet music as a transition to the reception the lobstermen had planned behind us. "Boat Drinks" dispelled the gloom and fed the camaraderie the service had woven.

Bode walked to the podium and stood next to me. I felt his hand on my back, and I took a breath to compose myself. It was then that I remembered the man who had been leaning against the building and looked over to where he had stood.

"Bode," I said. "I think Jimmy Buffet may have been here."

But the stranger with the aviator sunglasses had disappeared. "Life can be crazy sometimes," said Bode. "You just never know what's going to happen." I leaned into him then and exhaled. "You've got that right," I said.

CHAPTER
FIFTY-TWO

I SAW MR. STANLEY approaching, and he brought my mind
back to the present.

"Miss G, that was a lovely service. I was not entirely certain you
could pull this one off, but it was perfect." Whereupon he gave me
a slight bow.

"Thank you so much, Mr. Stanley," I beamed. "I agree. The
warm fall sunshine and fresh breeze were nice additional touches,
don't you think?

"Can you get these fellows to dismantle the chairs and podium
now? We'll leave the sound system up until the reception winds
down. The music is lightening everyone's mood, and there's no
denying it captures Cam's spirit. If you'll excuse me, I think I'd like
to mingle with folks at the reception for a bit."

"Absolutely, I'll take care of everything."

With that, my work was done. I looked at the guests congre-
gated around the beer kegs and steamers and walked over.

"Lizzie, that was very nice." I turned and was a bit surprised to see Ollie and Alice.

"Thank you both. That's so nice. I wanted the service to capture Cam, and I think it did," I told them. "Did you know him from The Old Port?" I asked them then. "I don't recall ever seeing you there."

"Oh, no," smiled Alice. "We don't do much outside the house. A few years back, though, Cam was real helpful when our son was having some difficulty in high school. It was unnerving because he had always been a solid student and had always done what was right. Then suddenly he seemed to be losing his way.

"His track coach called Cam, and the two went out on the *Jolly Mon* a few times. I don't know what happened out there, but whatever it was it seemed to set our boy straight. He's in the merchant marines now, earning a good living and taking care of himself. We were, and are, very grateful."

"What a nice story," I told them.

Many approached me to express their approval of the service, and I found it heartwarming. Eventually I found myself at the steamer table. I was reaching for a paper plate and a plastic cup of melted butter when my arm bumped against the sleeve of a navy-blue suit jacket. It seemed a bit out of context, for the tone of the service had been more casual. When I looked up to identify its owner, it turned out to be Daniel Dunkirk. My initial reaction was astonishment. How could Dunkirk have possibly known Cam? Why was he here? And was the man actually holding a beer?

Acknowledging him, I couldn't help but wonder if I might see him later that night at the cemetery, trying to sand his fingerprints from the gravestone. He was, I must admit, my first choice for a criminal.

As I slurped a few steamers down, the crowd began thinning out. I had suddenly had enough, too, and made eye contact with Bode across the way.

"One of the lobstermen is going to keep playing the Jimmy Buffet music over the sound system," I told him as he ambled over, "so we can go anytime."

"The *Lizzie G* is tied up at the dock. Do you want to go out for a quick ride?"

I smiled. "I cannot think of anything I would rather do. The air will feel wonderful, and I haven't seen nearly enough of you in the past few days."

We quietly slipped away and were aboard in no time. Bob was fast asleep under the starboard gunnel but awoke as we stepped aboard. He smiles a doggie smile whenever he sees Bode, and today was no exception. The two are quite a pair. He greeted me with the obligatory wet kiss, and we untied the lines and pushed off.

To my mind, the initial moments aboard a boat, when you feel the water all around you and breathe in fresh salt air, are the very best. The slight aroma of fish coming from the *Lizzie G*'s hold marked her as the very utilitarian lobster boat she is. I drank it in.

We motored out of the harbor, and Bode headed for Baker's Island. Its iconic lighthouse always looks to me as though it should be on the cover of a New England telephone book.

"Big news on the culinary front," I said. "I'm making beef stew for dinner tonight. Uncle Henry is coming by to eat with us before we head over to the stake-out. Ironically, Charlie, who has no idea what Uncle Henry and I are up to, was the one who facetiously referred to our date tonight as a stake-out. If she only knew!"

"Your plan is pretty out there, Z. Do you really think you'll catch the culprit this way?" I couldn't see Bode's face, but thought it had better not have a smirk on it.

"Actually," I said, "I do. Listen, we have to do something. It just isn't right to let the case go unsolved."

"Even if the deceased is Ty Waters?"

"No matter the victim, it's still a dastardly thing to do, don't you think?"

"Well, I, for one am not going to miss beef stew. Charlie and I will stay in while you do your sleuthing. Maybe we can put together that classic and contemporary/country music list we've been talking about for so long."

"Hey! Don't forget that Charlie has homework." I retorted. "Don't distract her."

"But the ideal classic/contemporary country songs need attention too," Bode noted with a twinkle.

"You two!" I said, dismissing the conversation entirely.

We were coming up to the eastern side of Baker's when we saw it—the beautiful silhouette of the *Jolly Mon's* sails imprinted upon a crystal blue sky. Her hull proudly breaking through the water, she left a thin white spray in her wake. She had made the final voyage for her master and had taken good care of him until the end. I knew I would miss both of them for a long, long time.

CHAPTER
FIFTY-THREE

B ODE DROPPED ME at the harbormaster's dock when we got back. As I disembarked I noticed Jennie and Geoff walking companionably up the street, laughing and looking relaxed and happy. Hmmm, I thought to myself, maybe this trip to Woodford Harbor wouldn't be Geoff's last! The lobstermen were near the end of their cleanup in the parking lot, and everything was almost back to normal. The day's events had changed me, however, and I knew I would never feel the same way again about this space; from now on it would be special.

I drove home quickly, glad to unwind from the morning's events. I could smell it long before I walked through the front door. When I was finally inside, the aroma took my breath away. I felt a bit like Bob as I began to salivate. Meatloaf and hamburger stroganoff are usually the pinnacles of my cooking abilities, so this was extraordinary! The beef stew I had assembled this morning smelled positively sinful. I might just add this dish to my limited repertoire.

Silently thanking Phil for his help, I went upstairs and changed into dark clothes—jeans and a navy-blue sweatshirt. I told myself I wasn't dressing for a stakeout, but in fact I think I was.

My cell phone rang. Charlie needed a ride home from school. I was already heading out the door when my phone rang again. Bode reported that he was on his way. Did I need anything? I did, indeed. Asking him to pick up Charlie, I returned to setting the table. It made me feel positively grown-up.

We usually sat in front of the TV and watched *Jeopardy* while eating from tray tables. But tonight was special—beef stew and detective work. Would we really catch someone removing fingerprints? Would Daniel Dunkirk get nabbed? What if it was Ollie or Alice? I didn't like the latter idea at all. They were so dear at Cam's service. They had supported each other their entire lives and had produced a wonderful son. They were to be commended.

Just then I heard Uncle Henry's car pull in. Glancing outside, I noticed he had driven his own vehicle and not his police car. I went to the back door and opened it.

"Hi, Uncle Henry!" I said, opening my arms to envelope him.

"Well, hello, dear."

"Can I get you a beer?"

"'fraid not. If we are really going to the cemetery to hide behind a tombstone to see who comes by, I think a beer would be inappropriate."

"Does that mean I shouldn't have a glass of wine?" I asked hesitantly.

"Well, dear..."

As I attempted to take this in, Charlie, Bode, and Bob alighted from the truck. As they crossed the porch, Uncle Henry turned to me. "Nice to see the two of them together, isn't it?"

I smiled in agreement.

"We lost our soccer game. It was so bad. Our forwards just couldn't put it in, and I'm afraid I let a ball get by me, but I think maybe our goalie should have been able to stop it. My goodness, it smells good in here. What's going on?" My little chatterbox was home.

"Hi, Uncle Henry! Oh, I just remembered, you two are going out sleuthing tonight, right? Mom, do you have a gun? Do you have a deputy badge? At least you're dressed in black."

"Stop now, honey. Don't be ridiculous—and by the way, it's navy blue. Why don't you go up and change, and then we can all eat some of this beef stew that smells so good!"

"Sounds good to me," said Bode and Uncle Henry simultaneously.

"Can I get you a glass of wine, Z?" asked Bode, reaching for a wine glass.

"No, I don't think so. Might be best not to have one tonight," I said, looking at the floor.

Bode's eyes widened. "Are you serious? Henry, what have you done to my girl? You guys seem to be really serious about this. I hope it works out."

"That's enough about all this," I said. "I don't want Charlie to know what's going on. It could be we'll be back here in a few hours with nothing to talk about but the Great Unsolved Mystery."

"Well, it won't be for lack of trying. Pepper has done a superb job of spreading that rumor about the state police and their new fingerprinting device," said Uncle Henry. "That woman has a knack."

"*There's* an understatement," I said, smiling.

"Well, *I'll* have a beer," Bode whispered to himself as he walked towards the drinks fridge.

I took four pottery bowls out of a back cupboard and dramatically unplugged the crockpot.

"This is unbelievable, Mom!" Charlie squealed, coming down the stairs. "Beef stew! It might be your last meal if something happens to you tonight; might as well go out on a high note." I looked at her askance.

"Really," she continued, "this is hot stuff! I don't know why you're all keeping it from me. Don't you think I'm old enough to be told what you're doing? Believe me, I can deal! Think of all the dastardly things I've seen at the movies and on television. Come on, tell me!"

"Charlie," I began. "First of all, what you see in movies and on television isn't real. It's time you begin to recognize the differences between real life and pretend drama. Most of the junk we're bombarded with is sensationalized, and one-dimensional. Real life is much more serious, and the repercussions it can have are broad and far-reaching."

"Whoa! Sorry, I was just chatting," said Charlie, defending herself. "Hypothetically speaking. No need for an ethics lecture here."

"Sorry, honey, I guess some things just hit a nerve with me. All the violence surrounding us as entertainment is one of them." I felt the need to defend myself as well.

"Girls, let's just calm down and enjoy this beef stew," interjected Uncle Henry. "It smells extraordinary, and I'm sure it won't disappoint."

We all relaxed then and dug into the simmering repast before us. And it did not disappoint.

Bode cleaned his plate quickly. "This is really good, Z, really good. If it turns out to be your last meal, you're going to die happy." I shot him a disapproving look, but got over it as I forked a sweet carrot coated in juicy broth into my mouth.

"So, Lil' Chuck, ready to start working on our top classical and contemporary country songs list?" asked Bode.

"Why don't we clean up the dishes first and see how it looks after that?"

"So I won't be here to know what goes on, you mean." I was impressed at Charlie's plan for getting me out of the picture—impressed and somewhat worried.

CHAPTER
FIFTY-FOUR

U NCLE HENRY AND I climbed into his car and left Bode pontificating about Willy Nelson. In a way, I wished I could stay behind too. I'd love to be part of the cozy scene in my little kitchen, my hands in warm soapy water listening to Bode and Charlie debate. Instead, I was going off on what might very well prove to be a wild goose chase. Even though I was with Uncle Henry, I knew I was stepping outside my comfort zone.

I turned to him. "It seems bizarre to me that the two of us are going off to sit behind a gravestone at Woodford Harbor Cemetery right now. In the abstract, this seemed perfectly logical. At this moment, however, it seems ridiculous. There can't be a murderer in this sweet little town of ours! Just when I think it's impossible, I cut to Ty Waters' body reposing in the refrigerator at the funeral home, collecting tennis balls."

"Lizzie, dear, you're babbling. I think you're trying to rationalize all this. Don't worry, it'll be fine; an interesting exercise if nothing else.

"We need to go about this in a serious way. I've chosen the gravestone I think is best for our purposes. When we get there, flatten yourself near to the ground in a comfortable position. Don't kneel or squat, as we might be in the same position for quite some time. No cell phone, either. The light from its screen would be a beacon in the dark—and heaven forbid it should ring! Obviously, there'll be no talking. We must remain stock still."

I mentally transported myself to my familiar kitchen, wishing this whole thing was not happening. But it was, and it was important now that I concentrate on Uncle Henry's directions.

We parked a few blocks from the cemetery and walked in silence along the perimeter. I followed Uncle Henry to a tall, rather wide, grave marker. The vantage point it gave to the tombstone where Ty was found was ideal. We would have a clear view of anyone arriving from all directions. It was a moonless night, and the last vestige of light was disappearing over the water to the west. We were in deep darkness.

We flattened ourselves on the dry grass, companionably close to one another. It was fun to be back in such an intimate position with Uncle Henry; I had spent a lot of time on his lap as a child, and his familiar feel and smell were comforting.

The lights were on in the caretaker's cottage off to our right. I wondered what Ollie and Alice were up to in there and hoped that no one ventured out. No, my money was on the nefarious silhouette of Daniel Dunkirk, skulking up from the south. "I know, Mom," I thought to myself, "but I just can't help putting him in that box."

I let my mind wander a bit, wondering what Bode and Charlie were up to. I thought about Jennie and Geoff, wondered when Mr. Stanley would retire, tried to imagine what my parents were doing just now, and how I would manage when Charlie went off to college. Going way back, I tried to imagine who Charlie's father might be.

It was a still night, and the leaves that remained on the trees hardly moved. A few stars were starting to appear, but they gave off very little light. My eyes had adjusted as well as they were going to, but the inky blackness was disconcerting. I heard a twig break.

There was definitely movement to the right of the stone. Oh, no, I thought, please not Ollie! Not Alice! As it turned out, sometimes a squirrel is just a squirrel. We relaxed and returned to our task.

After a while, I began to fear that I would doze off. It occurred to me that detective work was probably not my calling. Lizzie George, private eye. Not so much.

Suddenly there was another movement. I wasn't sure if I imagined it or if it was real. Imagined or not, I was now on ultra-high alert. I felt Uncle Henry tense as well. My eyes were straining to the left, and then I saw it. It was a man's figure moving ever so slowly towards the grave marker. I dared not breathe. I imagined that the silhouette before me mirrored Daniel Dunkirk's physique, but I knew in my heart that it was just wishful thinking.

The unidentified male's figure was about three feet from the tombstone when a blinding light erupted from the dark. It was brighter than anything I ever remember seeing, and it bathed the entire area in an otherworldliness. I shut my eyes briefly to recover my sight, but already the man's face was imprinted in my mind. It was the terrified face of Augustus Beethoven that stood before us.

Adrenaline coursed through my system. I don't know what was more shocking, the sight of Gus Beethoven staring back at me or the image of Pepper, Jimmy Olsen-like, emerging from the bushes, a massive old camera around her neck. I was speechless in every sense of the word. After what seemed like an interminable pause, Uncle Henry stood up, identified himself, and took over.

"Pepper, please step back and give Gus some space."

He turned slowly and addressed Gus. "Whatever goes on here, Gus?"

Gus looked around at the three of us, tears in his eyes. Though the man we had intercepted going towards the crime scene was Augustus Beethoven, it was nonetheless a shock to hear his voice.

"I'm so sorry," he began. His voice was its usual low baritone, steady and deliberate. "I am beyond ashamed to be standing here in your midst in this terribly compromising position. Yes, I picked up the shovel behind Ty Waters at Thistle's graveside service. It was sitting right there. I was so overcome with grief at losing her that I couldn't bear to be seen in public. But I wanted to see her one more time, so I came to the cemetery and watched from back here. When I saw Ty looking down at her casket I was furious.

"I was in a highly emotional state, and something inside me exploded. He had no right to be any part of her final moments. I hardly remember reaching for the shovel, but I suddenly found myself holding it. Ty must have heard me behind him, because he turned around in surprise. As he did so, his left foot slipped on a muddy patch behind the tombstone. He slid down the incline and whacked his head hard on the granite. I could see it all happening in slow motion, but there was nothing I could do to stop it. There was no sound, but his fall generated an incredible amount of blood. I didn't know what to do! I wiped off the shovel, set it back down, and retreated to my car.

"I don't really regret what happened, but I've spent an inordinate amount of time since wondering if I could have struck him with the shovel if he hadn't fallen. It would have been so easy, but it's so contrary to who I am that I think I would not have done so. I can't say that unequivocally, though.

"And now I find myself in the midst of this most disgraceful and embarrassing circumstance. Morally, I want you to know that in no way was this an act of hatred. Ty Waters was a shallow, meaningless, annoying lightweight. That he had the audacity to think he had any right to mourn my Thistle was the final insult.

"What I did was an act of love. How I adored and admired Thistle. She was everything good, and I guess I thought I was protecting her in some way.

"I am so sorry for my behavior."

Not a word was spoken as Gus slowly followed Uncle Henry down the hill and back to his car. I joined Pepper, who headed in the other direction towards her car.

Gus. So disappointing.

CHAPTER
FIFTY-FIVE

PEPPER AND I sat together in her car. Neither of us moved or said a word.

"What do you think, Pepper?" I finally asked.

"It's a real shame, Lizzie, a damn shame. I've never been so shocked in my life as I am right now. Gus Beethoven! It's so hard to believe," she answered slowly. "I wish there was something I could do to change it. It just doesn't seem right that a ninny like Ty Waters would end up ruining such a distinguished man's life. In journalism school I remember writing a paper on crimes of passion. 'There are crimes of passion and crimes of logic. The boundary between them is not clearly defined' was one of the Camus quotes I remember reading.

"Poor Gus. At least his actions weren't intentional or premeditated. They arose from his simple devotion to Bode's wonderful mother."

"Are you going to print the picture?" I asked hesitantly.

"I am only the messenger here, Lizzy, and one musn't shoot the messenger. I have to print it, and yes, it will be sensational; probably the most memorable photo we've ever run on the front page of the *Woodford Reporter*. Believe me, though, this does not in any way make me happy. But it's a matter of journalistic ethics to put one's personal bias away and simply report the news."

I was pleased to see the sincerity in her response.

She started the car and dropped me off at my front door. We gave each other an uncharacteristic hug, and I got out. The lights were on inside, and I could hear bass notes. It seemed like a long time ago that I had driven away from here with Uncle Henry. I felt a disillusionment starting to settle in, and I didn't like it.

As I walked through the front door, I instantly put a damper on a very happy scene. I met both their eyes. Bode got up and retrieved the box of wine on the counter; he returned with a generous glass. Charlie took my hand and led me to the couch.

"Sometimes we should be careful what we wish for," I began. "I didn't want this crime to go unsolved. Now, however, I'm not so sure." I proceeded to relate my night to wide eyes and closed mouths.

Charlie's reaction didn't surprise me. It was devastating for her to learn that a man she held in such high esteem could possibly commit so devastating an act. To her it was pretty black and white.

Bode, however, had a more ambiguous reaction. The fact that Gus had committed such a violent act shocked him. It was Gus's motive, though, that tempered Bode's reaction. What son could condemn a decent man's crime when it was a noble act on behalf of his mother? As Bode fell into thoughtful silence, Charlie began examining the situation from a sixteen-year-old's perspective.

"Wow, I guess the power of love can work in two directions. Mom, did Mr. Beethoven really kill Ty Waters? How could he if he never hit him with the shovel? I mean, he didn't even touch him," she observed.

"But did he intend to do him harm?" I asked her rhetorically.

"I don't think so. He didn't go to the cemetery hoping to see Ty Waters and kill him. It was just an accident," she went on.

"Yes, but it is an accident that wouldn't have happened if Mr. Beethoven hadn't been there," I replied.

"Well, how about the fact that Mr. Beethoven is a good man, and Ty Waters caused so much trouble for so many people?"

I was impressed with Charlie's grasp of abstract thought. And I could easily have gone down the road that killing bad people is less bad, given my affection for Gus. Instead I replied, "Honey, there are rarely black-and-white answers to ethical issues. That, combined with our morals and our behavior as it relates to ethical issues, makes life quite challenging at times. There are so many subtleties that influence a final judgement.

"That being said, however, there are no witnesses, and there is no blood on the shovel to implicate its involvement. Mr. Beethoven's appearance at the cemetery tonight could be construed as implication, but not necessarily proof. His confession seems entirely in keeping with the facts.

"Augustus Beethoven has led an exemplary life and will be afforded credit for that. This incident may tarnish his distinguished reputation a bit, but the respect he enjoys in Woodford Harbor will not change," I said with conviction.

"I'm going to do everything I can for Gus," said Bode. The determination in his voice was almost fierce. It was as solid a statement as I had ever heard from him. Gus had himself a strong ally and a loyal, loving friend. I imagined the bond now shared by the two was bringing a smile to Thistle's face somewhere.

"We had a Martin Luther King quotation in school today," offered Charlie. "It was something like, 'We must accept finite disappointment, but never lose infinite hope.'"

I looked at Bode, and I looked at Charlie. I knew that eternal and infinite hope was in each of us.

EPILOGUE

PEPPER PRINTED THE story and, as she had promised, included the photo she snapped of Gus at the cemetery. Her sense of duty to 'report the news' was lost on some, but others recognized her dedication.

In the meantime Uncle Henry took Gus into Portland to meet with the state police. Thankfully, nothing ever came of it. The lack of any solid evidence, bolstered by Gus's venerable reputation, made it unlikely that any trial would render a guilty verdict. Ty's death was an accident, pure and simple. Even Lt. Daniels realized that. Our beloved Augustus Beethoven was free to go—and Woodford Harbor was thrilled to welcome him home.

In fact, the town's response to his release was unique. The Driftwood's television was turned off for a time, replaced by a CD playing a loop of Beethoven's *Fifth Symphony*. The Old Port began serving a Beethoven Cocktail, which counted spiced rum and cherry, pomegranate, apple, raspberry, and blackberry juices among its ingredients. Charlie's class was assigned research papers on the life of Beethoven, Brown's had a special on fifths of spirits, and I swear I heard strains of "Moonlight Sonata" emanating from Uncle Henry's office. Amid all this affection being showered on Gus, I could not entirely forget the difficult hands that had been dealt to Ty and Dexter.

Ty's funeral finally took place on an overcast, gloomy Thursday morning. His plain wooden casket was lowered into the ground in the family plot, which was, blessedly, in a far corner of the cemetery and nowhere near the cottage where Ollie and Alice resided. The word around town is that those two have made arrangements to be buried with her parents when the time comes.

The service itself was a bit awkward, as one might expect. The twenty-some people huddled around the grave were mostly older women who did not, thankfully, wear tennis whites. I had searched the Bible, but was unable to find any verse that referenced tennis— no surprise there. I couldn't bring myself to allude to love at all, as in Ty's case it would have seemed more appropriately used in conjunction with tennis, than any notion of human emotion.

Bode stood with Dexter to give him as much moral support as possible. Uncle Henry had discreetly returned the box and photo from Ty's closet to him to do with as he saw fit.

Dexter did eventually go south and rebuild. It was slow and painful at first, but in the end he created a life for himself that was both full and happy, once again affirming the resiliency of the human spirit.

Many of our evening dinners are served later than usual, for Bode is often at Woodford Pines into the early evening chatting with Gus Beethoven. Nips of Woodford Reserve are often part of the protocol.

Geoff has been seen at The Old Port more than once, entranced, it would appear, by our own dear Jennie. I'm keeping my fingers crossed that he might be teaching at Woodford Harbor High someday.

I see Charlie becoming more and more independent. It's perfectly natural and is as it should be. I hate it.

Together, Bode and I are continuing our "Lovely Cruise" through life.

And me? I'm enjoying each day, always remembering to "breathe in, breathe out, move on."

Made in United States
North Haven, CT
13 August 2022

22693939R00146